MW01179065

Monkey

Monkey

MICHAEL BOYCE

For the mighty Terril
Thank you very much
All the best,
Michael

Pedlar Press | Toronto

COPYRIGHT © Michael Boyce 2004

ALL RIGHTS RESERVED. No part of this book may be
reproduced or transmitted in any form or by any means
whatsoever without written permission from the publisher,
except by a reviewer, who may quote brief passages in a
review. For information, write Pedlar Press at PO Box 26,
Station P, Toronto Ontario M5S 2S6 Canada.

ACKNOWLEDGEMENTS

The publisher wishes to thank the Canada Council for the
Arts and the Ontario Arts Council for their generous support
of our publishing program.

LIBRARY AND ARCHIVES CANADA CATALOGUING
IN PUBLICATION DATA

Boyce, Michael, 1958-
    Monkey / Michael Boyce. -- 1st ed.

ISBN 0-9732140-7-4

    I. Title.
PS8553.O934M65 2004   C813'.54   C2004-904707-8

First Edition

COVER Eva Sköld Westerlind, *Solitary Traveler Series*, 1998-99

DESIGN Zab Design & Typography, Winnipeg

Printed in Canada

THE CANADA COUNCIL | LE CONSEIL DES ARTS
FOR THE ARTS | DU CANADA
SINCE 1957 | DEPUIS 1957

ONTARIO ARTS COUNCIL
CONSEIL DES ARTS DE L'ONTARIO

40 YEARS 40 ANS

For Sandra

1

HE IS STRONG AND HE IS FAST and that is how he is. He is
quick to think and he will play you for a fool. He is not a bad man.
He is like a child sometimes who likes to play a prank or two. But
he is not a bad man who really means to hurt you. He does not
mean to hurt you.

Look at him move. He is so fluid and so fast, so supple and
so strong.

He likes to run and jump and climb and there's nothing bad
in that. That is not a bad thing. But when he runs and jumps and
climbs up the emergency escape ladders into places that are not
his own and into homes that aren't his own, then that is bad.

Up he goes and in he goes and where he goes and what he
does he does in there and just what is it that he does in there?
He'll watch TV. Look in the fridge. Get something to eat. Put
some music on and dance around to it. When he leaves he will
do so fast and easy.

You wouldn't know. You wouldn't know that he'd been
there. If you came in he'd be gone, long gone. Good ears he has
and good sixth sense. Never been caught not ever. What, never?
No never. Well hardly ever. Hardly ever been caught in there.

Sometimes he steals; just little things. They have no value really. They're just the sort of thing that you might pick up for fun. Or maybe someone gave it to you. Perhaps a friend gave it to you for your birthday. They couldn't get you anything that costs a lot, so they got you just this little thing, this little funny thing. It was just a token thing; a joke-like thing. It was just a curio.

It's a thing, the kind of thing that says something, but you forget just what it says. When you got it you knew it; there was something. It said something. But later you forgot what it said and what you saw.

When it goes then it is gone and you don't notice that it's gone. You didn't see it go and you don't see that it's gone. Usually it sits somewhere and when it's gone and it's not there, you do not care. You do not care to look there and you do not look there often. And when you do and it's not there you do not care a lot. You might wonder where it's gone, and you might not wonder where it's gone. But if you wonder or if you don't, you do not care in any case. But he does.

It says something to him. And when it's gone he knows that he has taken it away. Not just the thing, but what it said. Off he goes and takes it with him, takes it all away. He carries it around, but not for very long.

He might leave it there when he is there when he is where he is right now when he sees there's something else. He might keep it there at home in a box or on a shelf or on his mantelpiece. Now and then he looks at these things. Some he throws away. Some he throws in fights and he laughs and then he runs away.

He often laughs when he does fight and he often runs away. He likes to fight. But it's just a game for him. For him it's just a game. It is all just fun and games.

He likes to get others all wound up. He battles with their pride. And once they've lost all their control he likes to run away. He is not a mean man. But he is a cheeky one.

Now and then he likes to look and watch and see what people do. People do what they will do and when they are alone they will do it differently. That is what he wants to see the way they do it differently.

He is not a spy. He just wants to know. Inquiring minds just want to know. And he just wants to know. He's curious. It's in his nature. But, they wouldn't like it if they knew.

Oh, he can be bad. Not really bad, but still he can be bad.

He's careful, though, you know. He is careful where he goes. He is careful where he goes to do what it is that he does do. In the city there are places that are just like small-town places. They are in the city but they are places that are just like neighbourhoods, like places in small towns. Those places are the best places he can go to do what he does do. Especially those places where the students and the artists live.

Those places are the best because those people in those places, they are there far less careful there. They are not so careful there. They're just a little careless there. They care a little less in there.

Not that he would ever go in there when they were home in there. Not that he would ever let himself be seen in there, be caught in there, just staring there at someone who is home in there. He does take care when he is there, even when he is in there.

Where they live is more downtrodden there and it's less careful there, and so of course there are some creeps in there. Of course they are in there. The students are in there. The artists are in there. And of course the creeps are there, there are some creeps in there as well.

Not in any usual sense can he be said to be an artist. And not in any usual sense can he be said to be a student. And not in any kind of sense can he be said to be a creep. He hopes that it cannot be said that he is said to be a creep. He hopes not. And he hopes that no one else would think, not anybody else would think, he hopes that no one else would think that he was just a creep. He hopes not. He certainly hopes not. To be thought to be a creep would mean that you would then be hunted. It would not be good and it would not be nice to be hunted like a creep. No.

Would they catch him? — Maybe not. He is fast and he is good and he is strong and he is smart. He's smart, he's clever smart, he's tricky smart, Bugs Bunny smart. But smart or no his go would slow, it could make him go too slow, it could slow him down. And he does not like to be slowed down. So he is brash and he is bold, but he is careful too so he can go the way he goes and his going won't slow down. Nothing will slow it down.

But will he, would he, could he ever get caught? He's careful yes, but just how careful is he? Does he take the care he should? Does he take enough of it?

He was almost caught just once just lately. Just once just lately he stole something and it's not a good thing. He doesn't know that; he doesn't know it's not a good thing. But he knows that he was seen. He knows that he was almost caught.

He knows there was a man who caught a glimpse of him. There was a man who caught a glimpse of him just a little glimpse of him, but enough of just a little glimpse of him to see him move the way he moves like no one else does move, like no one else can move. He saw him move like no one else with speed like no one else does move, like no one else can move. And he saw, he knows, he took something.

It is a thing that would be missed and he is missing it right now. He wants it back. He wants it back right now. He'll get it back. He'll get it back. He's going to try to get it back.

2

AND SO THE MAN WHO CAUGHT a glimpse must catch the thing he caught a glimpse of, the thing the man he glimpsed, the man he caught a glimpse of. Little monkey.

How? How does he, how will he, how can he catch a thing like that? How does he catch a thing like that, that is like that, and is a man like that? The snake will catch it if he can.

If he can see it he can catch it. If he can find it he can catch it. How will he and how can he see it or find it? He can and he will look for it. He can and he will look for him. He will find him and will see him and will catch him, and then what will he do? He will work that out when he needs to. That's the way he is. That's the way the snake is.

Where then will the snake look? Of course he'll look where he has seen him, where he has seen the monkey. The snake has seen the monkey where the snake is living. You can think of that in two ways: he lives in his apartment, and in this part of town. Where he has seen the monkey is where the monkey is. He's in this part of town.

Perhaps the monkey lives there in that part of town as well. The snake can ask around and he will ask around.

Is he a thief, the man he glimpsed? He was, the man, he was a thing. He moved, the way he moved, he was, he was not like any other man; he was only like himself. Is he a thief? Certainly he is a thief to the snake he is a thief, but has he ever been a thief to anybody else? If he has, does anybody know, can anybody tell, can anybody say that they were stolen from today or yesterday or any day or ever lately?

He certainly is only like himself, and such a man who is only like himself would certainly be known to be someone who's only like himself. He would be known for it. He would be known, he could be known, because he is most certainly only like himself. He is only like himself and not just like another man and not just like just any man. He is not like any other man. He would be known for that. He would be known, he could be known, and anyone could know him as the man they saw as certainly a man only like himself. They might have seen him.

Did they know him? Did they see him? They could know and they would say when he would ask. They would say they knew him or they saw him. If he asked. And he would. And they would say for sure. Because he is that way, the snake, he is that way. He has a way to make them say because he is that way. He has a way and is that way and that is the way he is, just like himself that way.

He must be sly because he is. He must listen. He must look. He does look and he does listen. Always he does look and always he does listen and always he does see and always he does hear. He gets like that. He must be sly because he is. When he's looking he is seeing. When he listens he does hear.

He must hang around, but he does not. He does not hang around, and so he does. And when he does, he does get seen, he does get heard. So he must be sly because he's there and he must be there quite naturally.

How do you do it? When it is not natural to do it, how do you do it? When it is not natural, you must do it naturally. That is what he must do and of course he does it naturally, he does do it quite naturally. He is good at it, as good as anybody can be good at it, and he is good at it. And so naturally he does do it. He does do it quite naturally.

He should not stand out. He is looking for a sign. Looking for some sign. A sign of something strange and interesting to see. A sign that someone saw it. A sign that someone knows it. Knows it is a thing and that it's strange and interesting. Knows it is a thing to see. Knows it is someone to see. Knows it is someone to see who's strange and interesting to see. They would know and they would say and he would not stand out in any way.

When they tell him they would tell him and he would not stand out. When they say, they surely say, they nearly always nearly say, completely say, completely what they have to say. They say what must be said. They say it all, they tell it all and go away, and he does not stand out in any way.

The monkey is a one. The snake, he knows the monkey is a one. He's a one who does do things the way he only can do things. He moves the way he moves and the way he moves so quickly and so smoothly and so fast, he is so bold, he is so quick, into nothing does he crash. But he did break in and come inside; he came inside the snake's place. Into his place his little place the place he does call home, this man, this man came in and took something, he took it from the snake. The monkey took something.

He would not know the value of the thing that he did take. If he did it would be trouble. A special kind of trouble. Not the kind of trouble that most likely you would see. It is the kind of trouble that's a special kind of trouble, a kind of trouble that's a trouble only you can see, because only you can see it and see what it does mean. You can see it, what it means, and you can see it, what it's meant to mean, and you can see it, what it is. And what it's meant to be is what it's meant to mean. So it's not good that he took it.

When only you can see what it's meant to mean and what it's meant to be, then it's not a good thing when it's seen by someone else, you see. If someone else does see it and sees what it does mean, then trouble does ensue for the one who sees it too. The one who sees it too should not see it too. That is not a good thing. That means trouble. Trouble for the one who sees it too. If it's yours, then only you should see it. No one else should see it.

It was his and no one else should see it. And the monkey took it. And if the monkey sees it, then that's not good, and the snake will see right to it, to making trouble for the monkey. As sure as trouble can be made the snake will make some trouble for the monkey. If the monkey sees the same thing that the snake does see and only just the snake should see, then trouble will be made and plenty of it too. If the monkey sees it that is what the snake will do.

But probably he won't. Why should he, how could he, see it? It would be strange, it would be unusual, to see what someone else put there. The snake's the one who put it there. It would be strange, both strange and unusual, for the monkey then to see it there. He did not put it there, so why should he and how could he ever see it there? He will not see it there.

The snake must know and he will ask, and if he asks you, you will tell him. When you look at him and see him there, he's looking right at you, so very right at you, so almost right through you. You like it too, his seeing you, and it's like he looks right through to you, to deepest you, to secret you, your innermost, most secret you. It certainly does throw you.

And then, you're saying what you thought you would not say. He is so appealing. What he does is so appealing. He wants to know. He draws you out. His interest is appealing. In his look there is a warning, but his look it is alluring. And so you do the telling. You tell him what you know, whatever you do know.

And you are telling him right now what you thought you would not say. You throw your caution to the wind. You do not even hear yourself for talking. You don't heed your own misgivings. You're not careful what you say. And he makes you want to be that way.

You think, you feel, it will be best, and better when you're done. But when you're done it is not best nor better when you're done. It is not good, you realize, to say anything so free; to be so free to say so much, too much you say too free.

It will feel good, you think you know, that afterward it will. But I'm afraid it won't. It won't and it does not. But you are glad when it is over. You are glad when it is done. It was not for best, it does not feel better, and it won't feel good, not now, not ever. But you are glad that it is over and you're glad that it is done. And you are glad that he is gone away. You may have said what you have said, but you don't worry now because he has gone away. He has gone away and now you are OK.

And anyway it's not as if you really know that guy; you do not really know that guy. What difference does it make? It was strange. It was odd. But you do not know that guy, not really know that guy. It was strange. It was odd. It was strangely, oddly good and bad, and bad and good, and everything inside was stirring up inside, and the more that it was stirring it was scaring and it stirred itself exciting. It stirred itself exciting and it flushed you on the outside. Your skin flushed on the outside. Your skin outside it showed a flush. It was you for sure and you were blushing.

You do not know that guy. That guy you spoke about. Not really. You felt you shouldn't tell him. But you did. It does not matter anyway. But you felt you should not tell him. But of course you did, you told him. You thought you might feel better if you did and so you told him.

He is a funny guy, that guy you told him all about. You told that guy that scary guy you told him all about that guy the funny guy you told him all about him. He is a funny guy. You do not know him. Not really. But you did see him. And you did tell him that you did see him. You saw him do what he did do, that strange and funny guy.

You saw him making fun. Making fun of drunken guys. They were being rude of course. Being rude to some cute girl. The girl of course was used to it. Of course she was so used to it and able to get over it and easily she handled it. She handled those drunk guys. Then, from out of nowhere, he was there. He came from out of nowhere and he got there suddenly. Like a hero he was there, and he was, clearly, he was there, and he came from out of nowhere. Like a hero. He was there. Did she need him? She did not need him, but he was there, and he was, clearly, he was there, and he started to make fun of those drunken guys.

He was funny, he was smart; like Groucho smart; like Chaplin smart; Bugs Bunny smart; like biting, friendly, wicked smart. Taunting, he was taunting, and the boys they were not daunting. They were more than he, but, clearly, he was totally in charge. Then they laughed, they had to laugh, the whole of them they had to laugh. He made them laugh. All of them did laugh, except for one. And the one who did not laugh wanted then to fight.

The guy, he did not seem to mind, he did not seem to mind at all. To fight for him was as fine as not to fight at all. He seemed to like to fight. He was smiling when he knew. He knew the boy would want to fight. He knew he would not back away. The boy, he would not back away. And so the guy, the funny guy, he smiled as if to say that fighting was the best thing that could happen there.

And the girl did try to make it stop. She tried to make it all just stop. She did not want the two to fight. She was all right, she was OK, she did not need his help.

He was trying to impress her. She thought so, the boy, he also did think so. And probably she was impressed. He thought so, the boy thought so, and probably the guy thought so. He was like a knight. A shiny cartoon knight.

Then they started to fight and it was something else. He was like Zoro, but he didn't have a sword. He was a master of kung fu with his own invented style. A crazy style, a wacky style, a nothing-like-you've-ever-seen style. No one has ever seen a person fight this way before.

For us, it was a movie; like watching a good movie. He did

not hurt the boy. He made a fool of him. The boy was drunk. It was easy for the funny guy to beat him. But he did not hurt him. He ducked all hits and laughed and only tripped the boy and pushed the boy aside. The boy was getting tired fast, the guy could go all night, you could see that he could go all night.

The other boys who teased the girl, they took the boy away. The boy was angry, but the other boys, they took the boy away. He did not stand a chance against the funny wicked guy. That guy could really fight. He clearly loved to fight. He was a natural at fighting. And he didn't hurt the boy. He just played him like a fool. He could really move. He was so fast. He was so smooth. It was fun to watch him move. Like a silent movie star.

Charlie Chaplin was that way. So fast. So smooth. So funny too. That's the way, that guy, he was.

We knew he did it for the girl, that he did it to impress her. He said something that made her laugh and clearly he impressed her. And when he said the thing that made her laugh, he smiled and then he disappeared as quickly and as suddenly as when he did appear. We did not hear what he did say and we didn't see him go away. But he did it for the girl and the girl she was impressed.

The snake he is so cool and the snake he is so charming. And the snake is very careful not to be someone who alarms anyone he's talking to. He's careful not to trouble the young woman who is telling him the story she is telling him. She has said so much and she has told him lots. There is always some-one who always tells him lots because the snake is always charming. It is so good to be so charming and still not to be alarming to anyone who's living there.

Anyone who's living there is often young and often there to study or simply be an artist there or simply be someone who's always hanging out in there. There are many places there to just hang out and hang around and be around and check out both the sights and sounds of anything that goes by and anything that's there. And drinking this and drinking that and doing this and doing that and spending time and passing time and not much holding onto time.

Anybody might be strange and anybody might be odd and anybody feels they do or feels they don't belong. They are they, it's said by them who come to see them there, or come to visit there, to be like those who do live there, when clearly they do not live there to anyone who does live there it is clear for them to see. They are they to those outside, but not to those of them right there. They might be this, they might be that, and often they do know themselves to see themselves, if even they don't know themselves too deeply. But they are one and they are two and sometimes three or more. Some they know and some they don't, and they are them to them outside, and not so much to them themselves. And when they are, it will be over.

Now they know some and can see some and not see some if they care to not care to. So many living there together are not there to live together. They live together naturally. But they are not together.

So many strange together, not being strange together, and not being there together, means that they are being what you might call natural, and they are used to it, so they are not careful. Not always being careful. Not always being watchful. For the snake that's something good. Because he's strange because he's odd that is something good.

For the monkey this is also good. Because he's strange because he's odd this is also good. And for the snake it's good that being strange and being odd makes it good to come around in here. The monkey's come around in here because it's good to come around in here, because it's good if you are strange or odd.

And now the snake has been around and the snake has asked around and now the snake has also found that the monkey's been around. And now he knows a little more. He knows the monkey hangs around. He knows the monkey can be found. He knows the monkey talks to girls. And maybe girls talk back to him. And maybe girls have gone with him. Maybe they have been with him. Maybe one has been with him. Maybe one who's been with him will tell a tale of him, will tell the snake about him, will tell him more about the monkey.

There might be one who's been with him and she will talk about it now, she will tell about it now, tell the snake about it now, and tell him what he needs to know he needs to know some more right now. The snake he needs to know some more, and he needs to know it now. He needs to know important things, and he needs to know some more, and he needs to know it now.

There are some things the snake does know. The snake does know some things. He does know some important things. He knows there is a weakness. The monkey has a weakness. He knows that he is vain. And it often is a weakness if anyone is vain.

He knows he does not hide. The monkey does not hide, he likes to come outside. He likes to come outside and play around with boys and girls. He likes to fight with boys and stir up girls and make a big impression; to show the girls the way he is and be impressed with how he is.

He is that way, and in that way, he likes to show the way he is, and when he shows the way he is, is anyone impressed? Is any girl impressed? He is that way and is there one who is impressed with how he is? Is there a girl impressed with how he is? Is there a girl out there who is impressed, who wants to know, who was impressed, and wanted then to know and then did get to know him better? And then got to know him better?

3

THE TIGER IS IMPRESSED ENOUGH to want to know him better. But she is not the one the snake is hoping she would be. She is not the one he would be thinking of at all. She is a quiet one. And she is a deadly one. She has power. She has grace. She is agile too, fast and smooth.

All three of them have power, Monkey, Tiger, Snake, but in different ways. Her way is a prepared way and a forceful way. She is like a tiger. She does not look like one. She is one inside. Not one looks outside the way they are inside. They do not look like what they are. They are what they are inside; their outside is like anyone. They're like anyone at all outside, but they are different in themselves inside.

She strikes with speed. She strikes with force. She stalks her prey. Make no mistake — she does have prey, she will have prey. But she is good, so very good, so very, very just and good. What does that mean? She's a hero. Fights for good. Defeats the bad. No one fools with her; to fool with her is bad. She is good and she is strong and she is fast and she knows right from wrong.

She is the tiger and she is one but she is also one of them and who are they? They are who they are and no one knows just who they are. No one knows in total who they are. No one knows the whole of it, of who they are. But they are there and they help out. Whoever is in charge of the people there at large. They are there to help them out.

They are not the government but they are working when and where they can with them. They're a secret group of people and think they know what's right. They want to make it happen, to make the right thing happen. Sometimes governments and they are not in agreement. And that's a reason why they are a secret. Sometimes they don't agree. They do not interfere, but they clearly don't agree. They might lend a hand where hands are not meant to be lent. They must lend a helping hand when they know that it is right. But they do not interfere; at least not so much outright.

In secret and in silence they do what they must do; helping out and doing right and fighting all great evil in the hearts of all who live for bad. They try to do some good. And they do it very quietly. They do not say that they are there or they are one of them.

They are small. They are not big. Together they are who they are; there is no one who's in charge of them. They are doing what they do by all of them deciding what it is that they are doing.

They work together and alone, but together or alone, they work for what they all do say is what they all do want. They all do want, they say they do, they think they do, they all do want the same thing. They want to help to make things good.

What is good? They think they know. When it's hard to know then it is hard to know, but when they know they know they know and they are sure to act upon it, to act on what they know. They work it out. What's good is what is good when it is said that it is good, naturally. And when there's good you work for good or else you work for bad. Of course it's only said that way and there is much that's in between. But when it's said and you agree perhaps you do agree, and if you do and when you do then you do agree, and that is when they also do, they also do agree, naturally. Anybody could and anybody would and anybody will agree, and so of course will they.

For her, it's a vocation. It's not a job for her. It's a way of life for her. It is there. It is always there. And she is glad that it is there and always there. She does not rest from it. Rest assured that she is resting well in it by being there inside of it. It being there inside of her, it's just the same as being her.

She is who she is, and she is that. She is working that and being that, both through and through. She belongs there. She's the best there. Do not mess with her. She is deadly when she needs to be, she's a warrior for sure.

So what does she think about the monkey? He is cute but he is bad. Is he cute because he's bad? In the way that he is bad there is a way that he is cute. Because the way that he is bad could be a way that he is good. And he could be good — very good.

He is something else. Exceptional. Very bright. Very strong. Very quick to move very quickly. He can fight. He can really fight. If he had a way that was a moral way then he certainly would be someone that really could belong with them.

He could belong with us, she thinks. We are small in size but great in force. And we do good. At least we try. We try to make it better. We can help to make it better. He could help us help to make it better.

There are those who cannot help. They can only hurt. Some are mean, mean and malignant. Some are really menacing. And we need some help to slow them down. He could help us slow them down. He could be good. But he needs help.

He cannot yet control himself. He needs a goal, a lofty goal. He needs to have a way. He needs to learn a way to do the best of what he now does do without so much as thinking; it would do him good to do some thinking. If he could see that discipline is not just something from outside that does not have a life inside then he might see that discipline is something that is interesting. It could be good for him. We could work a bit on him. And maybe work with him.

They agree he could be good. She could be right. He could be good. And yes they say that she should do whatever she thinks she should do to help him be a help to them. And go ahead and work it out. Find out more and check him out. Be discreet. Can you hide successfully or will he know that you are there? Will he see that you are there and see that you are there to see what kind of person he might be?

No, she knows that he won't know. He will not know that she is there unless she lets him know she's there. And she won't let him know she's there until she wants it known she's there. She's a stalker who's sublime in her ways so natural for her to be the way she is.

He is so sure so very sure he's much too sure that it's just him, that there's no one else who is like him who is like the monkey. When he goes the way he goes he does not think that there could be anyone who follows him. He looks from time to time he looks to see but who could there be that's near to him, staying near and close to him while he is going like he goes? Who could go along with him or follow him? Who could do that? He does not think there is someone who could ever do that. No one could ever keep up with him. Over his shoulder from time to time he might just take a look. But he does not think that he will see someone there who's there to see.

But she is there and she has seen him and he has not seen her there to see him. She has been watching him, the tiger. Longer than the snake has known about the monkey, she has known about the monkey, the tiger. And now she knows about the snake as well. She is that good.

Well she knew about the snake in any case. She knew about the snake from way before. The snake he does not know her. The monkey does not know her. She knows about the snake. She knows about the monkey. She does not know them; really know them. But she knows about them. And that is more than they can say about knowing about her today.

Her group has known about the snake. Her group has thought about the snake. Could he be good? Could he belong?

Once they thought he might belong, once they thought the snake might go along with them. But the snake does not belong with them and he cannot go along with them. The snake does not belong with them or with anyone at all. The snake belongs to no one but himself.

The snake does have a group that he likes to go along with. But that group is not the group that the tiger goes along with. The snake belongs to no one but he goes along with them. They are not a force of good. They are more a force of bad. The snake does not belong to them but he likes to go along with them. He works with them. He works for them. And sometimes they are helping him. And mostly they are leaving him alone to do what he does best by doing it alone unless he needs or wants a lending hand and then they lend a hand to him.

She did not ask the snake to join. She knew there was no point in that. She didn't even say Hello, I know I see that you are good at what it is that you can do and what you do is what you are and you are good at what you are and would you like to do some good by being good at who you are and what you do and do some good? She didn't even try. It was clear to her at once to her that he was not that way and would not want to be that way and spend his power in that way to try and do some good. He could not be with them. He would not join a group like that. He would not come with them. He would not go with them. The only way that he would go was in the way that he would go by being by himself, devoted to himself and anyone that he was with was with him for his sake.

Maybe he was not so bad. Maybe he was just that way and maybe that was not so bad as bad as doing bad but was just not there to just do good. It might be that his group was bad but he was not so clearly bad so much as not that clearly good. He might not be so clearly good and maybe not so clearly bad. In any case, they did not ask and would not ask the snake to come along with them for they were clearly good it seems and the tiger too was good it seems and the snake was clearly not so clearly good it seems.

4

HE'S NOT CHEAP — THE SNAKE. He's not common, either. He needs to have a challenge. He likes to get around things. He doesn't like for there to be a barrier of any kind. He must be free to move and be and go whichever way he wants to go to any-where he wants in any way he pleases. His group likes that he is like that. They like to go where he can go and he can nearly go to anywhere. They like to go where they can't go, where they are not allowed to go, and he can go there usually. He can go wherever he wants to go to, usually. He can get through any door, any window, any lock and all alarms, usually.

He does not lock his own place up. He does not bother doing that. He doesn't need to worry. When you know the people that he knows you never need to worry. They have a debt to him and so they take good care of him. They are strong and not so nice the people that he knows. But knowing them it gets for him a chance to never worry that anyone would take from him or try to do some wrong to him.

He knows people, powerful people. People who owe him and do not own him. They are not so very nice these people. They are very dangerous these people. So why should he worry?

Who would dare do anything to him knowing who he has to help and who they'd have to deal with?

That sassy monkey took something; he took it from the snake. What nerve he has to take something from someone like the snake; the snake who knows who he does know, the snake who's like how he is like. The monkey took something, and the snake he wants it back.

The snake of course is no one's fool. And the snake of course he is no fool. He can see quite easily that the monkey has a specialty, and that it's valuable. The monkey could be valuable. He wants to get the thing he took, he wants to get it back, but he also wants to see if he should get the monkey too. The monkey could be very good to have around and help. If the monkey could go where he's gone and do what he has done, then the monkey could be very good to help and have around. The monkey and the snake could be a deadly team.

5

THE TIGER KNOWS ABOUT THE SNAKE but doesn't know the snake is looking for the monkey. She doesn't know the monkey's gone and stolen something valuable. But she has kept an eye on him. She has been watching him. She studies him. She's tracking him. And she's keeping track of what he does to see if when he does do things he does them in a routine way. Is there anything that he does do that he does do more usually then anything that he might do just sometimes or occasionally? And does he do it in a routine way, whatever he does do whenever he does do it? She looks for patterns in behavior. And she has been checking him for patterns. And she knows where he does go, where he often hangs out mostly.

She saw him go into the snake's place. That made her worry just a bit. Then she saw him leave again, and leave there rather suddenly. He left a little suddenly; a little bit more suddenly than what is normally the case for him as far as she can tell. And it worried her a bit.

And then she saw the snake peek out. And then she was concerned. The monkey was already gone but still she was concerned. If the snake had seen the monkey then he would want to know just who the monkey was and where the monkey was and if the monkey was someone the snake could make some use of. The monkey could be valuable and anyone could see that.

The snake could be so charming and make you want to know him and make you want to be with him and want to hang around with him and do with him the things he does and that could be a thing that's bad unless you're strong inside and know yourself inside and can be yourself inside and stay yourself inside and keep him from inside you and keep him there outside you. The snake is very tempting. He seems so reassuring and he's very much alluring as he goes about persuading you to come and join his group. His group is bad.

He will tempt you. He will have you. He will use you and be done with you. His group will simply own you and you will never own yourself again.

The tiger doesn't know if the snake can find the monkey, but anything could happen. Something might transpire between the monkey and the snake. The tiger does not want to lose the monkey to the snake. She must meet the monkey before the snake can find the monkey. She was going to wait some more but now she cannot wait some more. She must do what must be done and she must do it soon.

The tiger too is charming. She is very charming. It can be quite alarming just how charming she can be. Of course she can be sexy. She can be very sexy. She also is alluring. She's very much alluring. Being how she is, attractive like she is, she is of course bewitching, and it always is confusing and it makes it hard to think.

If you think that she is beautiful, both sexy and quite beautiful, then you will certainly agree that it's very hard for you to think straight whenever she's around. It is something that she does. It is something she can do. It all confuses you. Your thinking is not clear. Your judgment is not clear. She clouds your mind, and then it's hard for you to reason properly. Your attention is then drawn aside and she has you then quite easily.

She defeats you easily. If you are an enemy and you are caught like this, she will have you easily; she will have beaten you quite easily.

You will have to be quite strong, quite strong within your mind and in your body and your soul. You will have to have a will that wills itself alone. You will have to have a focus and be determined too. If you are a narcissist, then that might help sometimes, although it's true that being that will also mean that there's a weakness there in you. And if there is a weakness there that is inside of you, then she will find it out and stalk it down and use it against you. Vanity loves flattery and that can be distracting. And if you are distracted by the tiger, then you will be prey to her and will be vulnerable to her.

It's a good thing that she's good and that she fights for good.

She must meet the monkey before the snake does meet the monkey. She must meet the monkey now. She must get to know him so she can speak with him and be open and be frank with him. She must be a friend. She must truly be a friend. And she must help him see the peril of the snake. And he must come be on their side and fight for good and not for bad.

The monkey seems endearing, but the situation he's created could be dangerous.

And what if he is just a brat?

6

POOR MONKEY. DOES HE HAVE SOME FRIENDS? Not really, and he likes it just like that. He likes his secret life, his no-one-knows-him life. He is anonymous. Sometimes he likes to play that he is like a superhero. But although he might be super, he is not a superhero. And he's not a supervillain either. He's a super something else.

His identity is secret but he has no alter ego. Although his ego is an altar and he often worships there. The whole of him is secret but plain enough to see. He does not hide behind a mask like heroes have to do, pretending that they're normal when they're really something else. It's just that no one gets close enough to really know him.

He is not a lonely person. There are girls who really like him. He has fun with them. They have fun with him. He is always there with them whenever he is there with them and he is always at their place. They are never at his place.

But of course he does not linger. He does not stick around. And that is really fine by them. That is really mostly fine by them. He really can be tiring. He really can be just too much. He's always on and all the time he's really going on a lot. He's

always going on. He's really something else, and he's always
something else. He's never just a normal thing, an ordinary quiet
thing. He's always larger than life and he's never really small.

He's the kind of guy that kind of drives you crazy when he
stays around too long. He never is relaxing much. He's nothing
to ignore. And mostly people like to be with someone they
eventually can comfortably ignore. He would drive you crazy if
he stayed there long enough.

He's hit and run, an accident, a really thrilling accident,
and when he goes they do not mind they really do not seem to
mind. They know what they are in for. They see it from a mile
away. He is not someone to have and hold from this day forward.
He will not be had. That is very clear.

But he is fun he can be fun for any girl with time for fun; for
any girl who likes some fun and doesn't mind that it's just fun.
It's fun for her and fun for him. And that is all it is. It's fun. But
that is all it is.

He does not need to be in love, right now. He likes attention,
though. Maybe he will change some day. He is still young and
when he's not as young as he is young right now then maybe he
will change in that he'll want to be in love.

He is still young and still excited about everything he does.
His secret life excites him. It is extraordinary, and so of course is
he. He is extraordinary, and why then should his life not be? His
life is what it is and it is not ordinary. So why should he behave
as though his life were ordinary? He should behave he does
behave like it is something else and he is something else.

This monkey's full of energy. Why should he settle down?
He's not the type to settle down.

He only laughs at anyone who tries to have control of him.
He has no time for anyone who wants to have control of him. He
is too preoccupied with what he wants to do. He is a bit too
much you see for anyone it's true.

Why would anybody want to be with someone who's so
obviously so selfish and so vain? But he is tempting very tempting,

so full of life is he, so exciting can he be, entertaining he can be and funny he can be, so full of beans is he.

But of course, he is so charming and good-looking, and he moves the way he moves, and that body. What a body. And he's smart, he's really smart, he's clever, funny, bright and smart.

How can you help yourself and keep yourself from liking him? He really is exciting and he really is quite interesting. He is not a bad man. He is immature. But he is not a bad man. Oh, you'd love to slap him. But you'd also like to have him. He is a sexy man; a young and sexy man.

And yes the sex with him is good. He is not predictable. He comes to you with passion, with a hunger, with finesse, and he pays attention to you, listening deep and carefully to you, and then it's like he's trying hard to keep himself from ravishing you totally.

And when it's over and he's gone, you don't mind it that he's gone. You don't mind it when he goes away and you don't see him again. He's a bit too much. He's a bit too much. He has too much intensity. He's like a small vacation, a sexual vacation.

Anyway, it would not be a good thing to fall in love with him. Everything you'd give to him, your body you would give to him, your mind and soul you'd give to him, and most of all your heart to him you'd give away your heart to him and what would he return. He would give you pleasure with his body and his mind, but he would keep his soul from you and would not give his heart to you. He is just not ready yet to give his heart and soul away.

With the trinket in his hands, he smiles now thinking of someone who was someone he was with before, who was lovely to be with before, and he wonders what it's all about, that wanting to be with someone. He has the trinket in his hands. And while he thinks he tosses it and catches it and tosses it and catches it.

He throws it up, it's in the air, and while the thing is still up there, he does a little handstand and grabs it with his feet. He's something of a show-off. He cannot help himself. He's showing off to just himself, but still he's showing off.

He's not a bad guy. He's the monkey. He can't keep still. And while his body moves around his mind is moving too, thinking this and thinking that and thinking this way, thinking that way. Thought to thought and thought to thought and thinking thoughts, his flitting thoughts, are going just along that way. They play out in his mind that way, in the front part of his mind that way. But in the back part of his mind, in the part that's just behind his mind, there is something that is going on, something different going on. That's the place that is the place where nagging does go on, and there's something there that's way back there that is nagging him right now.

There is something nagging him. He is trying to ignore it. He doesn't like the nagging. He never likes the nagging. No one likes the nagging. What is it that is nagging him? What could be there nagging him. Everything is A-OK. But there is something nagging him.

Something there behind his mind keeps knocking at the door. It's knocking at the door and it wants to come inside. It wants to come inside and it wants to hang around.

It bothers him. It worries him. It bothers him that it worries him. He is not the kind of guy who usually does worry. He has no time to worry. And what is there to worry for?

There is certainly no worry when it comes to having money. He has enough money. For now he has enough. In any case he has enough money that it doesn't warrant worry. His inheritance was large.

His parents both have died and they left him lots of money. They died when he was younger than he even is right now. Not too long ago they died. But long ago is different when you're young from when you're old. And when you are much older than you were when you were younger, then long ago back then seems quite different from now. They died when he was young, when he was a young teenager. But now he is an adult, although he is a young adult.

His parents were professionals. His parents they were scholars. They came from what is often called old money. When anybody comes from what is often called old money, then it often means that no one knows just where the money came from.

It is a bit mysterious. What they did and who they were and where their money came from is a bit mysterious. But he's never been that curious. He can be really curious about some things sometimes. But he's never been that curious about his family. He doesn't know that much about it and he doesn't seem to care.

They were isolated. He was an only child, and they were isolated. He was brilliant as a child. He didn't have to go to school. They taught him on their own. They had their own ideas. They taught him everything.

And when he was sixteen they gave him his own place. They put him in a loft and they left him on his own. They left him so that he could do whatever he did want to do and do it privately.

He loved his mom and dad. He got on well with them. They were more like colleagues then they were like mom and dad. And that was very good for him and that was very fine with him. That was very fine.

He was very sad of course when he found out they had died. Apparently a plane had crashed. They had a private plane and apparently it crashed. When their lawyer came to see him, that is what their lawyer told him. The lawyer told him that his parents died when they were flying in their plane. The plane had crashed and they were dead and no one found their bodies. They could not find their bodies in the wreckage of the plane.

The lawyer told him everything about the money they had left him. They had taken care of him. They had been prepared just in case something did happen. They made sure to make provisions in case there was a tragedy, so that everything would be ok. He was set for life.

There was a letter that they left him and the letter explained more. The letter told him how the lawyer would be there if ever he did need him. And the letter told him he would get some help from people with his money.

The monkey was no fool; he would not be ripped off or duped or taken for a ride by anyone at all. But he knew that he could trust the ones his parents chose for him. He knew these people would be honest when they came to do their job. His parents were not fools. They would not be mistaken about anyone they hired.

The people were good people. They helped out the monkey a lot. His money was invested, it was very well invested, and he did not need to worry about ever having money.

As for who his parents' parents were, he didn't have a clue. He did not know an uncle and he did not know an aunt. Of course he had no cousins then, or if he did, he did not know he did. His mom and dad were all the family he had ever known. They were all of anyone that he had ever known and loved.

So now he is alone. But he doesn't really mind. Of course he's sad and misses them, but they brought him up to be a person who is quite content to be the only one who is around and love himself, enjoy himself and be his only company.

He is alone and by himself but he does not feel that he is lonely. He is too excited about everything there is that is always going on. He doesn't need to have someone. He's an independent person. It might come to be someday that he will come to need someone. Maybe one day he will need someone to keep him company. If he does then when he does he will deal with it.

Of course it just might happen that the money gets all spent or gets lost through bad investment. The money may not last forever it is true. He may have to get a job or figure out a way that he can earn it by himself. He might have to do something in order to make money one day. But for now, that is a bridge that he does not have to cross. For now that is a bridge that he doesn't even see. He has not come yet to that bridge. And if he does then when he does he's sure that he will cross it. He doesn't have to worry now, so of course he doesn't worry now.

For now, he's very cool. He's set up very nice, and he lives in a nice place. It doesn't cost a lot and it is a really nice place. He likes the way it is. It's a really nice place for him. He doesn't need his place to be a really fancy place. He doesn't like to have to pay too much attention to it. He doesn't like to be the type that fixes up a place. He spends more time outside than he does spend time inside.

It's important that it is comfortable for him and it's got to be that way just by being what it is. He doesn't have the patience to make it be that way. It's got to be that way and feel that way from the moment he moves in. And his place does that and so that's great, that's just the way he likes it, great. He likes to go outside a lot and when he comes back home and comes inside he likes it when it's comfortable and it's like that right away.

He likes to get up in the morning, get up early in the morning, and when he gets up in the morning right away he goes outside. He likes to go outside and he likes it in the city, especially in the city when it's morning in the city. He likes the city morning. He loves the city morning before everyone gets up and everybody goes to work. He gets up and he goes outside and runs around and hangs around and lies around on rooftops looking at the morning sky.

It is quiet in the morning and it really is sublime. When the big bad city's in repose, when everything is sleepy, the light it has a certain way of being sleepy too. The light it is exquisite when it is this time of day. The light is blue, it's much more blue, it's all so clear and blue, and it reminds him of the sky. And he looks up at the sky.

The air is clear. It's quiet there but sometimes you hear birds. Sometimes you can hear birds. The light is blue. The air is clear. The air is fresh and clear. And the sky is getting bigger by the moment.

The sky is opening itself up to a bright and clear forever going up and on before you, opening itself before you, going on forever for you, opening itself forever, going on forever for you, widening before you, and getting higher for you. And everything is soft, and everything is clear, and everything that is the world feels absolutely near.

The city vibrates always, when it's wide awake and going, when its engine's fully going, and the world seems very far away. It is a world, of course it is, the city is a world inside. But though it is a world inside there is another world outside and that world that is outside seems very far away when the world that is inside is going through its day.

But when it is the morning, very early in the morning, the motor of the city is idle and it's waiting. And while it is within that state, the state when it is idle, the city is a thing that's pure potential while it's waiting, and in that state of waiting it has a beauty he admires.

When he sleeps he does not sleep a lot. He sleeps some hours here, and he sleeps some hours there. He sleeps here and there and on and off. He likes to try and be outside for all the different times of day and all the different times of night.

He knows that in the afternoon, the mid to later afternoon, he knows that people are the least attentive and alert. This is when he usually will go inside somebody's home and have a look around. He is very careful to make sure that no one's there and won't be there, they won't be coming home at any moment soon. His instinct is tuned into that, he has a good instinct for that.

Did his instinct fail him at that place the other night, when the guy came in and almost caught him? That is what is nagging him. That is what is knocking at the door to get inside. And he does not want to let it in. It is a question that is good that he doesn't want to deal with. The answer to that question could present him with a problem.

It was a situation that was exceptional. And the fact of that is also something that is also nagging there at him. And it could make him wonder if his skill was still OK. And it could make him wonder if this was someone who had a skill that was equal to his own.

Was that why his instinct did not register at all? Was that why he did not hear him coming like he normally he always can from like a mile away? And was that why he did not feel him coming like he normally he always can from like a mile away?

He usually could tell someone was coming way ahead of time and long before they got there. By the time they usually got there he was far away from there. They would not see him leaving. He'd be far away from there.

But this one saw him leaving. He was the exception, the exception to the rule. He has never met someone; the monkey's never met someone exceptional like that. He has never met someone special in the way he is, and he has never met someone who is maybe like the monkey is.

There was something there about him, this guy he could not hear, this guy he could not feel. There was something there about him that left a clear impression, but the monkey wasn't clear what it was or what it meant. But it's clear the clear impression left him with a feeling and it clearly was disturbing.

There's a little bell that's ringing, an alarm bell that is ringing, but it's ringing very low. It's warning him, it's telling him, that he should watch himself. But he isn't really hearing it. He is a bit disturbed. He feels a little bit perturbed. But he doesn't feel the danger. He doesn't feel in danger.

The guy came in without the monkey knowing but the monkey got away. The call was close but still the monkey got away. There was no threat that he could think of, at least not clearly think of. But the thought of someone like him, who had almost nearly caught him, who was someone that he did not know, was somehow vaguely threatening. Mostly though the monkey's only curious to know. Who was that guy? What was that guy? That is what he'd like to know.

The monkey did consider that his skills were failing him, at first. But now he wonders if that guy could be someone with special skills just like he has himself. Maybe he has special skills just like the skills the monkey has. Or maybe he has special skills the monkey does not have.

What kind of a guy is a guy the monkey cannot tell is coming? What kind of a guy is a guy that he cannot detect? The monkey is so good at knowing when someone is coming in. When he's in some place he broke into he usually can tell when someone's coming in.

If he were alert as he always usually is, if he did not slip up in any way that he can tell, then it must be that this guy is quite exceptional. Perhaps he is the kind of guy that is the kind of guy the monkey is. The monkey's not exactly what you'd call an ordinary guy.

And as he thinks about this guy and studies what he stole from him, it starts to be intriguing, and a little bit exciting, to think that there is someone out there who could be someone who's similar to how the monkey is. It stirs in him a thing that's never been stirred up before. He wonders what it would be like to know someone like that, to know someone who's similar to how the monkey is.

Why would it ever be the case that the monkey was the only one who was the way he was, special in the way he was, special and exceptional? He was a special one.

It only makes good sense that if there is someone like that, who is special in a way like that, that naturally there also can be someone else like that who is special too like that. There could be two like that who are special both like that.

And if there could be two then there also could be three. And if there could be three then there also could be four. And if there could be four, then who could say how many more than four there could really be? There could be really more than four, there could be many more.

He knows of course that he himself is not like everyone. And he knows of course that maybe he is not the only one. But he has always been the one, the only one that he has known who was anything like him. His parents were quite special but they were not like him. They were quite smart and interesting but they were nothing like a thing like him.

They knew of course that he was odd and beautifully strange. But they did not point it out to him. They let him find it out by living his own life. He realized it when he got to know some ordinary people. And when he knew that he was strange they helped him know how beautiful it was to be that strange. And they helped him to affirm it and they helped him to develop it.

They taught him about people who would want something from him to improve their lot through him. They taught him all about the different types of people he might meet. And they helped him hone his skills to know and find out who was trust-worthy. And they made him strong within himself, and made him so that he could be quite happy and content to be his one and only company.

Ordinary people were nice enough sometimes. Some of them he found attractive and fun to hang around with. But sometimes he was feeling that he had a clear advantage over ordinary people. And that is why he more or less prefers to be alone. But if there were someone who was a bigger challenge to him, then maybe it would be more interesting to hang around with them.

So it was intriguing for him to think about this guy. And it made him feel a little better to think his instincts were OK and that his skills were still OK. And it made him think excitedly that maybe he could even get his skills to be a little better than they were. Maybe with a challenge his skill set might improve. He thought he might just like to try and meet this guy sometime. And the thought that he might do that intrigued him certainly.

When he looked at the thing he took from the guy who was someone he now thought might be like him he wondered if there was something that he could see about him there. Some-times he does see things about the person in the things he takes from people. But they are ordinary things he sees about ordinary people. Maybe he would see something extraordinary here.

He looked at the thing. He had been thinking all along that it only was a trinket. A knick-knack. That is what he usually takes. He takes them and he tries to see if he can tell something from them. Sometimes he will keep them, and sometimes he will not. Sometimes he likes to bring them back and wonders if they notice, and wonders what they wonder when they notice that it's gone, and wonders what they wonder when they notice that it's back. It makes him chuckle when he thinks of how confounded they could be.

He looks then at the thing and he can see that this thing has some kind of meaning. And he can see it there. He cannot see the meaning, the specifics of the meaning. But he can definitely see that there is some meaning there. It's plain to see that certainly this thing has got some meaning. It could be just a knick-knack, it could be just a toy, it could be just a trinket, but there is something there about it that tells you it is more. It is not a knick-knack and it is not a toy and it is not a trinket. It is something that has meaning. He cannot see the meaning. But he can see that certainly there is some meaning there.

What the thing exactly was did not exactly matter. Of course it did not matter. It never really matters. Although it always matters, it never really matters. It matters in the way that it is something made to matter. But what it is exactly is nothing much that matters. It matters that it is a thing that often makes things happen in a way that's different from how those things normally are happening. And it matters that it is a thing that has in it some feelings, that makes you have some feelings that are a mystery, that always have some meaning, that make you have some feeling, and make you powerful in the way that they connect you to yourself and also to the world.

The thing looked like a hood piece from a car from long ago, a fancy ornament from a car from long ago. But it was more than that for sure. You could see it if you looked at it. And anyone could look at it. The monkey was quite good at it, at looking at and seeing it. He looked at it quite closely and saw that it was there. He looked at it from far away and saw it there as well. He put it on his nose and balanced it and still he saw it there. With it balanced on his nose he went backward with a flip and it flew from off the tip of where he balanced it before, and as it fell toward the floor he caught it with his feet, and with it in between his feet he lay down on his back and he brought it to his face and he turned the thing around, he is quite dexterous, and he turned the thing around and round between his feet before him and he saw it still he saw it there.

He took it in his hands and he sat up and he looked at it at what he saw and wondered what it was. Maybe he could work it out, figure it out and find it out. There was a presence there.

There was the kind of presence that was there because it was something that meant something to someone. When something means that much to someone and they handle it and think of it and put in it their thinking and their feeling then the thing takes on a presence, it has a kind of presence. Of course it was a mystery exactly what was meant to be the thing that it was meaning. But there was there a presence that told you there was meaning there, despite the fact that you would say you could not say just what it was the meaning was or what it meant to say or what the meaning meant to be, you certainly could say that there was something there that meant something. What could it be?

He was curious of course, but to really work it out would take a lot of work and a lot more effort then he felt he could commit to give right now. The thing was curious and the guy was curious and it made him curious to know about him more. The thing was something else all right and the guy was something else all right and the monkey well he too was something else all right.

Well maybe it was not so good that he took something this time that was something else this time. He never did take something that was something else before. It must be something valuable. It must be something valuable and important to the guy. And if it's something valuable and important to the guy then he probably will miss it.

He will likely be the kind of guy who is missing it right now. And of course the guy walked in while the monkey was still there and he caught a glimpse of him, he must've caught a glimpse of him. And since he caught a glimpse of him he must be thinking that the monkey took this thing that he likely now is missing and he would be right in that to be right now thinking that.

Perhaps the guy has called the cops. Of course, he only caught a glimpse; he didn't really see him. He didn't see him well enough to give a good description. At least the monkey did not think so.

And the monkey knows that if that's true it's just because he's lucky. One more moment could have changed a glimpse into a look. A good look. And a good look would not be good luck.

Of course it doesn't help that the monkey dresses like he does. It's not exactly difficult to see him in a crowd. He may now have to change that, and he doesn't like to change that. He likes his eccentricities.

Luckily, the guy did not get more than just a glimpse of him and likely did not get more than just a little look at him. Probably he did not get what you'd call a real good look at him. So, with so little he can go by, there is little he can do. At least the monkey hopes so. More than likely this is true. At least the monkey hopes so.

Now, it's not like him to be unsure of anything at all. He has great confidence. Everything depends upon his overwhelming confidence. And if he loses just a bit of that, it could gum up all the works. It could slow him down. It could trip him up. It could blow his cool. It could do the kind of things that things don't usually do to him.

It is clear that he must go back there and spy a little on the guy. And he should maybe try and just return the thing he took. But probably he won't do that. He doesn't think that he should do that. At least he should not do that right away. He doesn't want to be inside that guy's place right away again, because he is unsure.

It's not like him to be unsure. But he tells himself it's good. He's only being cautious, and being cautious now is good. Sometimes it is not good. But right now it's good. This is what his instinct now is telling him is good. He can tell there is some danger there. He does not know for sure just what that danger is, but he does know, and he can tell, he sees some signs of danger.

How exciting. An adventure. This could be a challenge. There are different kinds of challenges and this could be the kind he likes. This could be the kind of challenge that really tests his limits and really makes him stronger and really makes him smarter and really makes him more of him, and makes him powerful.

What could happen was intriguing. His heart sped up a little bit when he thought about it all, about going back to try and find out more about this guy, and to find out just how special this guy might really be. He could be someone bad, he could be someone good, but either way he could be someone who was good for him to know. And the monkey wants to know.

7

OF COURSE HE DOESN'T KNOW that the snake is looking for him. He doesn't know the snake is waiting there for him to come back soon. And of course he doesn't know that the tiger's getting ready to go out there and meet him. She is wondering right now how she's going to manage that.

The snake is getting ready to meet the monkey too. And while he's waiting he is thinking now, and he's starting to believe it now, that the monkey won't come back.

He is pretty certain that the monkey's never had to deal before with any disadvantage. But maybe now the monkey's had his first experience of that. Perhaps the monkey was now at a certain disadvantage. Perhaps the snake has thrown him off. And the snake is thinking now that if the monkey is not used to that, then it could be to his advantage to know that it is true.

If it is in fact the truth that the monkey is not used to that, to slipping up and tripping up and being disadvantaged from losing all his cool, then it's likely that the fact of that will throw the monkey off, and it's likely that the fact of that will make the monkey slip some more and trip some more and likely lose his cool some more. And each time that he slips or trips or loses some more cool, he's likely, much more likely, to leave each time a trace that will make it all a little easier for the snake to track him down. Each trace the monkey leaves would help constitute a trail. And if he makes a trail the snake will follow it, and find the monkey at the end of it.

The snake's been out and hanging out and checking it all out, but doing it discretely. The snake is very cautious, so he tries to stay obscure. He knows the monkey hangs around there. He's heard he comes and hangs around there. In time he knows he'll come again, he'll hang around again. It's just a matter of time.

And when he does the snake is sure he'll catch a glimpse of him. And more than just a glimpse of him, he'll get a real good look at him. But the snake must stay unseen.

The snake won't just be standing there or sitting there or generally just being there just waiting for the monkey. He won't just wait around for him and wait for him to show, no, while he waits he also plans to scope the area.

He could employ somebody to do that job for him. He has people he can use to do that kind of thing. But he will not get someone to do that thing for him. He does not want just anyone to know about the monkey yet.

He does not want his people to know about him yet. And he does not want it to be known the monkey stole something. He does not want it known that the monkey got inside. He does not want it known that the monkey got away. He does not want it known that there is someone out there who could get away with that.

Undoubtedly it is the case that pride is uppermost an issue for the snake. More than caring for the thing the monkey took away, the fact the monkey got inside and got away is what is bugging him. Of course the snake does want it back, the thing the monkey took away. And he does not think it will take long or be difficult to do, it won't be hard to do.

He will get his thing back. If he has to, he will kill for it. He will kill the monkey for it. He would kill him for the upset and the bother of it all.

He thinks he has a good idea of where the monkey's living. He thinks he knows the neighborhood the monkey's living in. So he goes out in the morning, very early in the morning, just before the dawn. There is hardly anybody up and out and doing anything when it's early in the morning, very early in the morning. It's a good time to be looking for what he needs to find and it's much easier at that time to stay hidden and unseen. It's good to look around when there's no one else around.

He may not know exactly what it is he's looking for, but he's counting on his instinct and relying on his feelings to send him premonitions and help him on his way. And he's very sharp at seeing things and hearing things and knowing things and what is going on, even if it can't be known by ordinary eyes and ordinary ears and ordinary minds.

He goes out for a while, and then he goes back home, and he then waits and while he waits he gives his strict attention to everything around him. He is the kind of guy the snake that doesn't sleep too deeply. In fact, he hardly sleeps at all. The merest movement or the slightest sound will easily awaken him.

But still, he gets well rested; don't imagine that he won't. It's like a meditation that he goes into. It's like a self-hypnotic state that he wakes up from refreshed without memory or feeling of any kind of stress or any aggravation. It is like the best sleep ever. You've almost never known someone to be as rested as the snake.

While he rests, he pays attention. While he rests, he still is waiting. He is waiting and is listening and is paying strict attention. Especially in the afternoon, he is waiting very carefully. He is waiting for the monkey to come back to his place.

Why does he think the monkey would do a thing like that? It would not be a prudent thing for any thief to do.

But the snake has got a notion that the monkey's not a prudent man. The snake has got a feeling that the monkey's kind of rash. And the snake has got it figured that the monkey's kind of vain. And if the monkey's kind of vain and the monkey's kind of rash, then probably the monkey can be expected to come back.

Also, the snake is pretty sure that precisely since the monkey was almost nearly caught, the monkey's curiosity will get the better of him and will compel him to come back to see what kind of man could be the kind who almost nearly caught him. Because the monkey has his vanity, he'll feel it is a challenge, it will be as if he thought that he'd been bested in a way, and no doubt he is not used to that. And because he is not used to that he will want to come and face again the challenge and defeat it. Because almost nearly being caught is like a small defeat to him, and the monkey would neither like that nor would his vanity accept it. So, it will feel as if he has been bested in a way. Because he has been almost caught, in a small symbolic way, it is as if he were defeated, and the monkey is too vain to accept defeat like that.

It's clear then, that he must come back to reestablish confidence. His confidence was challenged when he was almost nearly caught. And he will want to know about the one who was someone who almost nearly caught him. He will be, the snake does realize, just as curious about who and what the snake is as the snake is about him.

How will it fare, how will it go, the snake is interested to know. When the monkey comes the snake must be careful not to let him see how interested he is. The snake must keep his cool. He must not let the monkey know how much he knows about him. He must not let the monkey know the snake is looking for him. He must not let the monkey know the snake is waiting for him.

What would be best would be to see the monkey come around to see the snake and have it be the snake who sees and not it be the monkey. Then the snake would follow him and find out where the monkey lives. The snake would get the thing the monkey took from him without the monkey knowing that the snake was even there. And then the snake would see about what there was to talk about between him and the monkey. And then the snake would let the monkey come and see him face to face. And then we'd see what we would see.

8

OH, THE SUBTLE TIGER. The tiger now is sizing up the situation in the same way that the snake is. She is just as good at sizing up the situation as the snake is; in fact, she's even better. The tiger's got one over him because she knows about him and the snake knows nothing about her. He doesn't know about her and he doesn't know about her group and what it is they do.

The tiger is a stalker and she's very good at that and she's very good at strategy. Before the monkey meets the snake, before the snake picks up his trail and tracks the monkey down, she knows that she must track the monkey down and meet him first.

So, the tiger has to prowl. She already has been stalking him and has learned about his way of going around and hanging around and breaking into places. Now she has a plan to put herself before him and to do it suddenly so it will be surprising and it will also be intriguing. She also wants to have it look as if she did not plan it. And so she goes and does it.

Early in the morning when the monkey has gone out and the snake is also out, the tiger goes out too.

The monkey now is out and he steers himself toward the place that is the place the snake lives at.

The snake goes out and goes away, he goes away from home. He's going there, he's leaving there, away from there, away from where he calls his home away from where he lives. The snake goes out and goes one way and then he goes another way and then he goes to where he was and then he goes back home. He does this lots of times.

The tiger's out and looking here and looking there and hearing this and hearing that and feeling what is what and picking up the monkey's trail, and it doesn't take her long, it doesn't take a long time for her to pick it up. And it doesn't take a long time for her to spot him moving here and moving there and moving this and that way. He's moving very quickly and every time he moves he seems to move a different way.

He's so obvious he's hard to see, but of course the tiger sees him. And it seems that she is right about him going where she thinks that he does want to go. And she wants to head him off at the pass and stop him now from going there.

All three of them can move so fast and quietly they do it and they smoothly do it too. So gracefully they move that way because they all have purpose. Purpose makes them move that way so fluid in the way they move so certainly they move that way, deliberately they move that way so beautifully they move that way. It would be something you could see if only you could see them, and if you saw them you would say that they were really something.

So, the tiger moving quietly and moving smooth and very fast, she very quickly gets in front of where the monkey's going to, so quickly he is going to, so interesting his movements are, she gets in front of him, and puts herself in front of him so he can run right into her and almost knock her down and get a big surprise from that, a big surprise from all of that. She is very sure of that and she is certainly quite right in that he certainly is very much surprised to find her suddenly in front of him. And almost he runs into her he almost runs right into her and almost knocks her down and he really is surprised by that just like she thought he would be.

The monkey is dumbfounded. How could it ever happen that someone ever could surprise him like the tiger just surprised him? It is so unlikely that he never even thought of it as ever being likely that anyone would ever be so suddenly before him, that there ever would be someone that he never had a sense of and that he almost would run into, would almost run right into and almost knock them down. And because it is so crazy and really so unusual it never even dawned on him that someone might have planned it and someone might have set it up so it would happen just like that just like the way it happened.

He was going he was going strong and strongly he was going and moving very quickly and moving very smoothly and moving in a way like no one else can move with every movement looking like it came from something different there inside of him, going this way like great guns and going there with purpose and that is why he moved that way so quickly and so quietly and moving with such beauty and such strangeness in his form, and here he was now struck quite dumb and once again dumbfounded by the sudden quick appearance of someone that he didn't know could ever be someone who would ever be in front of him without him even knowing that they would be in front of him well before they were and well before he ever would be running into them and almost running them right over and knocking them right down. It really was surprising.

There he was while on his way to meet someone who also did perform this kind of thing with him, the kind of thing that no one else had ever done before, and after getting all worked up to go and meet this guy, and getting ready then to go and meet this guy, getting ready then to go and check him out, she comes out of nowhere and surprises him just like that other guy surprised him. But this was worse because she really came from out of nowhere. And why did he not see her? She was standing there in front of him and how could she be there?

He was all bugged out and that is why he had just gone out

to see this guy, the guy he never knew was coming when he suddenly came home, then bam she's there she's suddenly there, then bam she's there like that, and he never saw her coming, and what is wrong with him that he never saw her coming? He wants to know, he needs to know because he always sees them coming — whoever, anyone and everyone, from a mile away, coming anywhere that's near to him with any kind of interest and with any kind of purpose, he always sees them coming from a mile away.

This is all so strange like nothing like the things that are the things that have a way of happening the way they have of usually happening when they are happening to him. Who is that guy who is this girl and how could this be happening? How could it happen twice? It took this long to make a move regarding what had happened once and just when he had made his move it's gone and happened twice. He really is dumbfounded.

Perhaps it is because that guy has thrown him off so much and now he's thrown him off so much he's thrown him off his game this much that he can be surprised this much by even just someone who happens to be there right in front of him, to be there right in front of him while he is going somewhere. That can happen all the time. It can happen any time, that when you are intent on going somewhere with great purpose and going there deliberately, that you can bump right into things, although, it doesn't happen much to him. But then again, he's never much been so intent on going to somewhere to go and meet someone like he is going to do today; he's on his way to meet the snake. It makes it all the more the case to him, it makes it all too clear to him, that he must meet this guy and he must deal with him, because this guy is throwing him so clearly off his game. He cannot have this happening.

He can't afford to have himself not noticing when ordinary people are getting in his way. Although looking at this person now, looking clearly at this person now, it clearly seems to him right now that she is not so ordinary after all, at least she doesn't look that way. Extraordinary actually, is how he would describe the way she's looking to him now, at least the way that she is looking to him now. And he questions where she came from and how she came from there. From out of nowhere she did come, or was he just distracted, and he didn't see her coming because he was distracted, and she didn't come from nowhere, she came here in a normal way, and he was just distracted, although he sees her now and she really looks like something, she looks like something else.

What's she doing here and doing here right now at this early time of morning, in this time when no one's out here, normally in any case, and moving in a way that he doesn't even notice, even if distracted she must be moving quietly, and certainly she's moving in a fast and agile way? It's obvious she was because she stopped here just in time, before he ran right into her and almost knocked her down, and standing there she's standing there and she has a funny look on her, and his hairs are standing up on end, the small hairs on his arms and neck are standing up on end, and the rush that goes right up your spine whenever you are startled, it's going up his spine right now because he's really startled and it's making him prepared to be prepared for something that might happen, but he doesn't know for what.

His senses are now heightened.

And everything just stops.

And that is an amazing thing whenever that does happen and it doesn't happen often. It very rarely happens and so of course it being that it happens very rarely, it really is extraordinary whenever it does happen and it makes you pay attention to everything around you.

When everything just stops and you look at everything and you pay attention to it, to everything that's there, it all comes into focus. And anything that's moving moves only in slow motion. Like when you see an accident sometimes when you do see one, they often happen just like that. Everything just stops, and whatever's there that's moving is then moving in slow motion.

You might go and say that afterwards, after what you've seen has happened, you might go and say to anyone, well it was just like it was happening all of it was happening like it was going in slow motion, like everything just stopped, and what I could see moving was moving in slow motion. You might go and say that.

And then there is the feeling that you have when you are there and everything has stopped, has suddenly just stopped. And an instant is much longer, it seems to last forever. And many things there are that seem to cross your mind in only just an instant, there are so many things. And the feeling that you have is like you are both there and you are not there, as if you slipped dimensions, and were looking into one, the one you used to be in, from the one you are in now. And each dimension has a way of living in its time. And each sense of time and tempo are very, very different. And there you are, you're out of it, but being that you're out of it, you see it with a detail, and you feel it with a detail that you normally do not. The world has caught its breath and you are in the midst of it.

The world had stopped and there she was a woman most remarkable and looking most exceptional and standing right in front of him and she was smiling now. So, he made sure that his mouth was shut.

When you are stunned sometimes your mouth hangs open like you are and it makes you look like you are stunned and he didn't want to look like that, like he was really stunned. So, he shut his mouth and then moved on, or rather made the move that was the move of moving on from where he was. But when he made that move or made to make that move she suddenly said, 'hello.' And of course he stopped again. And then he just said, 'what?'

It was a 'what' that said 'what the, what,' not just 'what was that,' 'what did you say,' but 'what is this, what's going on?' It all just seemed to be absurd, it really all just seemed absurd. And she just had to laugh. The whole thing was of course absurd and she just had to laugh. And so she did, she had to laugh and so she did she laughed out loud and once again that threw him for a loop, that laugh of hers just threw him for a loop and so he had to stop. He really had to stop and take a look at her, a good long look at her and try and size her up.

When the world stops, that is one thing — when you stop, that's another. He was going, going, gone and now he had to stop to take account of things. And doing that does mean something. And never has he had to do that thing. And that means something too. So he stopped his movement of himself moving out ahead of himself — the movement that he only had to follow. It was his go, go, going, and it ran out far in front of him and that he only had to follow. Now he stopped that movement of all that and settled back into himself and got moved back into himself, back to where he was, and tried to get his bearings and deal with what was what.

And then she leaned toward him and looked like she might kiss him. And he wondered was he drunk? And he wondered was she crazy? And he pulled back just a bit from her and leaned back just a bit from her.

She really was attractive, and he felt the pull of beauty and a lot of sex appeal, but his fire bells were ringing a full force five alarm, but his judgment was impaired and his reflexes did not respond (at least not right away). His instinct was to jump back but it also was to kiss her, and so there was a conflict, and so much for trusting instinct to save you from a jam, it cannot be relied upon to save you all the time.

And she was very close to him, much closer to him than he ever under any normal circumstances when he wasn't in control — so completely in control — would let someone get close to him — even an extremely attractive and mysteriously seductive and completely compelling woman such as this one was. This was all too weird for him it really was too weird and there she was all close to him and he could feel her breath on him and he could smell her smell on her and he was definitely into her and she was leaning close to him but was not really kissing him it seemed that she was sniffing him which really was too much for him and really was quite strange to him and it really turned him on and he really wanted just to grab at her to grab and take a hold of her and have some fucking sex with her — have some crazy mindless sex with her — have some dark and purely animal-like sex with her and have it now right now with her have it now right now right there with her.

But the five alarm was ringing and his warning system screaming, and that does mean really screaming, so much he had to pause and try to think a second.

And in that second that he took to try and think and have a look he noticed she was changing in a way her way was changing, it was a subtle thing but he could tell that she was changing and she was surely up to something. And as soon as he did see that there was surely something coming, the most amazing thing of all surely then did happen.

It was the most amazing thing the most amazing and perplexing thing that had ever happened yet and soon he had to wonder if he hadn't fallen into the twilight zone or something. Because now she had a hold of him and she was surely throwing him super judo style.

And as he flew right through the air the world again just seemed to stop. He could see the world around him and it was as if he stood outside himself and took a look from there to watch himself go flying go flying through the air.

Then everything became quite clear and all the fog was gone and his adrenaline was running running running. And he got his bearings back again and got them in mid-flight and he took control and somersaulted to a smooth and perfect landing.

Incredibly enough she was right there when he landed where he did. And she grabbed at him again. But now he was awake and in his element, and all his thinking at the level of just talking to himself was gone and he was moving in full form and thinking with his spirit and his mind full in his body. He was in full form, full beautiful form. And with great speed and great agility he sprung away from her sprung backward flipping out of reach of her two hands which were trying to grab hold of him. He landed where he did and she was there again. But this time he was ready and he spun around where he had landed and he kicked her in the side, thus moving her aside.

He was totally impressed to see her take and gather up the force of being kicked and transform her falling sideways into doing cartwheels which worked their way toward him coming back again toward him flying in the air toward him when she was near enough toward him like a cannonball toward him rolled up into a ball. And he had to laugh at that. It was audacious and inventive and he had to laugh at that. And he found it was a joy to meet with such a challenge, because it was quite rare.

He caught her up from underneath just like in volleyball and propelled her overhead feeling for an instant like they were a circus act — Ally OOP! — he even said.

But she managed to uncurl herself as her head was passing over his and she grabbed a hold of him, she grabbed him by his shoulders, by the clothing at his shoulders, and with a great display of strength and a brilliant management of the force of her propulsion which was amplified by him as he tossed her overhead she actually did manage to land and carry him up and off his feet so that now he went into the air flying over her.

She spun around to face him where he landed with both grace and ease and with a smile upon his face. There was a smile upon her face as well. She threw a punch at him. Extremely fast she was. But still he saw it coming and he pulled back so she missed him.

But the punch was just a ruse. His dodge put him off balance just enough for her to get him with her follow-up. Her punch became a spin with which she guided herself downward, throwing out a kick to just behind his knees to buckle in his legs.

He went into a handstand and sprung backward and away

from her. When he was upright again and ready for some more, he took a look around, but she was out of sight.

But he did not let his guard down yet and it's a good thing he did not. She sprung out once again from out of nowhere once again and tackled him and knocked him down.

Sitting on his stomach with her knees upon his arms she smiled from up on top of him. He lifted his legs up; he lifted them straight up, like as if to do a backward flip overtop himself and that way also throw her forward and off the top of him. And as he did just that she complied completely with the movement and used the force to gather up her own momentum to do a handstand on his arms which was the first thing that did hurt him and it made him wince a bit. And maybe also for the first time he felt a bit of anger welling up in him.

But as this dangerous emotion was starting then to swell it was just as quickly quelled again overcome by more confusion when she lowered herself down getting close to him again and kissed him on the mouth, kissed him full upon the mouth. The fact of it was not a thing the monkey disagreed with and the pleasure of the kiss was evident to him.

And this quiet riot of confusion in the feelings he was having threw him for a loop enough to give her the advantage of the moment and to use that moment then to flip herself back over and completely out of sight, and right out of the picture, as it were. And although he came up quickly and got right into his stance, it was too late she was now gone and she could not be seen. And this time she did not return.

9

THE MONKEY SURE WAS having a rather strange compelling time of it. Suddenly he realized that he was not alone. He never did feel lonely. But he was certainly alone. And now he knew that he was not, he was not alone. That was rather clear. There were two of them out there. And they were both of them like him, exceptional like him. That was very clear. And that's what made it clear to him that he was not alone.

And ironically enough, now that it was clear that he was not alone, he knew now that he could be, that he could now be alone and now he could feel lonely. He knew it and he knew it was a blessing and he knew it was a curse that he was not alone and that now he could feel lonely. Now everything would change and would it be for better or would it be for worse? He was not sure it would be better, he was not sure it would be worse. It could be good, it could be bad, but he was certainly intrigued.

The girl was gone, for sure she'd gone, he knew for sure that she was really gone this time. She would be back, of course she would, but just not right away. And just who was she anyway? And what did she want anyway, if anything at all? Why'd she flirt with him and why'd she fight with him and why'd she kiss him anyway?

He was certain that, his vanity did make him think that, she had set it up for them to meet up in this way. First meetings when they're set up are often set up to impress. If she did mean to impress him, then she did succeed.

He has done this sort of thing before. He has used some fancy tricks before just to make a big impression on some woman or another. He knows how it is done. He knows the whole routine. But he has never fought with women, he could never fight with them, he has never met a woman with whom he ever could be fighting with in such a playful way, in any sort of way before. And there never was a woman who presented such a challenge, who was so fast and was so strong and looking so remarkable. It really was intriguing.

It was clear that she was trying to make a big impression. That is why she set it up, why she set the meeting up. And that is why she kissed him like she kissed him when she did. And that is why she just appeared as though from out of nowhere. And that is why she disappeared and reappeared and disappeared. BAM! She's here and POW! She's there and ZIP! She's gone away. If she was trying to intrigue him, then it worked. That was very clear to him, that what she planned did work.

But he was worried and he did not like to be like that; he did not like to worry. He was never worried and he never worried, he never, ever did before, and now he worried. And the thing about it was, was that he had a reason to be worried, and that is why he worried, and he didn't like it. In fact he had some reasons, more reasons than just one, or more than even two, he had a few good reasons that he should be definitely worried now.

If he was right about her, and he was pretty sure he was, then it probably was the case that she knew about him first before he knew anything about her. That worried him. And it also worried him that now there were two people who knew something about him. And this worried him because it made him feel a little weak. He did not like to feel that way. He liked to feel that he was strong. He never ever felt like he was ever weak before. And that worried him as well. It worried him that now he knew that he was not alone, which meant that he could also feel that he was also lonely. And it worried him that he felt weak. And it worried him that now he felt like he was vulnerable. His body felt more vulnerable because it was now open to attack, and his general feeling of well-being also felt more vulnerable because now his confidence was shaken.

Suddenly he found that there were lots of things to think about and he had to get himself together. He knew he had to change now. He knew he had to think about it all. Now he had to think about more than just one person. Now he had to think about the fact that there were two. There were two of them to think about and know about and figure out. And one of them did obviously know about him somehow before he knew a single thing there was to know about her first. He did not think that he had ever seen her anywhere before.

Probably she did not know a lot about him really. Probably she somehow noticed him when he was showing off sometime. He could not let himself afford to be so foolish anymore. Damn! He would have to be more careful. Damn! He did not like to be too careful. The thought of it alone already made him feel restricted. It is certainly no good for him to feel that he's restricted. It could hamper him. It could compromise his instinct. He cannot let himself afford to be self-conscious.

He was starting now to wonder if he could trust himself completely. But to doubt himself at all bothered him so fully that he tried to shake it off. But he knew that it was futile to try and shake it off. To try and shake it off was a recipe for failure. To try and shake it off would only make it sure to stick. That's the way it is with anything at all when you try and shake it off; it makes it want to stick.

No, he had to look the situation squarely in the face and try to realize that whether he did like it or whether he did not he was inextricably and totally pulled into a game. And he must learn the rules and learn the strategy and he must do it quickly, and he must learn to play it well and win or else quite simply he would lose. And he could not let himself afford to go and lose this game. He did not want to lose. He would like to win and be certain he would win, whatever that did mean. And he wasn't really sure exactly what it meant to win, or to lose for all of that. He didn't really know the specifics of all that. But he didn't want to lose, whatever it did mean. And whatever it did mean, he did really want to win.

Regardless of how prudent it might be to retreat he did not want to do that. He was not the prudent type so why pretend to be. He would not try to be something that went against his nature. He would only play the game if he played it by his rules, if he played it in the way that was best for him to play and not do anything that was against his way of being, his normal way of being, his being natural. In fact, he would be it more so.

He would be himself and even more so would he be himself. He would amplify himself. He would throw himself into the fray and hold back nothing of himself. That was something of a specialty a natural way he had and he would never change it.

Of course it seemed apparent that he must be more cautious. For sure he knew he could not any longer take for granted that he was the only one. But now he knew that it was so, and knew there was a game, he knew he must not be the one who was losing in the game. He must not be the hunted one.

He figured that at this point he was better off by being in the open, but he must turn the hunt around and not be the one who will be the one who's hunted, and start to be the one who is the one who hunts, and start to hunt right now. He would not hunt like anybody else would hunt; he would not hunt the way they would. He would hunt the way he does. He would hunt in his own way; his own inimitable way.

He was rash and so he would be rash because he was, he was quite rash, and that was how he was, and the best way and only way to win the game was just that way, to be that way, to be the way he was, and to be so fully and completely just the way he was that he would win unquestionably and he would win for sure. You cannot lose if you are totally yourself and free and going unimpeded and not intimidated by anybody else who is doing just the same as that being merely just themselves like that and doing it full on.

Somehow he would then work it so the fact that there were others who were out there just like him would somehow make him stronger instead of making him feel weaker. Now he had a challenge and he dearly loved a challenge and anything he dearly loved would only make him stronger, and being challenged fully would also test his limits and help push the envelope of his skills and capabilities.

So therefore, with this new resolve, and it was a new thing in itself for him to make such a resolve, he went forward now to spy upon and find out more about the snake just like he'd planned to start with. Here he was now with a new resolve when he had never had to have a new resolve before. And he had a new sense of himself that he never had to have before. He formed a new conviction in a way he never had to, and all of this new stuff that he'd never done before, that he'd never had to do before, made him feel intoxicated.

He was very glad about the very strange encounter he had just had with the tiger. So off he went and took with him his new knowledge, his excitement and of course his new conviction.

10

THE TIGER, WHO WAS LOOKING at the monkey from where he could not see her or in any way detect her, was having a few doubts. She had hoped that their encounter would be fabulous enough and also weird enough to slow the monkey down and deter him from his course of returning to the snake. She had hoped that it would slow him down and make him stop and think, regroup and make a plan. She had hoped that it would buy her a little bit more time to work her way and worm her way into his daily life and make him wait to meet the snake.

Well, at least she thought that maybe now the monkey would show more caution after this remarkable encounter. Maybe now the monkey would think twice before he went back to the snake to try and have a meeting with the snake as soon as now. Maybe he would pull back some and only spy upon the snake to try and learn some more about the snake before he tried to meet with him. Maybe now the monkey would try to keep his distance from the snake.

But she knew the snake was on the lookout for the monkey too. She knew the snake was looking for the monkey, but she hoped he would not find him so they wouldn't have a meeting, not right now in any case. She had hoped that she could slow things down. But now it looked like maybe things were only speeding up.

What an amazing fighter the little monkey was. Or at least he really could be, if he learned some discipline. She admitted to herself that she was attracted to him. He was immature for sure, that was unquestionable. His energy was raw and it was undisciplined, that was also plain. But she admitted to herself that she was attracted to him. And she was totally impressed by his capabilities. And she admitted to herself that, even though she played with him by kissing him the way she did, that it also turned her on, and he also turned her on.

And when she thought about it now she thought that she would like to actually seduce him. She figured that she would have to do that anyway for the sake of realizing the specifics of her plan. But before she might have led him on, she might have played with him before. Now she really wanted to, she really wanted to seduce him. Of course she realized that this was something dangerous and a risky thing to do and her face reflected this by frowning while she smiled.

The monkey had been standing there obviously thinking about everything that happened and making some assessment about everything that happened. And she was hiding not too far away, but far away enough that he could not detect her (although even if she were not really all that far away she was anyway quite good at covering her presence). And she watched him as he stood there wondering about what he should do next. And then he just took off.

Obviously she knew where he was going and so obviously she followed him. This thing was not yet over. It was not over yet.

11

THE SNAKE GOES THIS WAY and goes that, back and forth and back and forth. Ever vigilant the snake is. Always patient is the snake. His focus is impeccable. It is like he has been hypnotized, but he did it to himself. It seems like nothing can distract him.

He is only waiting for something to catch his eye. Not just anything. He is so well trained. And he's so well disciplined as well. It's in his nature to be so disciplined.

All three of them are like that in the way that at their best all three of them are who they are and what they are is that, they are their discipline, the discipline of being one with what their nature is. At their best, but only at their best, and who is always at their best? There is no one who is always at their best. But when they are, when they are fully at their best, they are fully what they are, they are their discipline; the discipline of being one with what their nature is.

And so it is with him, the snake, right now he's at his best, and he's seeing everything yet nothing in particular and waiting until something stands out from all of it. He's waiting until something sticks out naturally from the mass of everything. He's waiting for the moment when that something becomes something that he is looking out for without trying hard to see it. When that happens — zap — his attention goes to it and grabs hold of that thing and his focus is on it and nothing can deter it, not when he's at his best.

He has the capability to be practically invisible by fading right into the background; he hides inside the quiet that he makes inside his head. It is as if he is not there even though he is right there. He might be standing right beside you. He might be standing right in front of you. But you would not notice him; you could bump right into him. You would have to be alert and be very sensitive to really notice him. So you would have to be someone who was like the tiger, then.

She would notice him because she is like a predator and she is like a hunter, so she can hear the quiet that someone's hiding in. She notices when there is suddenly a quiet that is suddenly around her that wasn't there before.

The monkey too might notice if he wasn't too distracted or if the person hiding were a threat to him. He would more than likely feel it then that something was not right and be on the defensive and then be more alert and then it would be likely that he would notice someone with any kind of power who was a threat to him.

But the inside of the head of the monkey at the moment was not very quiet; it was not quiet like the snake's head was. Inside the monkey's head there was a noisy riot of questions going on. So when the snake does spot the monkey, the monkey does not hear the quiet of the snake, and he does not feel that there is someone threatening nearby. But the tiger does.

And the monkey also does not hear the quiet of the tiger. As a hunter she can also be quiet in her mind, and she is trailing him from not too far behind, and she can hear the snake is out there, she can hear his quiet coming.

The monkey is distracted and that throws his systems off, his surveillance systems off. He does not know the tiger is following behind him and he does not know the snake has zeroed in on him. He's so thrown off by everything that's been happening to him.

But he is so committed to his purpose of just following his impulse to just keep going on. He is so committed to go full steam ahead and it seems that nothing will deter him from his course. He is so convinced it is the right thing he should do, he should trust his impulse and go and follow it. Go monkey, go.

Does the snake hear the quiet of the tiger? He's so focused on the monkey, he's so completely fascinated, that he doesn't hear her quiet, he doesn't notice her, and he doesn't know the tiger is anywhere near there.

And that's a thing that's happening that can happen when you have a skill that is remarkable. Sometimes when you do have a skill that is remarkable, you find yourself remarking upon the fact of it and taking pride in it and focusing on it. And when you do something like that, you naturally detract away some of its power and its capability; you become intoxicated and you lose some of the skill.

And that's what's happening to him. He is so proud he found the monkey, and that he sees the monkey while the monkey can't see him, that he cannot hear the tiger, and so he cannot tell she's there not far behind the monkey.

And another reason why he might not know the tiger's there is perhaps because the monkey's brain is really active with distractions that he has, and this state might be contagious to a kind of psychic hunter, which is kind of what the snake is.

Anyway, his pride for what he understands to be a definite advantage has put him actually at a disadvantage. He thinks he is so perfect but he has made a big mistake. He does not know the tiger's there. But the tiger knows the snake is there.

The tiger's being quiet and being very still. She is very clear and she is very calm and she will not make a move unless she absolutely has to. She cannot see the snake, but she has heard his quiet and she knows that he is there, that he is there nearby, and she hopes he cannot tell that she is also there or is any-where nearby.

She figures odds are good that he's distracted by the monkey. And of course she's right. And anyway she knows the snake does not know her yet. If he did he might expect her and might keep an eye out for her. But he has never met her, so why should he expect her? She doesn't think he would. And she's right about that too.

It is not too hard to be distracted by the monkey. In fact, it's difficult for them; it's difficult for both of them, for both the tiger and the snake not to get excited and to hold on to their quiet. The monkey is kinetic. He is like a force that naturally, and in fact, unknowingly, effects everything around him. He seems so reckless that the force of him also seems so reckless, but really, it is not. But it can make you feel that way, and it can make you act that way, it can make you be more reckless. So you have to pay attention and you have to stay clear-headed if you want to keep control.

The snake knows this is true and the tiger knows this too. So the snake knows that it will be hard to follow after him, to keep a tail on him and to do so unobserved and undiscovered by him. And the tiger knows it will be hard to follow both of them. She has guessed correctly that the snake is staying out of sight and must be hiding from the monkey so that he can follow him.

She doesn't want the monkey to be in danger from the snake. But she can't afford to let the snake know that she is there. So she thinks that she should stop right now, and she decides that she will stop right now and she won't follow them right now. She decides instead to disappear and fade back for a while and meet up with the monkey later when he goes back to his home.

She knows where he does live and she has made a plan. She will have to trust that things are under her control and that everything will work out right and that it is ok for now to leave the two of them alone.

She knows enough about the snake to know that if he's interested to know about the monkey, then he will cultivate that interest and probably do research by spying on the monkey and wait a little while before he makes some kind of move or presents himself to him. Of course, she doesn't know about the thing the monkey took from him, the snake, or what it means to him, the snake, that the monkey took it from him, the snake. She just assumes the snake saw him when the monkey broke into his home and has probably determined rightly that the monkey has some value and is interested in using him in some way that is bad. She assumes the snake is interested to have the monkey join his group. She hopes this does not happen.

But although it's true the snake might have an interest at some point to have the monkey join his group, that is not his issue at the moment. At the moment what he wants is to get the thing the monkey took. He wants to steal it back. He wants to take it back from him in the same way that the monkey took it from him. The snake wants to return the deed and even up the score and make it tit for tat.

The snake is oh so confident. Now at last that he has found him and is following the monkey, he knows that soon enough he'll know where the monkey lives, and then it won't be long before the snake breaks into there and takes his thing from there and evens up the score. After that he'll see about what the monkey might be good for.

Right now the monkey's also thinking just a little bit about the thing he took away from where the snake lives. He's thinking just a little bit about the tiger too, and the pure fact of the tiger is beginning now to register itself upon him deeply and he feels suspicious of her. He is beginning to suspect there are more things going on which involve him in a way maybe more than he first thought.

He was starting now to feel a little bit naïve and a little bit embarrassed by his naivety. But he also was excited because so much was going on at once and going on so suddenly, and what with all the intrigue that was present at the moment, it was really something else.

And as he looked upon the snake's home which was now there in plain view he wondered what would happen next and would it be exciting too? He was certainly excited when he wondered what would happen. And he certainly did like that. For all of what did worry him he was certainly excited. And he did certainly like that; he liked to be excited.

12

THE MONKEY DID NOT KNOW the snake was following behind him. The monkey's thoughts were on the snake perhaps a bit too much and they raced along and went along and ended up in front of him, in front of where he was and in front of what would happen next.

The snake already knew that the monkey was audacious and he knew that he was bold, and now he also knew that he was rash and he was reckless too. And the thing about that recklessness that turned out to be interesting was the fact that when the snake did see it, the fact that when the snake did feel it, that fact that when he did sense the fact of it, when it did become apparent, the fact of all of that did somehow seem to make it something that was contagious.

It made the snake feel like he was becoming reckless too, or that he wanted to. Just a little, just a bit, but just enough to make him lose his focus for a bit.

Now that is something that does not happen to the snake. It never happens that the snake feels anything like that, like being reckless just a little, not even just a bit. So, it was understandable that the snake would find it odd and find it disconcerting, and also find it interesting. And he wondered about that.

Could the monkey's recklessness be a trait he had that was a weapon too? Even if the monkey didn't mean to be that way or to use it as a weapon, it could be that it worked that way. It could simply be a part of him that was a part of his true nature that seemed to be a fault in him but which worked to his advantage.

The snake of course did realize that he must not underestimate the power of the monkey, or fall into the trap of thinking that he was undisciplined. And the snake did also know that he had to watch himself, he had to check his tendency to be too condescending and too much of a snob. It's not good to underestimate the power of your foes.

He knew the monkey could be valuable to both him and his group. It would be a good idea to try and win him over. A snake and monkey partnership could be really powerful. But the snake must still be careful and make a careful plan. He must keep his distance like he planned and only make his move when it was time to make his move.

The snake knows why the monkey is going to the snake's place; he's going there in order to regain his confidence. He knows that when the last time he almost caught the monkey it must have been a new thing and it must have thrown him off. So, the monkey's going back he knows to get himself together and the snake will let him do that.

If the monkey needs his confidence, then when he gets it back, he will be distracted by the feeling of the joy of getting it. And that will throw him off without him even knowing it. He will be less careful and, therefore, be more vulnerable. He will be relying on a confidence that's false. And that will cloud his instinct, and that will cloud his judgement.

The monkey is just going, just going with the flow. And he's going really fast. And although he is aware that he really should slow down, he's not interested in hearing that, he's not interested in knowing that, he's not interested in doing that, he's just interested in going, in going how he goes, going with his flow.

He simply has decided to trust in his conviction, the conviction that he has to go ahead and be impulsive. And because he has decided this, it is such an affirmation, that it sends a thrill right through him. And the feeling of that thrill and the chills it sends right through him also gives him strength in his body and his soul. The overwhelming feeling is like intoxication.

Now, just below the snake's apartment, he pauses for a moment, poised as if to strike, which is not like him at all. His heart is racing and his blood is rushing to his head — he feels quite out of it. He smiles from realizing the extent of his excitement. He takes it in; he drinks it in, before he makes his move. And when he makes his move he makes his move with grace, and he makes it with aplomb. It's thoughtless and sublime. If only you could see it you would see the beauty in the speed and in the sureness of the motion.

The snake watches him with interest and with the greatest admiration from a distance that is safe. He watches as the monkey climbs up to the third floor balcony with ease and great agility up to the third floor balcony outside of the apartment of the snake. He sees the monkey go inside. The snake has left his door unlocked, he has made a point of it, to keep his door unlocked. The snake has got some issues with his confidence as well.

13

THE MONKEY WALKS INTO the snake's place and his confidence is back. He doesn't wait to see if the snake is there or not because he doesn't even care if the snake is there or not. And anyway he can tell that the snake is not there. He can feel the snake is not there.

He feels victorious. He feels it so acutely that he laughs out loud a little, just a little, and his eyes tear up a little, just a little, from the feeling of the joy it brings to feel that he's victorious. Oh, how absurd, he tells himself.

He falls into a chair and just sits there feeling everything's all right and everything's OK. He is pleased. A certain calm comes over him and he feels a little sleepy. He shuts his eyes and soon enough, as strange as it might seem, he's fallen fast asleep.

He goes to sleep; he stays asleep for about a half an hour. When he wakes up, he's refreshed and not at all alarmed and not the least bit worried. In fact, a part of him is hoping that while he was asleep the snake had come and found him there, that he had found him sleeping there. He giggles at the thought of it.

Is he waiting for the snake? He wonders if he is. If he is, he knows that he will have to wait awhile. He won't be home that soon. He has a feeling that the snake will not be home too soon.

There are many reasons why the monkey and the snake should not meet in here. Now is not the time. And if it were the time it would still not be in here. It is not a good idea to meet the snake in here, not now in any case. The monkey and snake should meet somewhere outside. They should meet outside where there's lots of room for both of them to move around a lot.

As he thinks about the fact of this he thinks about the tiger. It makes him think that it was likely that it wasn't just an accident that they met up in that way. And he figures that she wants something. And he's certain he will see her soon; he will see her soon again. And he is sure that she is trying to make him pay attention. And it worked. And he is sure she must have planned it all. Which meant she must have somehow known about him. And he wondered how she did and what she did and what was going on? What was it that he did not know and what was going on?

Perhaps the tiger and the snake were acquainted with each other. Perhaps they knew each other well. Maybe they were partners and the two of them were working on a plan. Perhaps the two of them were cooking up a plan for what to do with him together.

Maybe there were more than just the two of them involved. Perhaps there were a bunch of them who all had special skills. There could be a group of them who were all working together. Or there could be a group of them who were all working together against another group of them who were working all together too. It could all be all mixed up. Some working for and some against and somewhere in between, there could be some who were not sure of who they were against and who they actually were for.

And of course there could be those who were against the both of them. And there could be those who were not either for them or against them. They could be like the monkey, free and independent.

Was that what he was? It seemed that he was that. Would he like to have a group of people to hang out with? Would he like to be with those who were more similar to him? Maybe. Maybe not.

Things often get confusing and often do get ugly when there are different groups and when all of them want power and want to have control. Especially if they think that they can only have it if the other ones do not.

He didn't have an interest in any of that stuff. But he had a feeling that the tiger and the snake had some interest in that stuff. And they might think that he did. Or they might wish that he did, or like it if he did have an interest in that stuff as well.

And it's good for him to know that, to know what is expected. It's good to know what people want and what they want to get from you. Then you can negotiate if you really need to.

The monkey frowned and thought about the thinking he was doing. It worried him to see his own encroaching cynicism. He felt already sucked into political arrangements, and he didn't want to deal with that. He didn't want a thing to do with anything political. He didn't want relationships that would be political. He wanted nothing whatsoever to do with anything that ever was a political relationship.

But to tell the truth, he also wanted something from the two of them. And he knew that what he wanted was something he could only get by knowing both of them. And so of course he knew that he would have to get to know them. They were different like he was but they were also different in their own way and they were different from him. He would have to get to know them to know that difference.

He was not worried anymore. Well maybe just a bit. He had taken something from the snake and he had to put it back. He could not give it back. He had to put it back. He didn't know beforehand that he would end up here today and just hang out and take a little nap. If he'd known, he could have brought it back and put it back and that would be the end of it. If the thing was really something that was something that had meaning, and that meaning was important, then he had been mistaken to take the thing away from someone like the snake. He didn't mean it to end up this way, but now he was in trouble.

That could be a problem. One he didn't want. And one he didn't need. And one he didn't really have the patience or the time for. So, he knew that he would have to be more cautious than he cared to be. But still he did not worry, he wasn't feeling worried.

He knew that he had value. He felt that it was true. It could just be his vanity. It could just be his ego. Of course he is a narcissist, even he knows that is true. But 'whatever' to all that. Instinctively he knew it. Innately he could feel it.

How did it feel? How did he feel, to feel that he had value, and know that he had value, and that he would be pursued? It's like the feeling that you get when you think all eyes are on you, and when you look around and see that it is really true, in fact all eyes are on you, then you wonder can you handle it, can you handle that attention, all of that attention? Well the monkey could. Of course, he could. He would eat it up. And that fact that he was like that could make things turn out better, for him in any case.

The monkey sat there soaking up the feeling of the room. When a person lives somewhere they put their feeling into it. You can get a feeling for a person by feeling what their home feels like. By making contact with that feeling you make contact with their style. And making contact with their style can make you understand their way. And if you understand their way, then you can tell a lot about what they like to do and how they like to do it, and how they like to fight — if they like to fight. And some do like to fight.

But the monkey was not someone who was normally reflective, who would sit and think about it, so he jumped up from the chair and moved around a bit and checked things out a bit and let his curiosity pull him here and there. He kept on getting feelings but didn't analyze them. His feelings were more interesting when he was nonchalant. When he made himself at home and acted naturally, he got a better feeling for the spirit of the home and the spirit of the person who made it be their home.

That is why he does it to begin with, don't you know. That is why he goes into their homes, into the homes of people that he doesn't even know. He goes into their places and he checks them out a little. It's like watching movies. It's like watching the TV. It's like a book that tells a story, or anything at all that shows how people live.

Anyone who does those things, who watches movies or TV or reads a book or anything that shows how people live, is also in a certain way, consciously or not, checking out their own lives and checking themselves out. They're seeing how they're different and seeing what's the same and learning if they like the possibilities of change, and whatever that might mean. At least, that's how he saw it, that's how the monkey saw it.

Right now he didn't want to think about his moral contradictions. But maybe for the first time he did have to admit that he felt a little bad, and he conceded it was wrong to go into their places and violate their privacy and desecrate the sanctity of all these people's homes. Even now he felt like it was wrong that he was there inside the snake's place. Perhaps it wasn't such a good idea to be in there at all, after all.

He looked around himself with more attention to the detail of the overall arrangement of everything in there, as if a more concerted effort would somehow validate his purpose and make it seem less frivolous than his previous adventures. He was trying to convince himself that he was on a mission to find knowledge. But he had no patience for such pretense even from himself. He must not kid himself.

Then he started to feel antsy. And he wondered if this place was making him uncomfortable.

This, he thought with sudden knowledge and conviction, is the home of someone with a calculating mind. The very ambiance of it, the total aura of the place, the place's atmosphere itself seemed to be encouraging a calculating mind.

It made him want to stop and sit or just stand still, which

was not like him at all. It was not natural for him. It made him think too much about himself and maybe even made him doubt himself. It threw him off his guard. That's what happened to him last time. It threw him off his guard. Wasn't that what happened to him last time? He had been too taken in by everything around him and it threw him off his guard and that is why the snake surprised him to begin with. Now he had to leave. Now he had to go.

He felt like he was being tricked and he really didn't like it. He's the tricky one. He's the one who does the tricks.

Of course, because he is a trickster he could admire the subtlety of the trick the place was playing. But he knew a trick could be a trap and really he must go. He would not meet the snake here — he must never meet the snake here.

He ran out to the balcony and leapt up on the railing. He perched there for a moment and smelled the morning air. It still was just the morning and was still a little early. He smelled the morning air and felt his head clear up.

Then he had a notion, he had a sudden notion, that he shouldn't leave this way. He had a strong compulsion to go out the front door, to leave by the front door, and go down through the stairway, through the exit stairway and go through the front door, go out the front door of the building. He felt this very strongly.

And normally, of course, he followed anything he felt, and he felt this very strongly. Yet, he ignored it anyway, and he jumped down to the ground — no mean feat for anyone — but for the monkey it was easy. And he started to go home.

14

HE WENT OFF so fast it was as if he hit the ground while running. The snake was fascinated. He had been waiting there and wondering what the hell the monkey could be doing in there all this time.

A complete calm had seemed to come over his place so he didn't really think the monkey was doing much of anything except maybe waiting for the snake to show, which of course he wouldn't do. And then suddenly the monkey had come out with the air of someone being chased and it gave the snake the notion, if only for a moment that maybe someone else had shown up at his place.

But he knew this couldn't be, because there wasn't anybody else who would dare to show up there unless they were a fool, a complete and ignorant fool, and certainly the monkey would never flee a fool. So, why did he fly away like that?

It must be something else. Something must have happened to the monkey. Something must have happened that was peculiar just to him.

The monkey seemed erratic to the snake. He seemed a little volatile. It almost made him want to kill the monkey and be done with it.

But that would be too rash and the snake was never rash. It

felt as if the monkey were responsible somehow for making him feel rash, or like he wanted to feel rash. How interesting, the snake thought. He could see that he was facing a challenge and that did intrigue him.

Eagerly, but not too eagerly, he followed the monkey to his home and it was pretty easy to follow him there. He would have thought that somehow it wouldn't be that easy. He would have thought that somehow the monkey would look back, that he would watch his back. But he didn't look at all, and he didn't check at all. It made it very easy for the snake to follow him.

That made the snake uncomfortable. He was ready to be cautious, to contain his eagerness, but it didn't really matter, it was a piece of cake.

Could the monkey be so rash? Could the monkey really be so arrogant? Was the monkey just so confident that he threw caution to the wind?

The snake could not believe the monkey was that bold, or self-assured, or negligent. How could he fail to take some measures to make sure he wasn't followed? It seemed particularly strange since he left in such a hurry. He looked like he was being chased. Well in a way, he was. The snake was chasing him, but the monkey didn't know it.

If the monkey was freaked out, why did he not watch out? He should be watching out because the snake was coming for him. It really made him wonder. Why did he not watch out?

Good question. The monkey, as it happened, was a bit freaked out by what happened at the snake's place. He was heading for his home and he was not looking back and he didn't even think of it.

He was not thinking anything. He was going, going, gone. He was trusting in his instinct. Maybe it was wrong. Maybe he was wrong. Who knows?

But for now, he felt conviction, and he felt it very strong, and he was going with it. Get out and get back home, it told him, and he did. He did not feel in danger and so he would not worry until he did feel danger.

15

SO NOW THE SNAKE KNOWS where the monkey lives. This is only fair. After all, the monkey knows where the snake lives. No one knows where the tiger lives, however. And that is where she is. She is waiting there where she lives. Just waiting and that's all. She is very quiet when she waits. When she waits, she is sublime.

Later, she has plans to pay a visit to the monkey but until then she just waits. And she thinks a little bit about what is going on. What has happened or is happening between the monkey and the snake? She would like to know this. But she can wait to find it out.

The snake can also wait. When it counts the snake can wait. He can wait forever when it counts, it seems. He is so good at waiting, it's like he invented waiting.

When he waits he's not so much sublime the way the tiger is. No, that is not the word for it. When he waits it's like he gathers all the quiet from around. All the quiet that is near and all the quiet from afar, is gathered there upon him. So much so that it blots him out. You can't see him then. You can't hear him then. He breathes it in. He breathes it out. He is the stillness in the air, and who can see the stillness?

Well the tiger can, but she's not there. The monkey could but only if the stillness moved a little bit. But does the stillness ever move? Sometimes, yes, it does. Anything that's held in silence gathers force, and when the force is strong enough then it develops presence, and in that presence there's awareness, and an awareness of itself — and that awareness of itself is what can make it move. It will move, maybe it will move only just a tiny little bit, just a tiny little bit, and it's such a sudden move, and that sudden move although quite small is just the kind of move the monkey's apt to see.

But the monkey wouldn't see it now because the monkey's sleeping. He's got all his clothes on. He collapsed right into bed and went out like a light.

When the time is right the snake will go inside. When the monkey leaves, then the snake will go inside. How will he get inside? He cannot climb the way the monkey climbs. But he can pick a lock like no one can.

Will the door be armed with an alarm? He does not think it will. But if he thought it might be, he would then be prepared. The snake is always pretty much usually prepared.

But the monkey is so rash and brash, why would he bother with alarms? The tiger doesn't have alarms and neither does the snake. They do not need alarms. So, the snake is pretty sure that there won't be an alarm.

Where is the snake exactly? In the stairwell of the building where the monkey lives. Yes, he followed rather closely.

He watched to see the door. The monkey's door. He's sitting at the top, the very top, where there is a landing that's going to the roof. It's above the third floor landing that's going to the roof. It's above the third floor landing that goes to the third floor. That's the floor the monkey's on. That's the top floor in this building. It's laid out like the snake's place. There are a lot of places that are laid out just like that around there. They are neighbours in a way. Though they are blocks apart, it is still in the same neighbourhood.

When the monkey leaves, the snake is going to know it. Just above the third floor and just around a corner, the snake waits out of sight. You wouldn't notice him, unless you bumped right into him, and even then you probably wouldn't pay him any mind. His silence makes your business louder.

The monkey and the tiger, they are a different story — but you, unless you're like the way that they are, you likely wouldn't notice much, if anything at all.

16

THE MONKEY SLEPT, and slept, and slept, and when finally he woke up he sat right up and stared out into space, his head was feeling empty. He did not mind the feeling. It was quiet and he liked it. He felt groggy and he liked that too. What did he have to do? — Nothing. So he liked it being groggy and staring into space.

His clothes were wrinkled 'cause he slept in them. He took them off and drew a bath. He had a big old bathtub with a nice high waterline.

He was up to his neck in water — hot water. It was a bubble bath, of course. He lay there in his bath and stared some more, his head all empty still — and liked it that way still — but less groggy. The bathroom door was open so it wouldn't be so humid after he got out.

Looking at the door, the open door like that, it made him feel excited. He looked at it and saw his room through it. It turned him on, that open door. He played with thoughts of being seen. What if there were someone who by chance was there to see him?

The tiger crossed his mind and then poof she suddenly was there before him smiling, naked, awesome, outstanding and becoming and moving there toward him toward him in the bath.

She stepped into the water and the wide-eyed monkey wondered for a moment was she real or was she not. Then she sat down there upon him and he felt her flesh inviting and knew she would not drown him but rather would seduce him. He knew she was for real all right and he let himself be taken and still he was not thinking, but feeling he was plenty.

The water, it went everywhere. It was hot but she felt hotter. Her kisses reached down deep inside and made him feel quite high.

The tiger is so daring she knew that she would do this. Her racing heart and heavy breath however, overwhelmed her. She was intoxicated by the boldness of her deed, the execution of a plan so intimate and brash. Maybe that's the reason why she missed the snake upon the landing. Sex can cloud the sharpest mind.

The snake was busy being quiet. Waiting was the snake. Waiting for the monkey, for him to come outside. When you're waiting so for just one thing, expecting just to see it, the appearance of another thing can throw you, so you miss it.

The snake did not reply then to a distant call to listen. But he did not disregard that call to listen altogether. Like when you're sleeping there are things that stir you only slightly, the snake stirred slightly from the movement of the tiger passing.

Something passed he realized that might be something new, something he should think about when it was time to do that too. It might not be related directly to the monkey, But then again, it might. Perhaps it was a friend. Perhaps it was the monkey's friend. He would wait and see. He was waiting once again, waiting totally.

The tiger entered easily. The door — it wasn't even locked. And she didn't even think about the fact that it might be. Her conviction was so raw. She'd never done a thing like this, not quiet like this, before.

She knew that it was bold, and that excited her. She knew it could go wrong, and that excited her. She doubted that it would go wrong, and that excited her. She was going to fuck the monkey. She was taken by the thought of it. How audacious.

She surprised herself a little. She liked that. She liked to be surprised that way.

Now, the monkey was surprised for sure. And for the moment, not complaining. This amazing, possibly crazy, mad, insane woman, so stunning and astounding, was blowing his mind with how devastatingly intense and yummy she was to be having sex with.

Normally, he was the one who was so much in control of everything that happened when it came to sex. Normally, he was the one who made the big impression, who was such a fucking turn-on. He got off on getting them off. But she was such a fucking turn-on. He felt for once on equal ground. He was moved by this and so was she.

First, they were performers trying to impress. Then they gave it up and started to have fun. From out of the bath they moved across the floors, onto the furniture, onto countertops and tabletops and everything and whatnot until finally they also got up into the bed. They said little in the way of words, but sounds they made a lot. They made sounds of approval, of encouragement and joy. They were ecstatic. They were grateful.

Every now and then, they would stop for just a bit and appraise each other for a while in different kinds of ways, and then they would embrace and go at it once again.

What could they do once they were done with doing all of that? They lay around a little while looking at each other, and touching just a little, coming back to earth.

Then the monkey said, 'well?' And it was over.

And then the next part started. The getting to know you part started. This can be exciting too. And monkey certainly was curious. He'd like to have some answers to some questions. So he started asking them.

Before she'd answer one he'd ask another one. And she laughed. And he knew it there and then that he really liked her laugh. But he also knew that there was more to this than meets the eye. So what was it all about?

She danced around it lots. How much should she say? Not all of it for sure. So, how much then? A little. Tantalize him. He thought he was alone and just one of a kind. Now he knows he's not. What will it mean to him?

So she tells him there are others. He knows he's not alone now, but she tells him there are others who have put themselves together, who come from everywhere, who can be anywhere, are living here and there all over. They've formed a kind of group and everyone's in charge, they all must have a say and what they want is good — they want things to be good.

But there are others too. There are some others in another group who don't want things to be good for everyone, just only for themselves. They can be bad. So her group then tries to make it so the good ones will succeed and the bad ones will have a harder time of doing their bad things, because they never could quite stop them. Of course they realize they cannot stop all badness, it'd be foolish to believe it. So, they try to slow things down or speed things up depending on who's who and who needs what, and what it is that should be done, what they think is best that should be done. They decide then only if they all agree, and mostly that's the case, that they all should all agree.

But sometimes there is someone who it's hard to say is either fully good or fully bad. Before they do anything with them they try at first to work it out, and it could go either way because that's of course dependent on what they've done and what they're doing — the ones they are not sure of.

Then she said she's told them, she told her group about him. She told them he was special. Would they like for her to ask him if he would like to know them, and know some more about them? They said yes, they would, and so now she's asking would he like to get to know them, or would he rather not?

He said he did not know. And he wondered was he being tricked and was she getting him between the sheets to try and get him in her group? Well, he wasn't sure about belonging to such a noble group. And was it really noble, or was it something else?

He wasn't really knowing if he wanted to belong, although he liked the thought of knowing he would never be alone. He liked the thought of thinking that he could have some friends and liked to think his friends could be some friends who were like him.

And then he thought hey, what about the snake, and he asked her if she knew him. He described the snake a little bit and asked again, you know him? Was the snake a member of this group that she belonged to?

Well, she said, oh yes, she knew him, but then she told a little lie, she said he was not with them but she did not tell him why. She said they had not asked him yet, they were waiting for a bit.

She knew she couldn't tell him all about the way the snake is bad, or about the group the snake hung out with. She knew that if she told him then the monkey'd be inclined to want to know precisely what that was all about. He'd be so deadly curious; he'd simply have to know. So he'd go do some exploring, and then he'd get in trouble, and then she did not know which way the monkey'd end up going — turning good or turning bad — which made her really sad and it frightened her a bit because she liked the monkey, see.

Now, the tiger was not someone to ever be afraid. Her fear, of course, was for his sake. Oh, the tiger. It would not do for her to get wrapped up in a man, especially in a man like this, in such a monkey man. She did not think she could afford the luxury to fear the losing of a friendship that had only just begun.

The tiger was aloof by nature but the monkey threw her off. Of course, the monkey saw right through her lie about the snake. He knew there was a problem though he did not know just what.

He asked her if she'd met the snake and she told the monkey truthfully, that she knew the snake to see him but they'd not been introduced. She said the group was thinking about asking him to join, but had yet to work it out, whether he was worthy, or was just too self-absorbed. The snake, she said, did not know her group was considering asking him to join, and she did not think, she said, that the snake knew they existed.

The monkey knew the snake would be far too calculating and far too controlling to ever be controlled or ever share control. The monkey saw right through it all. He knew the snake was bad and a force he'd have to watch for. Perhaps the snake was not all bad, not bad in every way. But for sure the snake was mean. It was best to stay away. Or at least not get too close.

And then he thought about the thing he took away from him. He didn't know exactly what it meant, but it was trouble he knew that.

He felt a little vulnerable when he thought about the snake. After all, the tiger'd found him and could have just as easily killed him, as easily as she'd loved him. So the snake might also find him. The snake had only seen him just a little bit it's true, but maybe it was just enough to make him want to know just who it was and where was he this guy who took his thing away.

It might be that the snake knew all about the group and maybe he would think they were behind the monkey's deed. And maybe there's another group the snake is in instead. Maybe he's the boss, in one way or another. He must be a boss, for who could boss the snake around?

The monkey now got worried. He didn't want to keep the thing around here any more. Should he tell the tiger all about the thing he stole? No, it would stay a secret; he would keep it to himself.

He did not think he knew for sure which way the wind was blowing. He was not sure he knew the way his interest was inclined. And so, he kept the tiger in the dark, he told the tiger nothing.

The thing he must get rid of. And also he should move. He should find another place to live, a secret place to live. He needs a hideaway. But he'll never run away. He'll keep hanging around, but less so in the open. Now that it made a difference, now that he knew that there was danger, he'd have to be more cautious, just a little bit more careful. He'd have to get himself a place where he'd be harder to be found.

And what about the tiger? The tiger was amazing, absolutely fabulous, and he must get her out of here so he can make his plan and make it happen, get his stuff together and get another place, and lose that stupid thing, it's a liability.

So, the monkey fell asleep. Amazing, no?

But you know what — it worked — because the tiger was just thinking that she really should get going, and after making such an entrance she knew it would be hard to make the proper exit. So she was quite relieved to see the monkey fall asleep. It was very easy after that for her to slip away.

17

THE SNAKE WAS IN THE STAIRWELL; he was still waiting patiently in there. This time when the tiger passed he noticed her a little more. And he wondered who she was. Could it be the monkey has a girlfriend? Why did that surprise him?

He did not dwell on it, however. He didn't waste his thoughts on wondering who or what the tiger was. He waited; he kept waiting, at the top of the stairwell. And the tiger, the stunning tiger, once again she missed him.

This can happen to a sharp mind even like the tiger's when they're as distracted as she was. She was preoccupied. She was not at that moment now a hunter like she almost always mostly usually was. Even she could slip up like she did and she did.

She hurried to get out of there, and she was a bit confused, even though her actions were still going according to a plan. And the plan was going smoothly — so then, why the worried frown? She really didn't know.

Could she count upon the monkey? No, of course she knew that all along. He would probably be tempted to get to know the snake. But still she had done something — she'd planted a small seed. She had let the monkey know that there were some options open to him. The snake might be exciting, but then again, so was she.

The snake might be a challenge that the monkey'd find intriguing, but he'd also find a problem there. So the monkey might need help from her and her group as well.

Now he knows there are two worlds, at least two worlds, that he can now belong to, where he will not be alone.

She really hoped the monkey would stay a friend of hers. The monkey and the snake together could be very bad indeed.

18

THEY ARE FORCES to be reckoned with, each and every one of them. Combined they could be trouble.

Strong forces can combine and become another thing, an independent force with a life that's all its own.

It can do a thing that is only just its own thing. It can be good it can be bad. It could do what they would not if they were on their own.

When forces good and forces bad are playing both together something that they make from it from playing it from being it can turn out either way — or be something in between — or be different altogether. This is powerful.

It can be creative. It can be destructive. It can be a thing, a living, breathing thing. Or, it can be a thing that is a thing that's not a living thing but a thing that has a power that lives inside of it; like a fetish, like a magic amulet, or like a magic ring.

The monkey did believe it best to do what he did do by doing it and letting it be done with as little thought as possible. Just like it was an instinct to do what he did do. He did believe it that his instinct was a thing that he could use. He believed that he could hone it. He believed that he could train it until he trusted it. Don't interrupt the flow is what he always tells himself.

So whether he did or whether he did not join up with the snake or join up with the tiger, or whether joining with the one or joining with the other was creative or destructive, was not for him a worry, not for the moment anyway. And so he didn't worry.

He was more concerned right now about getting out of there, because whether he did join up or whether he did not and whether it was him or whether it was her, she knew where he lived and the snake might know it too, which was a disadvantage. His whole advantage needed some improvement. And part of that advantage hinged on getting a new place, a place that was a hiding place. Hide and seek, he thought, and thought it was amusing.

He looked at the thing that he stole away that was giving him some trouble. It was not the only thing that was giving him some trouble, but in a way it was the main thing, the central thing, the pivotal thing, because it was the thing that started everything that now could be a thing that brought to him some trouble. If you could blame something at all on a thing that was a thing, then this thing was the thing that he would blame his trouble on.

No, he wouldn't blame himself. After all, he was only doing what he did and what he did was fine, or so he told himself. What he did was what he did — what could you do with that? He almost did get caught, and that was surely a drag, and that threw him for a loop. But almost getting caught was something he might have sorted out more easily it's true if he didn't take that thing. Oh well, what can you do?

This thing made the whole thing much more complicated. It made things much more serious. And anything that serious is something that's a threat. And that's what made these people and his getting on with them seem to be so iffy.

It was all because of this thing, or so he figured anyway. If he hadn't picked it up and taken it with him when he bolted, then things wouldn't be so complicated in the way they are right now.

He didn't know how he should deal with it, what he should do with it exactly, not just yet, in any case. And he didn't care to think about it but he thought about it anyway and the thoughts just got him antsy because he didn't really know what it was that he should do. And he felt like he should go. He should leap outside the window into the tree that was nearby. He was ready just to do that but instead he hesitated.

Oh, he hated that. How he hated that. He hated hesitating. He hated to reflect and he hated being cautious, having to be cautious. But he had to be, he knew it because he was worried now that one of them might see him — he couldn't be so careless as he had been up to now.

It really can't be helped that you get a little paranoid when there are people in your life who are a little iffy; when one of them has found you in the place where you are living; and the other one could find you just as easily. So, that is why he had to move — he had to get a new apartment. And, until he did, until he moved, he'd have to be more cautious, whether he did like it or whether he did not.

So, he didn't jump out of the window; he went out by the door instead. Out he went and fast he went. He was moving very fast. When he gets a notion that it's time to do something he's got to go and do it and he does it very fast.

When he got into the stairwell, suddenly he stopped. But why, he did not know. He only stopped, that's all. And he frowned; because he didn't know why it was that he had stopped. He had a sense of something. But he was sick of sensing something. He was sick of vagaries and all of his suspicion.

Oh, just go, he thought, he was fed up and he wanted to get on with it, and so he did.

He jumped down a flight of stairs. If you'd seen him it would look like he was moving in slow motion. It happens that way sometimes when you see amazing things, amazing things involving motion are sometimes taken in that way by the mind they say.

So, it was like that. If you'd been there and you'd seen him take that first jump down the stairs, it would've looked to you just like he was moving in slow motion.

He landed, then he jumped down the next flight of stairs as well, and then he stepped quickly down the rest, swinging around the banister to give him extra torque.

19

GIRL, YOU CAN JUST BET the snake was wide awake right now. And after waiting for so long, you'd think he'd be a little bit excited. Well, he was, but just a little, because the snake is one cool customer.

As soon as he was gone, the snake was at the monkey's door. It wasn't even locked. The snake marvelled once again at the monkey's pure audacity.

Once he was inside, he looked around a little bit. He checked it out. He tried to get a feel for the way the monkey lives and the way the monkey is. But there were no revelations, only confirmations.

It didn't take him long to find what he was looking for. It was lying on the floor in the middle of a room. He picked it up and put it in his pocket. The room was messy, much too messy for someone like the snake. It made him feel all edgy.

You see, places can be like that; they can be just like personalities. So of course, they can affect you, especially if they're different in a kind of way that's different and that rubs you the wrong way.

People aren't just people, they are also atmospheres; they are like environments. And they have an ambiance. And they also have a rhythm and a tempo. Their charm is like their melody. Their way is like their style. Likewise, an environment is also like a person, whether it's a room, or somewhere that's outside, or a bus, or a car, or whatever. Wherever there's a place there is an ambiance and it's like a personality.

So he didn't linger. He didn't stay there long. The snake got his thing back, he took it and he left. Then he went back to his home.

On the way he thought a little more about the monkey and that girl — that girl who came out from his place and who passed him in the stairwell and who had a way about her some kind of way about her. He didn't really notice it so much when she was there. But now that he thought about it, he noticed there was something there about her. Who was she anyway? Was she just a girlfriend? Or was she more than that? What kind of girl could be a girlfriend of the monkey's? Was there something special about her? Could she be as interesting as he was, or even maybe more?

Then he thought about the fact that the monkey left so fast. He wondered why the monkey left as quickly as he did. But perhaps the monkey always left a place in a big rush. He had left the snake's place in a rush. And he left his own place in a rush.

The monkey to the snake was a bit too unpredictable. But that was interesting. What a rare thing that was for the snake to find someone like that.

He wondered why the monkey took that thing of his. What could it mean to him. It had no value you could see. It had value for the snake. But that value was just personal. He figured it was random — just some souvenir. He hadn't treated it as though it had any other kind of value. The snake was glad to have it back.

A thing like that with special meaning had special power sometimes too. Like a fetish imbued with magic power. A good luck charm can be like that. Like a lucky hat — when you wear it things really do go better for you because that's what you believe so strongly. The thing was like that for the snake.

The snake went home and put the thing away and had a little rest and after he was rested he went out to get some food. He went out to a *fancy-high-priced-so-you-get-the-feeling-of-belonging-to-a-class-of-people-who-can-afford-this-even-though-it's-overpriced-like-crazy-but-obviously-you-are-paying-for-the-privilege-of-eating-with-your-own-kind* type of restaurant that happened to specialize in Thai food. The food itself was nothing special, but he wasn't paying for the quality of the food. The snake was tired of the company he had recently been keeping. He had enough of the students and local bohemians over the last little while, whilst he was looking for the monkey.

The snake was a bit of a snob. He sat like an aristocrat. And while he ate, he thought about what he should do next. He had to figure out the monkey, and he had to make a plan for what to do with him.

He was not a boss but neither did he have a boss, not really. What he had was a steady employer with good fringe benefits. It was like working freelance. This was good. It gave him a special position and he did not feel he had any obligations. He wasn't just sitting around waiting for orders. He had his own life. He could do his own thing. He was independent. No way could the snake be simply somebody's employee.

And yet, there was no way the snake would ever have someone working for him either — with him, maybe. And that is where the monkey maybe did come in. If the snake could strike a friendship between him and the monkey, and get him interested in the line of work he did, perhaps it would be possible to make some kind of partnership. That could be exciting, or entertaining even.

They could still be independent. They could be shadows for each other, or each other's secret weapon. It could be like maximizing benefits through their specialities.

The snake was pretty sure that the monkey was amoral. He was certain that he wasn't what you'd call some kind of goody two-shoes. I mean, how could someone that you'd call some kind of goody two-shoes be breaking into peoples' places and taunting people and going cruising for some girls? No, obviously the monkey's morals were what you'd call a little loose, and perhaps they're rather flexible as well.

To the snake the monkey seemed like he was just some kind of thrill-seeker. He was someone who was always looking for something new to do. He was a perfect personality to make a perfect partner, a partner for the snake.

True, the monkey's reckless. But that was good because the snake was cool. It was a combination that was good. Opposites attract. And opposite forces in conjunction create a greater force. The snake knew that was true.

Both of them had charms and both of them had skills and the two of them together could be complementary. And since they would be independent, really, just benefiting from mutual self-interest, really, then there was no reason, really, that the monkey should drive the snake too crazy, really. It was obvious, of course, that the monkey could do that, so for them to work together, and to do it properly, it would have to be set up and properly prepared.

The snake could handle that. They'd have to set the terms, and define some boundaries. The snake would have to keep the monkey at a good arm's length. He would have to keep his distance and make sure he kept it casual, and then it could be interesting, possibly quite profitable and probably fun as well.

20

THE SNAKE MIGHT BE deluding himself a little bit, but it is a good idea for him to be more cautious when it comes to dreaming up arrangements with the monkey. Any relationship with the monkey is bound to guarantee a somewhat bumpy ride. An arm's length might not be far enough a distance to keep him at if you don't want him to have any kind of an affect on you.

The monkey could be like a tornado, and you usually have to be more than an arm's length away from a tornado for it not to get at you. Still, if anyone could manage a casual relationship while working with the monkey, then probably the snake's the one who could manage that.

Maybe you are thinking that the tiger could do that. But it's hard to think the tiger and the monkey could have anything that's casual given the intensity of their relationship so far. It's true that their relationship might resolve itself into just some kind of friendship, but that doesn't mean that it would be only casual.

If they could work together, they could have a partnership. They would probably work close. And it could be a good partnership. She would like to work with someone who was equal to the task.

She wasn't interested in being just the monkey's lover anymore than she did figure he wanted that from her. Not in the usual sense of what that is construed to mean, in any case. But the monkey was if anything far away from usual. And he was rather unpredictable. So who knew for sure what he would want or what he did desire, or what it all did mean to him, if anything at all.

But she was not concerned or worried about that. Her concern right now was with trying to form a friendship and with the possibility of a working partnership. Her work was her vocation and she hoped that he agreed that it was a good and worthy one and that he would like to help.

She would like to have a partner. And the monkey could be good. And the monkey could be also good for the group that she works with. They might not work together every single time. The group might not want them to work together all the time. They might not want them to be partners actually. That didn't sit so well with her. Nevertheless, she knew that it would be good to have the monkey working on their side. And she was sure that they could work together even if just sometimes. They might work different cases, but perhaps they could confer and help each other out.

Anyway, she was getting ahead of herself here. She didn't even know if he'd be interested at all. It would be a shame if he were not. He had a great deal of potential. It excited her as much as it did worry her that he didn't have the discipline that he really needed to take the full advantage of the talents that he had.

Of course, she realized the monkey was not one for taking orders, and suggestions she might have would have to be made carefully and in the spirit of their friendship. If it were something that would clearly mean improvement, or if it were exciting, then he probably would listen.

The tiger wondered how the monkey would be with her now that she had slept with him. Most guys got pretty weird after you had slept with them. Of course, the monkey wasn't typical, and he already was weird, but he was weird in a good way.

Nevertheless, he would likely be aloof, and be a little cautious and perhaps a bit suspicious. She could easily imagine that the monkey might be worried that she wanted something from him, which wasn't really wrong. So, she couldn't really blame him if he stood back a bit to see what she was going to do next.

She hoped at least that he was thinking about what it all did mean and that consequently this would slow him down a little bit. She knew that thinking was not probably his favourite thing to do. Although she also knew that he was clever and fast-thinking on his feet.

And so, in fact, was she. But she also did like thinking. She liked to think about the different ways that anything could go. Not in a way to calculate or only to manipulate, but in a way like chess can be to understand the consequence and to try and plan ahead. Probably the monkey had no time for that. Well, perhaps he had some time for that, for just a bit of that, but not too much of that. She never had too much of that. She loved to do that often.

Suddenly, she had the thought that the three of them were interesting in the way that they all thought the way they did; they all had their own style. And their styles were just like them. Their thinking and their being were like their personalities; they were certainly consistent.

None of them should ever be underestimated. They all would have their different ways of making an analysis of a situation. And they were different but they could easily complement each other — just as easily as they could confound each other too.

She liked to think about their differences and wonder about them. She would daydream about them so that she could then imagine them doing different things and get a kind of feeling for the way that they do things so she would know a little better what she might expect from them. On the basis of such daydreams, she could make some plans.

Of course, she would always wait and watch and make an effort to be ready for when the time would come when she would have to pounce, but the daydream made her feel like she was just a little more prepared. It was important that she think about what they might do next and why they might have done what they did do sometime before, in order that she would then better understand all the possibilities. And she must always keep in mind that in fact she could be wrong. Her predictions might be wrong. And so, of course, her plans should be always open-ended. Expect the unexpected.

The tiger, the powerful tiger, the smooth and subtle tiger, whose carriage was so graceful, whose movement was sublime, was moving as though floating, so open, and so ready for anything at any time anywhere it happens, she's always with her wits about her. Well, almost always anyway.

When she's on, she's something else. And she is on right now; she is fully on right now. She is tiger moving, she is moving all around. Walking all around, taking all things in, she is ruminating. She is beauty, and she is strength, when she's in reverie thinking about things.

She looks up at the snake's place as she passes by. She doesn't let it look as though she's interested in who is actually up there. But in truth she really is because, in fact, she's tracking him. Of course, he's not there at the moment. He is eating at the restaurant.

The snake's not home, and she can tell, so she just keeps moving. She's just tracking him, that's all. Maybe she'll spot him somewhere. She'd like to get a notion of the sort of place he goes to. Does he go places? Does he hang out anywhere? If he does so, well then, where so? She'd like to know these things.

You can learn something about a person by where they go, and where they like to hang out at; like the monkey, hanging out all the time around the college students' bars and cafés always trying to impress and always showing off.

Now, the tiger's also pretty good at getting your attention.

She can also throw you off, just by being near you. But to make this happen, she must be centred in herself, or else it will not work. The thing about the monkey is it seems his centre is de-centred, like he has a shifting centre.

He doesn't act from inner calm like she or like the snake does. He acts out of chaos. So, only things that stop him in his tracks, which still his busy mind, and throw a calm into his being, can defeat him in a fight.

You see, the tiger's really good at working people out this way. She daydreams about them. She thinks about their strengths and turns them into weaknesses, and she thinks about their weaknesses and turns them into strengths. She tries to see what they might do in different situations. Each one is a positive and each one is a negative and she tries to blend them in her reverie, a dream of yin and yang.

It didn't mean that she would then be able to defeat them. But certainly she would be a little more prepared and know a little better what she should look out for. She could be so fixed, so clear and so precise, when she locked onto her target.

Of course, that strength of hers was something that could also be a weakness. That was the way of the world and its forces; always able to turn from strong to weak and to turn from weak to strong.

21

THE MONKEY FINDS A NEW PLACE with a big and open space. It's a further bit away from where he's living now. And there's less that's going on there. It's in the old part of the city, the first part of the city.

He'll be less conspicuous down there. And the open space is good. He can do more things when he's in an open space. He can change things around more if he likes. He liked that. And it was great for moving around. He liked that too.

He likes to move around. A big open space with nothing in it. That feels good. Liberating. Moving around in a big open space with nothing in it. He'd like to keep it this way. Just a bed. A table to eat on. Sound system. TV or not TV? — He wasn't sure.

There was lots of room for all the stuff he had to bring in there and lots of room besides all that for him to move around. He'll keep his stuff, for sure. But sometimes it is nice to think about giving up your stuff. Sometimes it's nice to think that you don't need any of that stuff. Stuff can be a burden. Stuff can have a hold on you. Stuff with all its history can become a part of you. You hold on to it and it holds on to you. It can be good. It can be bad. The interdependence of objects in mutual relations.

He had to laugh at that. He really loved the feeling of being unattached to things, even though he also loved the feeling that he got from having things, and the feeling that he got also from getting things. But he didn't like the feeling of feeling bound by anyone or held down by anything.

What about the tiger? Would she try and bind him? It doesn't matter what she tries. And the snake? Whatever. This was all exciting, but he'd better turn the tables around a little bit. He was feeling much too vulnerable and too much like a target.

He liked this place with nothing in it. He liked the feeling of it. Virgin territory. No vibe. A clean slate. He liked it all so much that he stayed there overnight.

He lay down on the hardwood floor. He stared at the high ceiling until he fell asleep. And when he woke up in the morning the place was filled with light. And it was beautiful.

He was in the middle of the room. It was a big and open room. And big windows let the light all in. And the light was warm.

He watched dust particles floating in the air, pretending they were other worlds with other people there. Yes, it did feel good for him to be inside of there.

But he felt a little stiff from laying on the floor. So he rolled around a bit. He did some flips and turns. He did some push-ups, too.

He thought he'd put some bars up high so he could swing around. And he'd build a climbing wall. Perfect. He liked to play like that. It's not a workout for him. That would only bore him. For him, it's just like play. He's got a lot of energy. And he's got to burn it off somehow. Physically. Jumping around, dancing, whatever. He keeps his body busy.

22

HE RAN HOME — JUST FOR FUN. When he got there he could see that right away the thing was gone. This pissed him off for sure. Which was kind of funny, actually. After all, he didn't want it. But he was mad that someone took it.

It could have been the tiger, but no, he knew it was the snake. That really pissed him off. Now he knew for sure that both the tiger and the snake knew where he did live and that both of them had entered as easily as pie. Both got what they wanted and left without a care. And no doubt both of them were making more plans for what to do with him.

Well, he wasn't going to let himself be someone else's plan. He was glad the thing was gone. But this matter wasn't done with. Which was not so good. Probably. So he had to make some plans himself, for what to do with them, the tiger and the snake.

Perhaps the snake had something going on that was different from the tiger's thing, but maybe just as interesting, or maybe even more so. But right now the monkey knew that his own position was a weak one. He had to move into a strong one.

He was pretty certain that he'd see the snake again real soon. If the snake went to the trouble, if it were indeed a trouble, to find and get his thing back, then maybe he will want revenge, or maybe something else. Obviously the snake has something in his mind. It's not likely he'd just take the thing and leave it at that. He must've been pissed off that someone took it from his place, and it was clear that he did know who that someone was and where that someone lived.

He had found the monkey. Not good. Did he follow him? Did the tiger tell him? Were they in it together? Doubtful. His intuition told him no. But where was his intuition when he really needed it — where were all his senses? Why did he not know that he was being followed? That was very strange. It's not what he is used to. Well, he'd best get used to it.

He got worried for a moment. Then he smiled. Actually, he liked this. He liked this feeling of a game, of playing cat and mouse. OK then, he would play. At least now he's in the game by his own design, and not just by default. A rush went up his spine. There was buzzing in his head.

He was going to move his stuff over to his new place, but now he thought it best to leave his stuff right there. He didn't want the tiger and he didn't want the snake to know about the new place that he had got himself. And he also didn't want them knowing that he had moved away. So he thought it was a good idea to keep both places for a while. It was a little bit expensive, but worth it for right now. He could stay here for the most part, then his new place could be more like the hideout that he needed.

He would need to take some time to figure out their patterns. If he figured out their patterns, then he could guess beforehand where they'd go and what they'd do. So to figure out their patterns, he'd have to get to know them better. And to know them better, he'd have to hang around with them.

They knew where he was. He knew where the snake was. But he didn't know where the tiger was, or the group she talked about. He would have to learn a little more about her group and, if the snake did have a group, then more about them too.

He would have to string them all along for a little while. Play footsie with them all. Be a friend. And yeah, why not? He wanted to know more. And he might enjoy their friendship — if they really could be friends, given all that's going on and what there is to come.

He didn't want to be the one who was at a disadvantage. He would have to watch his back a little more. He wasn't used to that. And he didn't want to be like someone who was paranoid. But he'd like to be more sensitive to what his instinct told him.

God, how do you train your instincts? Your instincts are your instincts. They go along, they're going strong, it's you that's just not heeding them. So, how do you get in tune with them?

Think less, and be more like an animal. After all, you are an animal. A peculiar one, it's true, but an animal no less.

He liked the challenge. Someone had successfully followed him without him knowing it. Unusual for him. He must've slipped up somehow. There had been so much going on. There was so much that had been happening. So many things he'd not experienced before. Definitely, he was thrown for a loop.

Fool me once, shame on you. Fool me twice, shame on me. Now he knew. And now he knew he must respond to new things in a broader way.

He liked to go-go-go, but it was good to stop a minute also. After all, there's nothing wrong with wait and see, sometimes. It creates suspense, and suspense can be great. Like in sex, for instance. Like delaying your orgasm. You don't have to rush through it. Waiting on it, sustaining it, can get you really high.

It's not a holding back that's like suppression or repression. It's suspense. Suspended animation. A brilliant frozen moment, suspended and yet filling up with energy on the verge of going pop. Yeah.

Or it could be like savouring delicious food or drink. Chewing slowly, letting the taste sink before gobbling it all up. That's what finding something new could be.

The monkey had a calm that was peculiar to him. He had a silence of his own. He had a way to wait and watch and wonder all his own. He could be still. But even when he was still he still was being busy. He was like a sponge.

Quietly, he'd soak it up. Into his being it would seep. Understanding at the level of his body. His muscle and his tissue and his blood and his bone, and all his inside organs, and the outside ones as well, would together be conspiring to know what it all meant.

Then he'd know. And then he'd act on it. Not by thinking with his head, or rather, only with his head. He thought with his whole body; with his body, mind and spirit.

He had made a mess of it this time. That's ok. The monkey liked a challenge. They were so few and far between. He would sort this out, somehow.

He would get a bed for his new place. Just a futon to make do. He would get a few other things too. And he would make sure he wasn't followed.

The monkey liked to dress up every now and then. He liked to wear disguises. He hadn't done that in a while. He used to do it all the time. When he first moved into where he lives, into his neighbourhood, and before he was so bold, he would dress up different ways. He figured it would help should he ever get in trouble.

He got very good at it. He was rather subtle. There was no need for full-on costumes like you'd use on Halloween. Sometimes, just a little bit of putty, or some cotton in his cheeks was enough to do the trick. He would change his voice a little.

But the most important thing he found was his attitude, and of course, his clothes. He would dress up like a business man and try to act like one and go out to a store and buy some kind of thing. He'd buy some milk and say hello and see how they were to him. They were usually polite. Then, he'd go back there a day or two later in some other kind of guise, like a punk rocker for instance, and also act like that. While he was buying beer he would say hello to the cashier. Do you remember me, he'd ask. No, they'd say, and look a little worried then at him.

On the street as well, he noticed people looking differently at him depending on the way he dressed or even how he walked. He pretended once to have a leg with something wrong with it. Some people gave him a wide berth and others seemed annoyed by him because he slowed them down.

Unless people know you well, they normally just notice the superficial things. There are even those who know you well, who will only notice surface things. Have you ever had someone who said to you that "you look great" when you feel absolutely awful?

Maybe he should take again to wearing some disguises. He hadn't done it in a while but he could do it again easily. And it might be even more effective now since people were a bit more used to seeing him look a certain way.

The monkey felt a little sad that people knew him now. But he kind of liked it too because he also did get lonely. But there was a romantic thing about being such a secret.

Where he was living people were starting to know him. There was talk about him sometimes. He played with too many dumb guys, fighting them and razzing them. And he'd known too many girls. True, a lot of these people were students who weren't around there long. But nevertheless, there was a bit of a buzz about him, and this was not a good thing for someone with a need to keep his profile low.

He had been showing off too much. He would blow everything if he kept it up. For sure it must've helped the tiger and the snake to find him all that easily.

Perhaps he wanted to be found. Maybe that was why he hadn't been so cautious. He should have been more cautious. Maybe he was bored and lonely and he needed to be found and have some excitement for a change. Well, ok then, he got it. So now what?

The tiger, the tiger, what about the tiger? What should he do with her? It had been two days now since their sexual affair. And he had a funny feeling he would see her sometime today. He felt there might be contact with her in some way today. He knew it.

And since he could not contact her, she would contact him. And how? She might drop in unannounced. She might drop down from the sky, just like she did the first time. She could be outside right now. But he really did not think so.

23

THE MONKEY IS A TRICKY GUY but yet so normal in a way. He's a survivor, for sure. And he's usually pretty positive. Sometimes he feels down, but he doesn't mind it when he does. Each emotion has a power and depression's one of them. So, depression also has a power. When you are depressed you cannot be seduced. And if you cannot be seduced then you also can't be tricked. And the monkey likes it when he can't be tricked.

He is tricky, but he doesn't like it if someone plays a trick on him. Not that it's an easy thing to do to play a trick on him. But it's not impossible. And the way things have been going it might be a little easier than it was before because he's thinking far too much. He is not depressed but he is thinking all the time.

Well, you know, there is a lot that's going on. Normally there's not this much that's going on for him. Sure, the monkey's always busy, there's always something going on, but he's always had control of everything before. It was just like entertainment all that stuff that went before. He just went along, just being himself, just doing what he did without much thought about it all, or about himself at all.

Now with these people in his life, with the snake and tiger

in his life, he thought about himself much more. And thoughts about himself were surely a distraction. It was like a hall of mirrors. He had made mistakes already where he never would have made them any time before and now he had to exercise some caution and he wasn't used to that.

But it was kind of exciting all this difference and change. But it was also somewhat tiresome. And for the first time ever he felt a bit of a loss for the way that things once were.

The monkey was not one to ever be nostalgic. He's never known the feeling. So it was interesting.

He never much thought about himself or how things were, and now that he was doing that, thinking now about himself and how things are around him, he found that he was also now starting to think about the way that he did used to be and the way that things did used to be. And he thought about the differences brought on by all this change that he both liked and didn't like. And it made him long for how things used to be and how he used to be before he started thinking so much about himself and how things are around him. It's funny how it works that way.

Before, the monkey always just went with the way that things were going. Now he had to stop and think and remind himself to do that; to just go with the way that things are going. Now it was a thing to do and a way to be, because since he had to stop and think and remind himself to do it, that meant that it was an idea about how he should do things. How he was quite naturally was becoming now a recipe for how he'd like to be. So he could only be the way he was if he remembered how to do it. He had to tell himself to be like that and guide himself to be like that, and there was something weird with that. There was something in the fact of that which meant he couldn't be himself unless he tricked himself into being like himself.

He had to trick himself to be himself, to be just like he was when he did the things he did when he did them naturally without stopping first to think to remind himself to be that way.

Was he better being more himself that way? Wasn't he

right now just being more himself right now by being just himself right now even though he's different right now because now he could see that he had changed and knew now he was different? What was that difference? Was it a fundamental difference? Or was it just a change in how he did behave? Was his behavior the same thing that his nature was?

Maybe he was still just going with the way that things were going but that now they're going in such a different way and he's changing naturally with them. You just can't really count on things going how they go in always the same way. And whatever you are thinking about the way that they were going might just be presumptuous. Maybe you were wrong about them all along, and maybe you're wrong still. The changes and the differences might be more within yourself and a part of your perception of the way that things are going and the way that things are being.

And even if you're not thinking about the way that things are going and the way that things are being, you might have made in any case some assumptions that were tacit about the way that things are going and the way that things are being. Why else would you then be surprised if the way things are have changed? You wouldn't know that they had changed if you didn't in some way have a sense of them to start with. Try to tell him that. Maybe he is getting it.

If you have a notion about the way that things are going and the way that things are being, but you don't really know that you have a notion about them, then maybe you are going with the way that things are going, and when they change you might not realize that you still are going with the way that things are going. What has changed is the way that you now think about these things and the way that you do now also think about yourself.

That is what the monkey was starting now to see. And he thought that it was interesting.

Perhaps the monkey had invented a version of himself and

didn't notice it before. Maybe that invention was just another way of tricking himself secretly, of tricking himself into a way of thinking about the way that things are going and the way that he is being. This could be something dangerous and this could be something good.

It could be something dangerous because now he was responsible for making himself long for something that was not really ever there, for something that he's making up based on wrong assumptions about the way that things were going and the way that things were being and the changes he imagines in the way that things are going and how they are right now. He was a bit confused. He was making these things up for the sake of an emotion, and what was that about?

Things weren't really different, but there were some different things. And one thing that was different was his new-found melancholy. And the other thing that was much more interesting was the fact of his division in himself.

This can be a good thing and this can be a bad thing but regardless of its being good and regardless of its being bad it can be absolutely vital and necessary too. If he can fight well with himself then he can fight with anyone.

Some people think it's good to just stop going and just wait until you naturally start going once again. Some people think that when you go up against yourself in such a way that stops you in some sense, that it is a good idea to not resist that stopping, but rather to respect it and to do it with some care; just stop and wait until you just start up and go again.

So often things will happen when you do not think of them and sometimes they are good things and sometimes they are not. Some people recommend that you stop thinking if you want something to happen. And other people recommend that you concentrate if you want something to happen. Two quite different ideas about how to make something happen. Which one was the right one for the monkey?

Well now the monkey knew that he had a history and that

things were changing in it, that he was changing in it. And now
he had a memory of how it used to be, of how he used to be, and
whether it was real or only just a trick, a trick that he was playing on himself without him even knowing it, regardless of all
that he could make use of that, of that sense of how it was and
how he was before. What use of it he'd make, he wasn't really
sure, but there it was, and it seemed to have a function just by
being something meaningful when thinking about new things
and what their value was.

He felt a little sorry that things weren't how they were, but
things now were exciting, and he really loved excitement, and
things now were more complicated, and he was more at risk.
Well that was all OK.

Because these things were complicated, he was developing
his thinking. And because he was at risk, he was developing
some caution.

Of course he'll take the proper steps to reduce his vulnerability. He had a new place, and he would keep his old place for a
little while. And he wondered what they wanted, the tiger and
the snake. This was new to him as well, you see, wondering
about people and what it was they wanted. Wondering about
these people and what they wanted with him fascinated him.
But perhaps it fascinated him a little bit too much.

He could see that he could be rather self-indulgent about
it. It was like gossip, wasn't it? Gossip was so tasty a treat and
it was filled with speculation about things and people and what
was going to happen. It was like fortune-telling that way too.

He could see that once you thought about the way you are
and the way you were and what other people wanted with you,
that it was not anything but natural that you would think about the
future and how you might be then and what would happen then.

If you changed once, and your world could change once,
and the way things are and the way they go could also change
once, and you could meet people with designs upon you once;
then you could do all of that twice and more and more again

and again. Not only that, but you could develop a taste for it. You could want it. You could love it. And, of course you also could just dread it.

And if there were ways, if there seemed to be ways, that allowed you to find out ahead of time how things were going to be, then weren't you likely to give it a try and wonder about it all? But of course, you couldn't know for sure until it really happened. But you could be prepared for it in case it really happened.

And of course, all that preparation for what was maybe going to happen, could so much distract you that you kind of maybe lost some sight of where you were there in the present there. And again you could get tricked.

The monkey felt like he was lost in some kind of big time tunnel. It was all a lot of fun, but man it made his head spin.

If he got drunk then he could just forget about it all. He could get drunk and just drive it all out of his mind.

That wasn't like him, either. If ever he got drunk, it was for the fun of it; he never did get drunk so he could drive things from his mind. 'Don't drink and drive,' he said, and 'ha!' He never had to ever drive anything from his mind.

The monkey got up and went outside and had a look around. Then he went around the block a few times. He was making sure, just being careful — in fact, maybe too much so.

Do you know the saying 'Couldn't see for looking?' He knew it. So he sat down on the curb and he bit at his thumbnail. He had a way of doing this without breaking any of it. He sat there doing nothing in particular, and thinking nothing special. Sighing. He waited till he was definitely bored. Then he got up and started walking nowhere special.

Walking nowhere special was a very good idea. Now he was relaxed. The anxiety eased off. He was more just like still waters. This is very good. Just letting his flow go. When something breaks still waters, ripples do occur. So just be natural, and be cool, and if something suddenly feels different, that's a ripple. Something's in your pool. It's just like human radar. Forget about it all. But be very quiet. That's the way it works. The ripple will get closer. And will get bigger too. Wait until it moves you to action. Let it be the cause, the motive. It's a natural cause and effect system.

Oh, the monkey could be very Zen. True, he was a noisy rascal. But he could be very Zen. He was into Tao. And after all, the noise is also Tao.

The monkey took to the rooftops. He hadn't done that for a while and it really did feel good. He felt like one of the super-heroes he used to read about in comics when he was just a kid. Moving through the big bad city all along the rooftops. You have to be in a dense area for it to really work. But he could jump really well. He could jump a 10-foot gap with no trouble whatsoever.

He moved very quickly along the rooftops. He could cover a lot of ground a lot faster than if he were at street level. And he could look down on the street and see what was happening. He pretended he was looking for criminals. In the comics, super-heroes always fought supervillains. It was like battles of the titans. A superhero would go out for some air and before you knew it there would be some spectacular villain on their ass.

The hero was always reticent and ambivalent about their power. They were burdened by it. It was a big responsibility. The monkey felt no burden and no such responsibility. He truly revelled in his power.

But he did feel separated from everybody else. But he also knew that you didn't need to be super-powered to feel that. You just only had to be different in any way at all.

There were so many ways to be different that it made you wonder about just who was really normal. But even different people hated other different people. Just like superheroes and supervillains. There was never any guarantee that anyone would ever like anybody else or treat anybody right just because they shared something in common, like their difference. There wasn't any guarantee of anything at all.

The monkey leaned against a smokestack and stared up at the twilight sky so blue like a blue indescribable blue so rich it made you ache a little bit, and the first twinkling stars, and Venus, bright silver against blue, nothing could beat that.

He took all of it in. And he wondered how he'd find the tiger? He knew where the snake was. He found that out by accident. But how could he find the tiger? He's not a hunter by his nature. His looking skills all come from his curiosity. Intrigue drove him more than hunger ever did.

Well, he could look around. He could snoop around. But he had a notion that this would not accomplish much. And he knew he would get bored of it eventually in any case. These people weren't the type to just hang out the way he did. They only would go out if they had specific purposes in mind. They weren't like him in that way. He liked to just hang out. And, of course, that was just the thing that made him easier to find. But damned if he was going to change just on their account.

No, the thing to do was to use your natural talents and to turn your natural ways into talents. He would take his natural way of doing things and find the strength in it.

If hanging out made him easier to find then it could also make it easier for him to find someone. He would draw the tiger out and he would draw the snake out too. He would lure them out as bait lures fish. He was not a hunter but he could be a trickster.

He could play dumb. He could play the fool. He could pretend to be vulnerable. He could be open and available because that came to him quite naturally. So, that's what he would do.

Now he had a hiding place. And he was going to be more cautious. But he would do it on his terms, using his own method.

The monkey could have focus; he could be alert. The slightest movement anywhere could always catch his eye. When he is relaxed and not preoccupied like he had been lately. But now he knew the score so there was no reason for him to be out of it anymore. Always expect the unexpected.

So, the thing to do would be to draw the tiger out somehow.

First he'd draw the tiger out, then he'd draw the snake out too. Even though he knew where the snake did live, he would rather draw him out.

He could just wait at his old place for either one to show, but he couldn't really do that. He's not the type to do that. He couldn't wait around for anyone like that.

He would like to know where the tiger lives. He doesn't like that she does have the advantage in that way. Although it's true that soon, neither the tiger nor the snake will know where the monkey does live either. They will think they do, but they won't know all about his secret hideaway.

So the monkey will need to make something of a big show of himself. Easy enough for him to do. But while making this big show he will have to be alert. If he draws the tiger out then he will have to be quite tricky to find out where she lives. If he draws the snake out then he will have to be quite tricky to find out what his game is so the monkey then can know how he can win that game.

24

THE TIGER IS SO SMOOTH. She really is so smooth. She is so smooth; she doesn't even know how smooth she really is. But even the smoothest person can also be a sucker. And she was a sucker for the monkey.

She did not want to be like this. She did not want to like the monkey quite so much as this. She should stay away from him. She knew that would be best. But she also knew she wouldn't, and she also knew she couldn't, really. For one thing, she was committed to recruiting him. She wanted him to join the group. For another, the monkey was a challenge. And she always liked a challenge.

But she must be careful, certainly. The reason that a challenge was a challenge was because you did in fact risk failure. She never failed at anything. Things came mostly easy to her, and maybe they came too easy.

She needs to have a challenge or else she will get bored. And she doesn't handle boredom well. It's true she could be quiet. It's true she could be still. But one thing that she couldn't be was bored. She didn't value easy things the way the monkey did.

The monkey loved the things the best that came to him the easiest. He did not value effort. If he met a challenge and he passed it, it was true that he was proud. But he did not like a challenge in such a way that he would seek it out. He was bored more by a challenge than by something that came easily. He grew impatient with a challenge.

Not the tiger. She had great patience for a challenge. And the monkey was a challenge; there was no doubt of that. The monkey was a challenge and the tiger had a lot of patience for dealing with him too. But also, she was nervous.

She was nervous because most challenges for her were not things that she was a sucker for as well. She was not often if ever a sucker for anything or anyone, except maybe for a challenge, for the prospect of a challenge. She certainly was sometimes a sucker for a challenge. But for a person? That was rare.

She did of course like rare things, but this rare thing was trouble. She knew that it was so. And yet she felt compelled to see him. She had to see him once again, but should she be a certain way when she sees him once again?

The last time that they met they screwed for hours, so the next time that they met could be a little awkward. It could be funny. Not ha ha funny. Strange funny. Maybe awkward funny. Maybe not. She didn't really know how it would be, truthfully. And that was something also.

The unpredictability. What does she think of that? Unpredictability. Well, it was exciting for her. It can be thrilling for a hunter, really. It keeps you on your toes. And she liked to have that feeling of being kept upon her toes. It did keep her alert. She liked that feeling of being kept alert. But the monkey also had a way of clouding things for her. How did he do that, anyway?

It was just the way he was. And that's the fascinating thing. It wasn't something that he did. It was just a natural consequence of the way he was. She found that quite alluring. The natural monkey way. It was like chemistry or physics, the affect he had upon her.

Maybe he was like that when it came to her as well. Maybe he was also a sucker for the tiger. Maybe she did something to him just by way of being her. No doubt.

She took some comfort in that thought. If she could believe that he was more or less in the same boat that she was, then it would be more OK that she was nervous about meeting him, because then so was he. Probably.

But she didn't know for sure, damn it. So, she'd have to see him once again to re-establish equilibrium within herself again, and to see what's what as well.

But how then should she do it? Should she just drop by? She figured this might serve to keep a slight advantage over him. She did know where he lived. Last time she just walked right in. She walked right in and nailed him. She really could have killed him.

He must know that's the case, and it must make him somewhat nervous to think about the fact. Nobody liked to feel vulnerable like that. If she showed up again like that, it might be too much for him. She might scare him off completely.

Sure, he doesn't want to feel vulnerable like that. She knew he couldn't like the fact that she could get to him that easily.

Yes, seduction can be fun. Yes, they did have a good time. But right now that doesn't mean a thing. He probably thinks it was a trick, she was sure he did consider it to be something of a trick.

So, no, she should not just drop by. That would be invasive. That would be too much. She should give to him some space right now.

But maybe she could show up somewhere else instead. Away from his home. But make sure that it didn't look like she had tracked him down or anything. She shouldn't show up like she meant to, it should appear to be coincidence, or serendipity.

What games she had to play. But still she had to play them. After all, she was actually playing all the time. She had a plan, so she should stick to it. She was a sucker for the monkey so she should really stick to it.

There was her plan for the monkey and then there was the way she felt about the monkey. And though they seemed like they were different things, they were actually the same. They had to be. Or else, it would be trouble for her, for sure.

She didn't know how. And that, in a way, was the whole point. She didn't know how it would be trouble, and she liked to know what kind of trouble it was going to be and see it coming from a long far way away.

So how then should she meet the monkey? Well, it was so clear. He would have to actually be the one to meet with her. He would have to find her. He would have to track her down. He would have to chase her till she caught him.

She had to laugh at that, that old cliché. Well, clichés were clichés because at some level they were true.

The best thing to do would be to let him follow her to her place. She did not like this, really. She did not like for anyone to know where she did live. But it was for sure the best way for her to gain his trust. Because she knows where he lives, he should know where she lives. It would even up the score.

Of course that would make her vulnerable. More vulnerable, in fact, because she was already vulnerable because of how she felt for him. She'd be vulnerable and afterwards she might have to move.

She was prepared for that. She'd done it many times. Many times she had to move for one reason or another. She liked her place, but she could move at anytime and it wouldn't be a problem. Actually, she liked to move around a lot.

She lived very simply. She didn't own a lot of stuff. She didn't really like to own a lot of stuff. It just got in the way. She was not domestic. She liked her place, but her comfort came from inside, not from the things around her.

She could just about be anywhere and find some comfort there. It was a great strength that she had. She was adaptable.

Her places were quite comfortable. She made them how she liked them. But they could be anywhere and that was fine by her.

So it was easy for her then to move. She didn't have much to move around, and anything she had to lose could be easily replaced. This made her feel free.

She was very mobile. She was not held down by what she owned. The most important thing to her was how she was inside. How her being was. Her discipline. Her way. Her mission. Her plan. What else did she need? Nothing.

So, she'll let him come. And she will let him find her. She'll let him think that he has evened up the score himself. Fine.

If he turned out to be trouble — real trouble — then she could move. She could disappear. She could handle him. Real trouble was a good thing for her, actually. If he were a pain, a big pain in the ass, then that would free her from him. She wouldn't be a sucker for him anymore.

That's the trouble that he was right now. She was a bit of a sucker for him. That was fine while he was on her side. But if he went over to the other side, if he turned bad on her, then she'd fight him — and defeat him.

That would be too bad, because she really liked the monkey. She hopes that he is good. He could be good. He could be really good and really doing good. But she didn't know just yet. How vain was he, how selfish? How bad could he be? She had to know. She had to find it out.

It was her job to find it out. It was her mission to try and bring the monkey on board. If he were bad then he'd be dealt with. Not just by her, by her whole group.

They would not allow it, having people like him being bad. It is just too much. It's bad for everyone. If he is bad, then it's really bad; because he really could be really bad. He'd be really good at being bad. Maybe even better than the snake, and the snake is really very good at being bad.

Soon the snake would have to be dealt with by her group. But the snake was hard to deal with because he was not alone. He had his own group and that made him trickier to deal with.

If the monkey joined that group as well then that could mean big, big trouble and something would have to be done and it would all be a big, big mess for sure. Probably a war would start. Maybe not a war that you would hear about so much, you might not read it in the papers or see it on TV or hear it on the radio, or whatever on the Internet. But it would be a war in any case, and would be a war that's just as bad and just as vital for the future as any other kind of war could be ever said to be.

So the tiger then would have to let the monkey find her and let the monkey find out where the tiger's home was.

25

YOU MUST UNDERSTAND what it is like when two people like the monkey and the snake meet after all that's gone on between them. And that's an interesting thing too, because what has gone on between them is not very much really. But it amounts to a lot considering the way they think about each other, and how they figure that they factor in — each of them with each of them.

They all know that each one expects now something from the other, and they all know that they're going to try and sort it out and be on top. And each one has some advantage, but it's the same advantage, so it isn't really much of an advantage after all.

Each one is tricky, for example, and so how tricky can they be to one another really? And that is why the monkey thinks it's best to not be tricky. The monkey is the trickiest of the three by far. So, perhaps the best trick for him to pull would be to not be quite so tricky. That is a trick, of course, because it plays with expectation. A trick that tricks you into thinking that there is no trick at all.

The monkey might forget, but he always will remember that his power is his knack for being who and what he is. He's got the hang of it, that trickster, of accepting who and what he is.

So, although he's nervous, he doesn't mind, because it is to his advantage if he doesn't mind. He'll just incorporate it and trust in it, you see. That way he stays the way he is undivided against himself. When he's unified, his strength is greater. Refuse not what you are, use it all instead. It is there, it has a purpose, your mood and energy, channel it and use it, deploy it, don't deplore it.

What does it all mean? That is the question. Precisely that. What indeed? And he knows there's more than just one answer. He knows the answer's up for grabs. It means this and it means that and so he swings from this to that and that's what keeps him going, and he likes it when he goes.

So he goes there to the snake, and he knocks on the snake's door.

26

AND THE SNAKE is there and waiting.

Oh the snake can wait, it's true, but when it's time to strike the snake strikes fast. The snake watches and waits and looks like one cool customer. The snake is such a charmer.

There are so many ways a charmer knows how to make a strike. Violence isn't something you can always see. It's not easy to feel sometimes, as well. That's the thing about the snake; he can strike and leave no trace. And when the snake did leave a trace, it was deliberate. You wouldn't know it that he struck you unless he wanted you to know it.

The snake's been thinking too about the monkey, and just how he might get him. That is, how can he get to him, how can he affect him?

Well, he reckons friendship is his best bet. But, how can he do that? He thinks it won't be hard. The snake really can be arrogant and a little over-confident at times.

But friendship with the monkey, he knows it must be honest and sincere. No problem, the snake is truly and quite genuinely interested in the monkey.

His approach must not be obvious. No problem, the snake

is never obvious unless it suits him to be obvious.

So, what then should he do? Should he send the monkey some kind of invitation? The monkey now must know that the snake went in and took his thing back. That means nothing, really. That's just tit for tat. One break-in for another. One theft for another. Although the thing was his to start with so it wasn't really theft to go and get it back. No matter. It's the thought that counts.

The snake had gotten over it, he wasn't angry anymore that the monkey took his thing like that. It wasn't personal. The monkey couldn't know the value of the thing, that was something private. It was just a gesture, like touching coupe — an old game played by old and noble adversaries. It was like sneaking into the enemy's camp while they were sleeping, touching them and leaving a trace that you were there. Now their score was even at this game. Of course, neither one came in while the other one was sleeping. That would have been much harder, that's for certain and for sure.

For a moment, the snake entertained the idea of trying it. But it was not a good idea. Maybe later, but not right now. Now called for something else.

An invitation? It was bold. It meant: I know where you live, so what? — you know where I live too — we're even — let's meet — on even ground. The snake was pretty sure that the monkey would read it to mean that. But what actually should it say? What actually should he write, and where actually should they meet?

Well, it actually should say something rather simple actually, because what it really meant was more important than what it actually did say. It should actually just simply say come and meet me somewhere, but where should that somewhere be?

It could be anywhere, but it really should be somewhere that made some kind of sense. The snake liked that idea. Bit of a ham, really — the snake. A cool customer, for sure, but vain as well, it's true.

But the snake was in for a surprise because there was a knock now at his door. It didn't matter what the snake wrote in his note because he didn't need to write a note. He didn't need to write a note because the monkey now was knocking at his door.

The snake doesn't get all that many small surprises. The snake doesn't get all that many big surprises either. But this was one to come. A knock at his door was a small surprise, and that was odd enough. But a knock at his door from the monkey was a big surprise. And we're not sure he will like it.

Of course the snake will never show it. The snake was one cool customer. But when he opened up the door and saw the monkey there, he was certainly surprised. And we're not sure that he liked it.

27

SO AFTER ALL THE THINKING, here they are together. After all the wondering which way the thing could go. They know it could go this way, they know it could go that way. It has been thought about a lot. After thinking when they will, and if they will, where they will, and what's the best way to prepare for it, the thinking doesn't matter, because now they have to deal.

The snake he had a plan. He always has a plan. The snake for sure is one to plan and the snake for sure he had a plan.

Not to bother planning is the best way you can win a planning game, because a watched pot never boils, and it can drive you crazy planning for that pot to boil when you are watching it.

So do not bother planning, then. But then again, don't leave the pot upon the stove and walk away for good, because it will boil and then what will you do if you aren't there to turn it off?

When everything is right out there way out in the open it's best to just dispense with tricks and go straight to the point. No planning, no playing, just getting to the point. At least that's the way the snake looked at it.

And the monkey hoped the snake would look at it that way. The monkey figured that with everything being sneaky like it was and people being second guessed and grabbing the advantage, you could get lost in all the thought about it all. The best thing then to do was to bring it out into the open. Then you knew what you were dealing with. When you drew specific lines, then you could deal with things specifically.

Of course, that being said, the monkey played his best tricks on people when he was right in front of them. He didn't work in the shadows. He worked best in plain sight.

But for the snake, even plain sight could be a shadow if he did things right. So even going straight to the point was just another ruse, just another of his plans.

28

SO, HOW TO START THINGS off then? They sat around, the monkey and the snake. The snake invited in the monkey and he smiled a certain smile. They sat around and drank a drink. They drank a drink of scotch and sized each other up.

The snake poured a lot of drink into the drink of scotch. It can be interesting to see how much someone can take, and when someone is taking lots, you can see them at their best, and you can see them at their worst. The monkey drank the drink right down just like it was water. The monkey drank the same way that he did a lot of things. The monkey always did the things he did the way he usually did, which was with gusto often, and this was no exception.

Different people act in different ways when they're drinking and they're drunk. And you can tell something, although it's hard to know what, about a person who knows their drinking limit, and when they do get drunk you have to wonder did they mean to or was it oops I drank too much and now I'm drunk and can't speak right or walk too straight or do anything that isn't done now in a sloppy way.

So, it was a test, and the monkey knew it was, and the

monkey drank the way he did and if it made him high, a little high, he didn't mind because being drunk made little difference to him. He was drunken master drunk. Do not resist — that was the key. That always was the key for any monkey lock. Do not resist — go with it. That always served the monkey well. You had to be a certain way for that to work out right and the monkey was that way.

So the snake had poured a drink for the monkey and he poured him quite a lot just to see if he could take it and to see if he was fool enough to get a little drunk and then be at the mercy of the snake. But of course the monkey is a fool. But of course for him that works.

Some people just don't like that he can get away with things like that. They think it has to be a certain way; a way so anyone can do it and anyone can follow it, with lots of work and lots of effort, lots of unrelenting effort. And if anybody's way works without all of that effort, without going through all that, then they think that it's not fair. And then they get real mad and try to prove it's wrong and try to prove they're right and then they say OK, if that's the way you are then you can just fuck off, I'm not going to help you or give you anything because every-thing's too easy, things come just too easy to you and it's just not any fair.

Oh, but you know the monkey doesn't care about that kind of thing or any of those kinds of people or that kind of life, and lucky for the monkey what they think about his way means nothing to him either and affects him not at all. But what the snake thinks could affect him, although in a different way.

Nevertheless, one way or another, the best thing that the monkey has is himself and his own way. So gulp the whisky down he does. He likes it — yum, yum, yum.

Thanks, he says, and would he like another, asks the snake? And the snake is just a bit surprised at how fast the monkey drank the drink and wondered if the monkey were a fool, a lush, or totally out of control, or what? And again, the snake felt a little like the way the monkey had a way to make you feel like maybe you were just careening out of your control, and actually not minding that, but nonetheless still feeling it, like you were losing all, and feeling the temptation of giving way to that, and the feeling that was freedom to give into that, which made it hard then to resist because you just felt caught up in it all and swept up in it all, and it seemed like so much fun, like driving faster and faster till you saw a tree in front of you and oh no, could you, would you swerve in time?

Well, the monkey could, but maybe not the snake. He was not the type to go completely off half-cocked like that. And what was it, and how was it, that the monkey could do that to somebody, make them feel like that? It was very interesting, and the snake could only wonder if it was something useful in some way; useful like a weapon.

It was a good defense, the best defense in fact, because it wasn't a defense as such, it was just the way he was, the way the monkey was. And it was naturally to his advantage for him to be that way because it was a brilliant, natural defense, like the thorns upon a rose's stem.

So the snake now knew that it was not his best bet to try and throw the monkey off, because doing that might mean that he would only throw himself off.

29

THE MONKEY HAS HIS OWN PLAN, but he only knows it now. Now that he is feeling drunk, well, drunk a little bit, his plan comes to fruition.

He looks over at the snake, who is sitting just across from him, whose legs are crossed the way that is said to be feminine, like academics often do, and his foot is swinging, and he looks back at the monkey with a look of great bemusement.

And the monkey jumps upon him. From his chair he leaps upon him. The snake goes flying backward in his chair. And the monkey rolls away. He's drunken master monkey, now.

And the snake is furious. His body coils and recoils, his punches crack like whips. The monkey sways and stumbles, twisting this and then that way, dodging all his punches, but looking like a drunk who's just trying to keep his balance.

The snake makes contact on the monkey's lower ribs. The monkey takes it on the left side. He makes like he will fall right over going forward. He falls into the snake and he hooks his elbow, right arm elbow, into the crook of his right knee, into the snake's right knee. He spins back up around completely and the snake falls on his ass.

The monkey keeps going in his spin then tumbles down on top of the snake. But the snake moves quickly oh so quickly and gets quickly up and off the floor. The monkey falls down anyway hard upon the floor. And he doesn't seem to mind it. He rolls toward the snake to try and knock him down again like he's a bowling ball and the snake's a bowling pin.

The snake has got to laugh at this. He easily leaps over him, and pirouettes to land a kick right in the monkey's back. But the monkey parries it in time with the back of his left arm, rolling back the other way, he twists around and lifts his legs and kicks the snake right in the stomach and the snake goes flying backward once again and the monkey's back on his feet swaying back and forth.

The snake then decides it's best to stand his ground and let the monkey come to him. The monkey runs toward him and tries to tackle him, he grabs the snake around the waist but the snake is on to him, his stance is very strong and he doesn't budge from where he is, and with speed great speed he bends at the waist, and grabs the monkey around his waist and lifts him upside down.

The monkey's legs are dangling in the air and he's forced to let his own hold go. The snake drops him on his head, Ouch! — and jumps back a little bit. The monkey cushions the impact by using both his hands, but still it hurts his hands, and still it hurts his head; but he doesn't feel it all that much because he is a little drunk.

The monkey somersaults away and gets up quick and throws a big roundhouse kick forward right leg and follows through and spins into a backward roundhouse kick from the other leg, and follows through and throws another high roundhouse kick right leg. None of them make contact but the snake moves back some more. And the monkey stops and stands there in a low and swaying stance. His hands are up for boxing.

The monkey's got a smile upon his face. He is enjoying this. The snake can see it is the case and he must admit that he is too. This is a very odd thing. They are really fighting. But there's a lot of sport in it, right now in any case.

He's about to say something but he doesn't get much out because the monkey sees it as a chance to go swinging madly at him. The snake is used to fighting with precision — not this sloppy stuff. But he knows the monkey's powerful and he can't let him connect, because when he does he really feels it, this guy is powerful.

And connect the monkey does. First, he gets him in the stomach, then he hits him in the jaw, and he's driving the snake backward. The snake is losing all control of his stance and of his blocks, and he cannot find an opening to strike back at the monkey.

But with a sudden and blind fury, most unusual for him, the snake just grabs out at him and he gets him by the shirt and he pulls and tries to throw him, but the monkey's hanging on and the two of them are spinning round like they're playing at square dancing, and they're knocking some things over, and the monkey sees they're near the door that opens to the balcony and when he gets a chance he swings the snake right through it. But, of course, the snake does not let go, and so the monkey goes right through it too, and they both stumble from the shock of it and land, BAM! into the railing, finally letting go as each sprawls out on the balcony.

This is an opportunity for both to have a little bit more space. The monkey jumps up on the railing about to jump down to the ground below. But then he has a change of mind and he climbs up to the rooftop. And the snake of course does follow him by going up the other side.

30

THE TIGER IS OUTSIDE there waiting. They have not come out there yet. There is no sign that they are fighting.

She wonders, will she, could she, go up there and join them? Would she, could she do that thing? It seems it could be rash. But that could be a good thing.

That is something that she thinks a lot about these days. These days, she thinks that rash acts are, in fact, acts which could be good acts or be bad acts, but regardless of how good or bad they are, they might just be essential. Sometimes, in any case.

She listens to the birds. There are many, it would seem.

Then there is a noise that is nothing like the birds. The noise comes from the snake's place. Should she go up there?

It looks like she won't have to. She sees them on the balcony and it looks like they are fighting.

Now what should she do? She watches as they climb up to the roof and face each other there. The monkey starts to run, and the snake runs after him, and the tiger follows down below.

A riot of emotions is causing many conflicts, but she manages to stay them, and to make a clear decision. She will watch them from below, and she will not interfere, unless the monkey needs it, absolutely needs it, she will not interfere.

This could be a good thing. Now the lines were clearly drawn. Or were they? She must be very careful not to make assumptions about the fact that they are fighting. After all, that is what she did with the monkey first, as well. But that's not what she did the last time she saw him.

This just might be their way of getting to know each other better. Well, she had to laugh at that, but there was some truth in it, some probability.

It certainly was forcing hands and that would make things different, and would surely speed up matters. She was unclear if this was good or not. And this was not the time to ponder.

So, she followed close below making sure they would not see her, although their attention was most clearly set on one another. Still, she would not falter in her sense of protocol. And when sometimes she could not see them, she listened carefully.

She followed them no problem, they were mostly only running; the snake was chasing after the monkey. The monkey seemed to be actually enjoying it. She was not so sure about the snake, but maybe he was too. This kind of worried her.

It worried her that they were fighting and that monkey might get hurt. But it worried her much more that they might be only playing and that they might just get along. She could not interfere, in any case, unless she really, really had to.

After all, she also had to know if he was really capable of handling someone like the snake. And the bonus thing about this was she'd get a preview of the snake and the way that he did fight, which could come in handy if she ever had to fight with him. So she stuck to what she thought was right and watched them from below.

There was only one more thing that worried her; and that was who might see them. They really should get off the roofs, not just because of danger to their physical well-being, but because of danger to their anonymity as well. The tiger was beginning to become something of a worrywart.

31

THE MONKEY WASN'T REALLY DRUNK. He was just a little drunk. He was just a little tipsy. He could hold his liquor. But he let the feeling amplify as though he were more drunk. It would be more real and therefore more effective for the style of fighting that he had decided would be best against the snake.

A river can be tamed because it flows in one way only. It can be hard to tame a human because they can flow in many ways. But humans have got to learn to go along with their flows smoothly, or else they turn against themselves and end up blocking their own flows, or lose their flows completely and become a great big mess, a stiff and awkward mess.

For a river it is easy; it only has one flow and it always goes along with it and it never can be wrong. But if humans go with just one flow it can do them good or bad.

If a river meets another flow, it still will go the way that it has already been going. Sometimes it is contained and sometimes redirected, but it also keeps its flow. When a human meets another flow it can stop or go or can resist, it can turn another way, or try to go right through it, or hold itself against it, or try to influence or change it, or even try to stop it, for now or for forever more. Or it can try to complement it.

This is what the monkey now was doing in his fight. He let the feeling he was having of being somewhat drunk drop his inhibitions so that he would not resist the snake's attack on him. He would complement the flow of the snake's attack, and finish off his movement by pulling it around and pushing it away from him. It was a basic redirect.

It was an act of will, which was another difference between humans and the flowing of a river. Animals can do this too, especially carnivores who stalk their prey. But they don't do it with philosophy, which is something it would seem is just peculiar to humans.

The monkey and the snake fought now, but not with just their instinct. They fought with principles and knowledge, with skill and strategy that had been thought about before and was being applied now. Their fighting was philosophy, as much as it was fighting.

The snake, of course, was just as versed in principles of fighting. He could also redirect, and redirect the redirect. And so he did. And for a while it looked like they were dancing on the rooftops up above. It looked just like square dancing every now and then. And with the smiles on both their faces, you might not realize how serious their fighting really was.

The tiger was confused by this, watching down below, and a little worried also because it looked like they were having fun, and she would rather that they didn't. She would rather that they really fought with hatred on their faces. Then at least she thinks that she would know a little better where the lines were drawn.

Of course, emotions and the psyche, the movements of the mind and also of the spirit, all of these are flows. And all of it adds up to a complexity of being, and being is the flow of flows. When they say go with your flow, it is your flow of flows that you must go with. And it goes in many ways. So try and be alert. And try and be relaxed. And the best is just to do it and not to try at all. Trying is an effort, and it should be effortless to go the way you're going, to follow and to lead.

Of course, that being said, it's easier to say it than it is in fact to do it. That is also a condition, of what it's like to be a human.

32

THE MONKEY AND THE SNAKE had gotten to a point where their anger and frustration had all but disappeared. They still were fighting sure, but the pitch of it had definitely changed. It felt more and more like sport. And they were not throwing punches much and when they did they weren't as hard as when they first began to fight. They mostly grappled, tossed and pushed and wrestled with each other trying to throw the other off his balance.

Eventually, they both fell down and rolled along the rooftop. The roof, it happened, was inclined and so they rolled toward the edge of it. So, of course, they would fall over it, but they didn't realize it.

They were laughing as they rolled toward the precipice, apparently oblivious of the danger to them both. But the tiger saw it coming and she ran toward the edge — to do what, she did not know. She could not give herself away, but she had to be there just in case she could help in any way. She saw a metal garbage can nearby and she took the lid and threw it at the wall. It made a noisy clang that reached the ears of both the monkey and the snake.

It gave them both a start that made them stop and break apart and look toward the sound and see the edge that they were near and they realized how close they were to nearly falling off. They looked at one another and they laughed. They were a huffin' and a puffin'. The snake got up and offered up his hand to help the monkey up.

The monkey took his hand and jumped up to his feet. He went over to the edge and peered down over it. He didn't see the tiger there. She got quickly out of there when she saw she had achieved what she had meant to do. But she was still nearby. She was hiding once again.

The thought did cross the monkey's mind that the snake might push him off, so he braced himself a little just in case that might occur. But the snake came nowhere near him, in fact, the snake was heading up again up onto the rooftop to a much more level plane. The monkey followed him up there.

The snake asked the monkey if he'd like to go along with him to a place he likes to go to for quiet and good tea? The monkey said, 'yeah, sure, why not?' And the two left to go to there.

They went along the rooftops for a little longer, and then they climbed down to the ground and walked through alleyways and a little on the street. They didn't talk much while they travelled and they both moved very fast.

It was harder now to follow them, but the tiger still did manage. When they came down from the rooftops she decided to go up.

The snake and monkey every now and then would check their backs, just to make sure that there was no one after them. What would make them do that? Maybe they could feel a little bit of presence from the tiger. But they didn't pay attention much to the feeling anyway. They were distracted by the prospects of their potential partnership.

33

THE MONKEY AND THE SNAKE were sitting in the tea room secluded in a booth.

The monkey thought it strange, and the monkey thought it odd. He thought that it was odd to be here inside this place, inside this kind of place, and be in here with the snake. Drinking tea in here was something odd and something very strange. He felt really out of place.

He felt like they were superheroes sitting in their costumes in the middle of a restaurant that was for people who were rich, and very mannered like the rich. Of course, they weren't actually in costume, and he was not so sure that they were anything much like heroes either. He was pretty sure at least that the snake was not at all a hero, although he wasn't all that sure that he was a villain either. But, regardless of all that, he felt too conspicuous.

However, no one there could see them. They were secluded in a booth that had a curtain drawn on it. The snake was known in here and the staff did visibly defer to him. They led them to this booth that was apparently his booth, his special private booth, that was reserved always for him.

At first they didn't say that much, the monkey and the snake. The monkey took a moment to make himself feel comfortable, and the snake just seemed to watch him while he did do that.

The snake ordered some special tea from a special menu just for tea that was handed to them both. The monkey noticed that the tea was generally expensive. He was a little bit uncomfortable. Not because the place was for expensive tastes, but because it had an atmosphere that made him feel confined. He guessed it was supposed to be a place that offered comfort and a peaceful ambience, but he found it somehow more unsettling than he found it to be peaceful.

He knew the snake was watching him and was checking his reaction and his general disposition, so he tried to keep his cool, but then wondered why he bothered. His feelings vacillated. One moment he would feel like he wanted to rebel, and then another moment he would feel like he should just give in and try to be polite. He watched his own confusion while he watched the snake there watching him.

The snake could see the monkey was a little bit uncomfortable. He guessed he was not used to being in these kind of rich surroundings. But he also saw him struggling with himself to keep relaxed. This seemed to indicate to him that the monkey might be interested in trying to fit in. Thus, he took it as a sign that the monkey could be lured by it, and by larger prospects too.

The snake could offer lots of prospects all of which involved rich taste. If the monkey had a taste for that, then the snake could have a use for him that would help them both acquire it.

They said nothing to each other until their tea arrived. The monkey found the tea to be quite complex in taste. He sipped it carefully.

He felt very much on guard. But he shook off his suspicion. It was like the time when he was in the snake's place, the second time that he was there. The atmosphere in there was getting underneath his skin. It was as if something were saying, don't you want to be like this? And you might think that you did want to, even though it wasn't natural, for you to be like that at all.

The snake knew better than to ask the monkey any of the questions that he had about his background and his history. So he waited just a little bit until they settled with their tea and then he started telling him instead about himself. He didn't tell him anything that you would say is personal. Instead, he talked about his group and the arrangement that he had with them.

He called them his associates and said he got great benefit from their association. He said that they respected him and left him on his own. Their relationship turned out to be of mutual regard, and naturally there also was lots of mutual gain as well. They did not try to order him around, or in any way control him. On the contrary, in fact, they trusted his capacity to be inventive in his job.

What exactly was his job, was what the monkey asked himself, and he wondered if he ought to go ahead and ask the snake out loud? But he didn't have to do that.

The snake could guess he'd like to know that. And of course he'd have to tell him, if he wanted him to join him. And that was what the point of this whole meeting was about.

The snake did not, of course he didn't, think that it would be so easy as all that, to make it happen right away. But he had a good idea that the monkey would be interested, that he could get him interested and peak his curiosity. He had to let the monkey know how exciting it could be to do the things he does for them, for his associates. And he had to let the monkey know that what he did was his idea; they just offered back up and facilitated payment. He had to let him know that he would be completely free. He would not be beholden to do anything they told him to because they wouldn't tell him to. They would look for his ideas.

Of course, the snake was an idea man. What he did was mostly strategize. But once he did the strategy, he loved to execute the plan, and he always went along in order that he could do precisely that. And his associates would send along the extra people that he needed so that everything would happen and they all would profit from it. But with the monkey working with the snake he wouldn't need to use their men, not half as much at least. And they would both have even more independence then, that way.

He tells the monkey that he's something like an independent agent making missions happen in the interest of the group, but for the benefit of everyone. He tells the monkey that he's something like an operative, like a secret agent ninja, a mercenary that's for hire to take things from, and generally destabilize, some other groups that his group's in contention with. He tells the monkey that it's just like being in a governmental agency, except this is something that's gone beyond the level of mere government; this is at the level where things really are controlled.

He thought that might sound interesting, that it might get to the monkey and pique his curiosity, and the snake was right about that, the monkey's curiosity was most certainly piqued high. But his warning bells were ringing also like a full-fledged five alarm.

He never thought the snake would be involved in something at this level. Of course, the tiger spoke about her group before and he thought about that now, and he guessed she could be up there at that level too. And he also guessed that these two groups were probably quite different, and that likely these were two groups that were in contention with each other.

His whole world now just seemed to get immensely too complex. But there was something that was also quite attractive about that. He could see a game before him with many hazards in its play, but the prospect did excite him and he knew that he must play it.

The snake could see with some relief that the monkey was intrigued. He could see that he was trying now to keep a lid on his excitement. And thinking that the snake had sold the monkey on the prospects of a partnership already, he also therefore felt excited, and he also therefore tried to keep it down and hide it from the monkey.

The monkey figured that the snake would think that the monkey bought the snake's pitch and was sold on it completely. And he wanted it that way. In a way it was the truth. But it was not the whole of it. There was, in fact, much more to it.

The monkey knew that he would need to be very good at juggling. And he knew that he would have to be trickier than ever. Because he would have to be someone who could manage both the snake and the tiger's group at once. And just the thought of a good challenge and the possibility that, although there was great risk, he could have a lot of fun, made the warning bells stop ringing and made his concentration great.

So, the snake made the offer that the monkey first had dreaded and now received with glee. The snake suggested that he introduce the monkey to a few of his associates and make an offer to them that the monkey work with him, the snake, and be the snake's new partner. And the monkey did agree that this could all be very interesting.

So, then they made a date for them both to get together, and for the two of them to go and meet the snake's associates. Two days from then the monkey would go over to the snake's place, and they would go from there to a place the snake would take him to and have a little meeting with the snake's associates.

Things sometimes happen quickly and this was a time like that. It was, of course, exciting, as new things often are, especially when they're new things that are not yet defined. When they are not yet defined, then their prospects can seem greater than what they actually might be. And they both were quite excited, but they were for different reasons.

The monkey went to leave and snake said that he would stay. He waved away the monkey's money that the monkey offered for the tea. The monkey thanked him for the favour and said until the next time. And then they parted company.

When the monkey got outside he felt like he was free at last.

34

THE TIGER WAS OUTSIDE still waiting for her moment to get the monkey on his own.

She saw the monkey come outside. She saw the monkey leave the tea room. She wondered what had happened. She saw the snake was not there with him, she guessed that he had stayed behind.

She wondered should she keep on following the monkey. She would have normally. But she didn't know what they had said, or what agreement they had come to, if they had formed a friendship, or the start of one at least. She wondered what the basis of their relationship was now.

She also hesitated because the snake had stayed behind. Maybe he was only waiting for the monkey to be far enough away, and then he'd go and follow him. It was a possibility. And if he followed after him, then he also might spot her and see her following the monkey. And that would not be good. And more specifically, if he were following the monkey, it would not be good because that would wreck her plans.

She couldn't just appear in front of monkey, and then have the snake find out, and then follow after both of them, and so then find out where the tiger lived. She did want the monkey now to know, because it fit into her plan, but she never planned for letting anybody else know where she lived — especially the snake. That would not be good at all.

She kept following the monkey but she was not now so sure about whether she should wait or not to follow through with her whole plan. But she knew that if she didn't go ahead with it, it might get harder after this.

If the snake had made some offer that the monkey had found interesting, and if the monkey got involved in things, the kind of things the snake did, then all of it might be too late, and her plans would go to hell. And who knew what else would happen? So she would have to go ahead now and proceed with her whole plan.

She made as sure as she could make that the snake was not behind them. Then she made her way to get in front of where the monkey was. She would have to show herself and make like she was unaware that he was anywhere nearby. She would have to make it seem like he discovered her. She was interested to see how he would handle it. Would he follow after her, or do something else instead? What would happen all in all?

The monkey was not moving fast, so it wasn't hard for her to get in front of him. First she crossed the street. She would then be on the other side when she got in front of him. She got quickly out in front, staying inconspicuous, and then she slowed her pace and came out clearly into view. She walked casually along and let herself hang out.

The monkey saw her nearly right away. The tiger was not too hard to see. She had a presence that was strong and was clearly unmistakable. If you saw her you would be surprised that she could go unnoticed. But she could keep her profile low when she needed to, and she mostly needed to, so this was just a ploy, her showing off this way — and of course it worked.

So, the monkey saw her and it made him all excited. Of course, he was already in a state from his meeting with the snake. He was full of expectations and the hope of some great prospects. And now seeing her like this made him feel all the more excited.

There she was, the tiger. It was too good to be true. She was next on his agenda and for once he'd spotted her before she'd spotted him. At least, it looked that way to him.

He had planned to deal with both of them and planned to turn around the tables. Up until now they were the ones who were always in control. They seemed to always be the ones who were having the advantage. He was hoping that he'd find her next, and find out where she lived, and now much quicker than he ever hoped his chance had come already.

He saw the whole thing like a game, one fraught with many dangers. And he wanted to get on with it. He wanted to be playing it, and play until he won it.

But he was a bit suspicious, seeing her like that. And so conveniently like that, just like a happy accident. He was pretty sure the tiger was a strategist, that she'd been playing him ever since the moment that they met. But she really was amazing, and the monkey didn't mind that she was playing him a bit. He could play along and play the fool.

He ran across the street and managed to catch up to her. And when at first she saw him, she acted startled and surprised. She seemed a bit defensive, like she was ready for a fight. This didn't make much sense to him because he knew that she was sensitive, and that she probably could tell that he was coming up to her. She was not the type to be caught up to all that easily. This deepened his suspicion, and his interest too.

She kept walking, and he walked with her, and he said 'hey, how are ya?' and she smiled at him, and then she grabbed at him and pushed him back into an alleyway and up against a wall and started kissing him. This he found agreeable, and also found it funny, and he couldn't help but laugh at it.

Everything she did now, he saw as just her play, so it didn't throw him off at all, like it might have done before. Of course, he genuinely did like her. Of course, she was amazing, and he was absolutely smitten by her beauty and by her sex appeal. But he felt a little easier by doubting her sincerity to its full extent. He was sure that she did like him, but he knew that she was playing him in spite of how she felt.

She put her leg between his legs and pressed gently up against him. She asked him if he'd like to come and play with her at her place?

This really seemed to be too good to be true. First, he thought that maybe she was going to do him right there in the alley. Now he realized that what she was offering instead to him was something more than just the pleasure of her body. She was offering a closeness that was much more risky for her. It would make her much more vulnerable.

So, he knew the stakes were higher now and that her interest must be serious because she was making equal ground. He did not fail to register the significance of the words she chose to use. Would he like play with her, indeed? Yes, he would, he surely would; he wanted to go play with her.

She knew that she was playing it a little ostentatiously; some might say that she was going a bit over the top with it right now. But she thought that this was best. Sometimes it's best to be more obvious about the broad part of your plan, because it makes it easier to hide the greater subtleties of it.

She was sure he knew that she was only trying to lure him to her place, and that the gesture was transparent as a ruse for something else. But he did not know the details of what that something else might be. And she also knew that he must feel a bit suspicious about her. And probably he thought that she was trying to manipulate him, which of course she was.

But she thought that maybe she would manage to avert some of his doubt and ease a few misgivings when she demonstrated to him that she clearly was sincere about the things that really mattered, about her deeper interest in a serious relationship that could grow into a partnership with benefits for both of them. She was playing it with gestures that were, for the moment, rather large, but when she switched to being serious, she would change her tack, and by contrast, when she got more real, it would then resonate more deeply by the comparison.

Of course, he did accept her offer, and she was quite relieved. Not that, even for a moment, did she really think that he would really turn her down. She knew that he would see the value of knowing where she lived. And she also knew he really did like to be with her. But the thought had crossed her mind, what if the snake had gotten to him, and in effect already lured him and secured his interest fully, so that there would be no room for her? But she could see that there was room for her and that he was still intrigued. And so was she, for all of that.

35

THE SNAKE WAS FAR TOO CAUTIOUS to let himself believe or to entertain the thought that it would be a simple thing to have the monkey as a partner. He had to worry about trusting him. Well, that was OK. The monkey would still be better to work with, and also more effective than any of the agents that the group provided for the snake. That would make things easier.

There was a risk in anything, and of course there was a risk that the monkey would turn out to be an adversary. The worst thing that could happen would be if the monkey liked the snake's gang and got along with them and liked the kind of work they did, and then decided to compete against the snake for their better favour. That would not be good. It could be harder to get rid of him once he was well entrenched within the group.

And what if the monkey didn't like the group and turned against the snake and the group as well? Well, that would be much easier for everyone to deal with because then the snake would have the group to help get rid of the monkey. But he didn't think that either of those things was really going to happen. And at the moment anyway, he had mostly a good feeling about the way that things would go.

He knew the monkey was undisciplined, and he thought that was a good thing for the moment because it meant he could be trained to do things properly. At the moment he was just pure potential, really. He was pretty young, so it could be relatively easy to teach him a few things.

The snake liked the idea of being someone's mentor. He never needed friends before, he always felt superior to anyone he hung out with. Everyone he knew he always felt like they were just someone who was only working for him. But the monkey could be something else, that is, with the proper training.

He could be an equal. He could really be a partner and he could really be a friend. That could be interesting. With the two of them together, they could be very powerful. So powerful, in fact, that they wouldn't really need the group. Or they could also just take over.

That could be really interesting. Of course they'd have to do it slowly. It couldn't be a sudden hostile takeover. That would never work. What should happen is the snake should get more involved and get more inside the group and get a more specific position of responsibility. Then with the monkey as his chief lieutenant he could work to have complete control.

He had a very good arrangement at the moment being independent, but it would definitely be better if he were the big boss. Then he would never have to worry about the group being in his way or turning things around on him. And the fact of that would probably keep the monkey more into it as well. But the snake wouldn't let him in on this, not at this juncture anyway.

The snake would wait. He could be very patient. He would wait and he would be careful and execute his plan exactly and precisely. It would depend upon the monkey, and that made it rather risky.

If the monkey did accept the snake as his mentor and became beholden to him, if the monkey really did become the snake's good friend, then the snake could see his way to establishing some power. Otherwise, he would stay at an arm's length with the group and enjoy his independence.

It was good for him in either case, but he did have to think about his future, and he did have to keep an eye on the monkey and make sure things didn't turn around and turn against him either.

36

THE TIGER AND THE MONKEY got into a cab and went to where the tiger lived.

The tiger lived not far from where the old ports used to be. She was not far from where the river was. Her place was once for industry, but it had been converted. Now it was a big and open space with high ceilings and high windows that was very comfortable for living in. She had everything she needed.

The monkey was impressed and he thought about his own place, the new place that he got, and how similar it was, and how forward he was looking to moving into it and hanging out in it. He liked the open space. He liked to move around in it. He got down on the floor and rolled around on it then got into a handstand and walked around like that. He wasn't even showing off, he was just enjoying that there was the space that would allow him to do that.

She tackled him and knocked him down, and they wrestled on the floor a bit. He felt a bit the feeling in his body from the fighting he did earlier, and that feeling felt a little tired and a little bit worn down, and he also felt some bruises, but he didn't really mind, and he didn't let it stop him from wrestling her with gusto.

She was strong and he was strong, but they were only playing, and they started to take off their clothes, each taking off
the other's clothes and they started to make love. They rolled
around and fooled around until she got up from the floor and
extended him her hand and she took him off to bed where they
fooled around some more. They did this until they felt like they
would like to go to sleep and so they did.

Sleeping together and having sex together is not really the
same thing. And when you stay and sleep together after you've
had sex, it's something somehow different from when you leave
after you do. It does seem that the two of you are somehow
more together, when you actually do stay there and sleep away
the night so that you wake up in the morning and you see that
you're still there, the two of you, the both of you, are there, and
you are definitely there at where one of you does live, and it is
now the morning, and there are always things you do, that are
your normal things to do when it is the morning, but now
there's someone else who's there, and you're doing it with
them, or with them there to see you. And so you are not then
alone like you might more often be. And so it registers on you
that it wasn't just a dream, and it wasn't just a night that had
an ending that had sex, but that it is a morning too. And you
have to face your partner in the deed. And that is when you
always really wonder what it means.

You do, or you might, wonder when you wake up, after such
a night when one of you has left and you are there alone, you
might wonder what it means to you and what it means to them.
But it seems somehow more unreal when one of you has gone,
because they are not there for you to see and to notice in their
face and in their general countenance, what it is they feel and
what it is they think about the fact that you have done what
both of you have done, and what it means to them, and whether
they regret it, or if you do, or if they think it's wonderful, or if
you do, or if they think it's one way, and you think it's another. It
can be rather complicated, and so you take more of a risk when

you actually stay and sleep there.

It's like animals allowing themselves to show that they have trust. It shows more trust than even by allowing sex to happen because that is more your passion which always can displace your trust. But after, when the passion's over, and you fall asleep beside someone you may hardly know at all, you are certainly more vulnerable, and you're saying something by your being there together, beyond the fact of having sex. And you are willing to face up to what the morning's meaning has to say.

So they woke up in the morning with full knowledge of this thing. Of what it means to wake up in the morning after having had a night of sex and see each other there, still there, in the morning. One of them belongs there and one of them is a guest. So the question then arises, is it better that the guest does leave, or is better that the guest does stay?

The monkey was not sure. Did he want to stay or did he want to go? He felt like he would like to stay because he wanted to know more about what was now in store for the monkey and the tiger. He wanted now to know what her next move was going to be. He knew that she did want something more than just to have some sex with him. So when he woke and saw her wake and turn around to face him, he saw that she did smile at him and he knew then he was staying at least to have some breakfast.

She decided now that she must be completely open to him. The sex and the seduction were like a ritual with large elaborate dances that each party knew were dances, but for which they all the same did throw their all into them anyway. But after all that dancing, there had to be more meaning, something with more meaning. There would have to be some kind of thing that brought their minds together in a way much like the way that their passion for each other had brought their bodies there together.

So, she told him everything. She told him all about her group and she told him all about the snake and how they had been interested in both him and the snake, and how their interest in the snake had changed into suspicion and changed into dismay.

She told him that her group was very interested in him and saw great potential in him. She said that she was worried that he wouldn't realize that the snake would try to use him to only further his own aims. She knew the snake was charming, she knew the monkey might find the prospect of knowing him alluring, but she said that if he joined with him, her group would then consider him to also be a risk like him, and possibly an enemy.

She tried to spell it out for him what the snake was all about, and what the snake's group was about. She told him how they interfered in everything and anything that they shouldn't interfere with just to make more profit and to make themselves more powerful. They specialized, she told him, in subterfuge and sabotage in any industry, and in trying to be the masters of corporate control. What they did was tantamount sometimes to organized extortion. They want a piece of all the action and they behave just like a mafia. But they have connections up in government, which makes it somewhat harder to have to deal with them.

That is why the group that she belongs to does exist. They also have connections up in the government. They also have connections with certain corporations. But they are there to try and make sure everything's done fairly. They are in a kind of war against the other group, the group the snake belongs to.

She is like an agent, just like a secret agent. And so, of course, the snake is like an agent too, just like a secret agent too. They tried to get him on their side, but he was clearly not that way, not the way they are. It seems that he was born to be someone who's on the other side. She was supposed to go and try and get him to convince him to come and be on their side, to recruit him for her group, but he already belonged to that other group. He was already a part of them, of that other group.

She knew the monkey was an independent guy, that he was his own free agent, as it were, and probably he never knew that anything like this was even going on. She thought he was amazing, and when she found out more about him by watching from afar, and when she actually had met him and discovered that for sure he was someone quite exceptional, she told the group about him and they said they'd like to meet him. And now she wondered if he wanted to at least see what they were like and see what they did do, what they were about, and what they had to offer him and see if he did find it to be interesting like she did. She found it to be interesting and she thought it was exciting. And she knows he likes excitement.

She said she knew that he had seen the snake and that the snake would have an interest in the monkey as a partner, that he had probably invited him to go and meet his group, just as she had just done now with respect to her own group. She said she knew about the monkey and she knew about the snake. She said the monkey knew about her and he knew about the snake. She said the snake knew now about the monkey and he knew about her group but he didn't know about her, not specifically about her, she didn't think he did, at least, and she wanted it to stay that way.

I know you, she said. And you know me, she said. And I know about the snake, she said. And you know about the snake, she said. And the snake knows you, she said. And he knows about her group, she's sure, because his group knows her group. And perhaps the snake has heard a rumour about someone like the tiger, but he has never met her and he has never seen her, so as far as she could tell he does not know about her, and she would like to let it stay that way for a little longer. And she wondered and she asked him if the monkey mentioned her to the snake at all.

Well, the monkey had a thousand things running through his mind, and a lot of them were questions, and a lot of them were answers to the questions she had already been asking him and asking him without a chance to really let him answer them because he had been waiting for the moment when she would finish saying all the things that she was saying, because she had a lot to say, and a lot of it was set-up and basic information, and there was a lot to think about, and of course he had been doing that, he had been thinking all about it for a while and getting himself ready by making his own plan for dealing with her plan and dealing with the snake's plan, and he already did have a pretty good idea about most of what she said, he didn't know the details, but he knew the gist of it, and he knew which way the wind blew when it came to both of them, and he knew it blew quite differently when it came to both of them. It had not crossed his mind that he would tell the snake about the tiger. And he hadn't even thought about if he should or should not do that. And he realized it now and he saw it all quite clearly that there was power in the knowledge of knowing who the tiger was and it gave him an advantage and offered him some leverage in keeping her a secret. But he wondered should he let her have the confidence of knowing that he would keep it all a secret, or should he make her insecure about the fact of her position and her vulnerability.

Well, he thought it would be best to put her mind at rest. He didn't really know if it would always be the case, but he told her that he hadn't and he wouldn't tell the snake about the tiger if she didn't want him to. He didn't tell her that he really thought that it would probably be best for him as well to keep this secret from the snake.

But neither of them knew that the snake had seen the tiger, when she had left the monkey after the first time they had sex. Of course he didn't know that she was in fact the tiger, who of course he'd heard about, she was something of a legend, just like the way that he was. But he thought perhaps she was a girlfriend. So there was a possibility that he might ask him about her and catch on to who she was. The monkey might not be prepared for the moment when the snake might ask about her, and it might throw him off.

Anyway, the monkey told the tiger that he wouldn't speak about her to the snake. He did admit that the snake had just invited him to meet his group just like she had done. He also said that he would like to meet up with her group. He didn't say he would or wouldn't still go meet the snake's group. He didn't have to say it; she could easily tell he would.

It struck him somehow that the two groups seemed more

similar than they might be ready to admit. Except that one did make the claim that their work was just. Perhaps the other one would too. It would be interesting to see the way each group defined themselves as different to the other.

The snake had not said anything about the tiger's group. That could mean a few things — or not anything at all. The snake was proud and arrogant, so he might not even deign to think about what might be competition.

The monkey liked the tiger, and he also liked the thought of being like an agent, just like a secret agent, and he also liked the thought of being like a hero, a solo superhero. But he also liked the thought of being not like anything at all, because if he were an agent, or if he were a hero, he would have a lot that he would have to answer to. Probably, there would be much more responsibility than he might ever care to have, or be able to live up to.

He did not want to be beholden to either of these groups. But he did not tell her that. He told her that he did not want to be beholden to the snake or to the group the snake belonged to. But he would check them out. And he told her then that maybe, and he did so hoping that it would lend encouragement to her, maybe he could find things out that could be useful to her group. Maybe he could be something like a double secret agent. He could be a mole. He could be a monkey mole.

She did not think that this was possible. She did not think it in his nature. But she didn't tell him that. For now she was just glad that he was interested in meeting with her group at all. Soon he might discover that the snake was not so charming as he thought he was at first. And the kind of things his group did might not seem to be exciting after he found out about it from first-hand knowledge of it, and he got a taste of it from doing some of it. But after he had worked for them, they would not let him stop. They wouldn't let him quit. They wouldn't let him walk away like it was a simple job. And that is when he'd need her and she could be of help and her group could then secure him to work with them against the snake and against his awful group.

They set a meeting then for the monkey and her group. She would like it for that meeting to be before he met the snake's group. Would he concede to that?

The monkey said all right he would. He was going to meet the snake's group some time tomorrow night. He was going to meet the snake first who would bring the monkey to them. That meant that he would have to meet with the tiger's group tonight, or tomorrow in the morning, very early in the morning.

He needed to go home first and maybe change his clothes and think about it all and be alone for a few minutes. Then he could come back here to the tiger's place and she could take him over. Did that sound all right to her?

It was quick notice, but that was fine, it was better that he meet her group under some quick notice than meet the snake's group first. And she knew her group would see it the same way as that way too. Tonight would be the better time.

If he was going home then coming back, then that would give her time to set it up with her own group, and then take him with her there. So, she said that it was fine and good, and that was great, and she would set it up, and would he like to have some breakfast first, and he said that he would like that.

So they made some breakfast there together and they ate it there together and they had some fun together and they didn't speak of anything in any depth together or cover anything at all that was relevant to any plan or to the snake or anything that was serious about the details of their being there together. They had some food together and they had some fun together and it was good to be together and the monkey really liked it and the tiger liked it too.

And then the monkey left her place and went back to his old place, to get a change of clothes and sneak off to his new place.

And she got herself together and started on arrangements for the meeting they would have. She had no time to think about it, she had to do it fast. And so she did.

37

THE MORE PEOPLE in your life there were, the more chances in your life there were for there to be some trouble there, some trouble in your life. The more people in your life there were the more your life could be complex. And that could be a drag. Or that could be a thing that you could think was interesting. Or it could be somewhere in between. Or it could be none of these. But you likely would agree that it could just as easily be as difficult to be alone as to belong to any group.

The monkey thought about this when he finally was home and was home there all alone, all alone in his new place, in his secret hiding place. The monkey liked excitement but he liked to have his space, and be quiet in that place, in a space that was his own, where he was by himself alone. This was a thing that he had just recently discovered, and he found it interesting.

Here was something new that he knew now that he needed. He didn't realize before that he needed time like this, time to be alone, to be there on his own and feel he had a space that was a space that's all his own, because he never had to be alone before, because he always was alone before.

Every now and then of course he would have some company,

but he always felt alone and apart from everyone. And he might have been there with someone together physically, but mentally and spiritually, or maybe, psychologically, he was not really there with them, he was always somewhere else. He was not really there. He was not fully there. He was something like an actor, playing it the best he could, as if he were there fully, as if his heart and mind were there fully. But his heart and mind were not. They were not there, his heart and mind; they did not come to life until he met his friends.

Were they actually his friends? He thought they were, he felt they were, it seemed they were his friends. He hoped they were his friends. He liked to have some friends. But it was different now.

Before he always had the time to think about whatever. Whatever there was to think about he always had the time to think about it comfortably and it always was quite simple to work out anything because there wasn't anything that ever was there that wasn't easy to work out. There wasn't very much that he had to think about at all, not really much, not ever.

Now that he was not alone and he realized the fact that before he was alone, and now it was the case that he could feel alone, that he could feel that he was lonely, he needed now in spite of that, or actually because of that, to have some time alone, and enjoy some time alone. He needed time to be alone to think about some things, to consider everything.

He was alone no longer, and it was strange and it was good. It was strange because although he felt like he was not alone, still he felt he didn't really feel like he now had some friends for sure or that now he had a family, a sort-of, kind-of, family, or that he could now say that he now knew someone who was really even anyone that he could say he trusted or could say he loved for sure. Certainly he liked them and he thought they were exciting and he thought they were enticing, especially the tiger, there seemed to be there with her something. But he wasn't really sure, not even with the tiger, that their motives were sincere or that their actions were not grounded in something too abstract, or something too self-serving to warrant trust or love. Because he knew, of course, they wanted him or needed him just to serve their own ends really.

Even though they genuinely might like him and be genuinely inclined to try to get to know him, and want to hang out with him, still they had a use for him, there was an end in sight, and since they had a use for him and there was an end in sight, that just made everything between them then more different between them than it might be so between them if they had no use for him and there was no end in sight. If they liked him just the same and wanted to hang out with him in spite of there not being any way that they could use him to further their agenda, then he might be more inclined to want to trust them fully and perhaps to feel some love.

If they were all just who they were with no affiliation and were only finding out just now that there were others there like them, the way it was like that for him, not yet employed to help out any group, just interested to find out only who they were and what they were together, if they were, all of them, just more like him, if they were all in the same boat, then it might be easier. For him, at least, it seems that it could have been much easier.

But they wanted him for something. And how about him? Did he want them for anything at all? Well, yes, it's true that in a way he did want them for something. He wanted some companionship. He wanted them as friends. That has its own demands. That has its own agenda.

He would like them all to be the way that friends are like when they are all just finding out about each other, getting off on one another and thinking wow, how cool you are, and seeing how just knowing you and knowing me is changing everything in a way that's really interesting. You know how it is when you're tripping out on friends and you hang around a lot and you're practically inseparable and you start to act alike, a little bit alike, so it gets so you're not sure who owned the gesture first or who owned the saying first? They are changing you and you are changing them and you feel their care and their concern and the interest that they have in you and all of that like that is something else like that.

But it wasn't here like that. It wasn't like that here.

It was very interesting because before he never needed anyone and now he felt like maybe now he did need someone sometimes to be his friend and maybe also to be his lover too, and that could be a good thing and could be very interesting, and just as he was finding out that maybe he did want that, he was also finding out that he really didn't have it, that he couldn't really have it because he really couldn't let himself really truly trust himself to really truly trust them.

Could he really let himself really trust himself to trust them? Well that was a funny question that he had to ask himself. To trust them he must trust himself. Now that was interesting.

Well, could he? Well, he wasn't sure he could, but he was pretty sure he could. He was pretty sure that he could trust himself and that was something in itself that he really had to think about because he never had a doubt before. There was nothing in himself to doubt until they came along.

Of course, there also wasn't anything to stir a confidence inside himself for all of that as well. So, in a sense, he gained something by way of losing something else. He doubted himself earlier but now he had gained confidence inside himself now. So now it is something that can go back and forth inside of himself now. There's dynamics between those states of being now. There's a dialectical relationship between those two things now, that's there within him now.

Well, maybe they will be his friends, or one of them will be, but could they, really, how could they really be his friends? How could they ever really be, given how things are?

Well, he didn't really know that, the answer to that now, how they could or if they could, or if they couldn't either, because these were just the first friends that he ever actually had. So, he had to grant that maybe there was something about friendship that he didn't understand. And maybe it was not the truth, not the total truth, that in order to have friendship you had to trust the people who you thought could be your friends, so absolutely totally. Maybe that was true. You had to trust them and you had to trust yourself, but maybe not so totally, absolutely totally.

They still might be his friends. He would have to wait and see now wouldn't he? He would have to carry on and just go on and continue — as you were, really — that kind of thing.

He has to make a plan. But it'll be a sketchy plan. That's the kind of plan that suits the monkey best, a sketchy plan.

38

THE MONKEY AND THE TIGER went to meet her people. The monkey met up with the tiger and they went to meet her people.

Meeting up with people can be very interesting. Sometimes it is a thing, which is a thing that's interesting. When membership does matter, it often is a thing that is an interesting thing.

It seemed to the monkey that the tiger acted nervous. She seemed a little nervous to the monkey and it felt a little funny for the monkey too. He was a little nervous too. It was the kind of nervous feeling that you can get when you are going to meet the parents of your lover for the first time, it felt a bit like that. Anticipation and some apprehension and some just why am I bothering to do this anyway?

But for the monkey it was also boring in a way. It was boring insofar as he had never had to prove himself to anyone before, and he didn't want to start proving himself now. He was fine the way he was. And because he was that way, fine to be that way, it gave him power in a way.

He didn't want to be, at least not necessarily, a part of her group anyway. But they probably did want him, so that gave him the advantage, as far as he could see. They had nothing that he wanted, and because he didn't want it, he didn't really need it, and because he didn't need it, there was nothing that they had on him, they would have to try and offer him a reason to join up. If he wanted to join up, and they knew it, then they would have the power. But they clearly wanted him, they were interested in him, they were trying to recruit him, and so he clearly had the power. It was his advantage — for now, in any case.

So they get there and they go through the security routine and it all seems calculated to make a big impression. Then they go into a room, a not too fancy room, but a comfortable room, and a room that says we're serious, but we're not a corporation and we're not a bunch of salesmen. No, it doesn't feel like salesmen and it doesn't feel like business, it's more like academia, it's more like education, it's more like a science research laboratory, it's more like government and it's more like military, like intelligence, that is to say.

Everybody's nice at first, although they like to be respected and taken seriously. They make that very clear in the way that they are sitting and the way that they are speaking and the way that they do look at him. But they are making a seduction, that also is quite clear. They are making an impression, an impression that they hope is good and will get them what they want. It's quite important, really.

What did the monkey want? Did the monkey want to join? Sure, why not. He didn't need to join. He was fine the way he was. At least the way he was before, he certainly felt fine. He was alone before, but he didn't feel alone before. Now he felt alone. That is, now he can, in any case, he can feel like he's alone. But he might get over that. Everything's still new to him, all these changes, that is to say.

Well, he didn't like to say that anyone was anyone he needed, and he didn't need these guys, even if he did feel lonely now, sometimes he felt that way. So, because of that he felt empowered when he met the tiger's group.

He met with them and everybody seemed a little awkward

and they seemed a little nervous and they seemed a little formal, a little bit too formal. They sat around a table in a fancy conference room. It was an oval table that was big, and there were windows in the room that were also rather big. They were high up in a building, and the view was rather nice, and the monkey swivelled in a chair and looked out at the view.

He looked out at the sky and he saw the city there, stretched out there before him. He looked at everybody who was sitting there around him, who were speaking to him now, and who seemed to be too formal. But he didn't pay attention to the things that they were saying; instead he paid attention to the vibe that he was getting.

He noticed some weren't talking but were watching him quite carefully and he guessed that they were people who were actually in charge. His guess was good, he was correct; they were the ones who were in charge of trying to determine his potential as an agent. They were, in fact, in charge of checking out his vibe.

He could see this was the case and he didn't change a thing about the way that he was sitting, or his general disposition. He was slouching like a teenager will often slouch when sitting. And his attitude was showing some disregard for trying to make a favourable impression.

He gave every indication that he was really listening to the people who were speaking. It was kind of like a pitch that they were making, a really low-key pitch, but full of seriousness. He could tell it was a prelude to a set of prying questions. They had to warm him up and make him feel that they were something worthy of his interest, and then they'd turn the tables and make him prove his worth to them.

Attitude was everything, and he made it rather clear that he wasn't going to try and sell himself to them. But he wasn't being arrogant. And he wasn't really bored, although superficially, it might have looked as though he were. But these guys who were there watching him could see through any smokescreen that any candidate might put up to try and hide discomfort. They could see that he was comfortable and could see his confidence, and could see that he was playing down his interest in them too. He wasn't really bored; he was an individual who would not blindly fit himself into the formal scene around him. His casual demeanor was a contrast to them for that reason.

Seeing how things were and the way that things were going, the monkey started getting antsy. Once things are established and you know how things are going, you then can be inclined to be a little bit impatient. This is what was starting to happen to the monkey. So the monkey drained himself of his own want and he drained himself of his own need and he listened to their voices and focused on just their wants and focused on just their needs.

The whole thing was quite simple. They were gathering an army. He was another soldier, potentially, that is. They would start him as a warrior and maybe work him up to be an officer, or some other type of leader, a strategist, or trainer. But in any case he'd surely be an asset as an agent for their special operations.

He was honest and up front with them. Why be any other way? He had no secret gambit.

He told them, well, he didn't know that he was fit to do the kind of work they did. But he was curious to know if maybe it was so, if he was the kind of person who was suited to do that, to do the kind of work they did, any of the work they did, and to see if what he did for them might be something that would help them out and make anything they did easier to do, or make anything a thing that was better than it was for anyone and everyone who needed it that way.

But he'd never played in groups before, and he never had a single person, let alone more than just one, tell him what to do and when and where to do it. And he couldn't really say that he was amenable that way, to being told what he should do and when and where that he should do it.

He didn't know too much, he said, about the world the way

they knew it. He never saw it like they did, divided like it was for them, into people who were good and people who were bad; with Special Forces fighting for the way they wanted things to be. It was interesting to see that they divided things that way.

Of course, although he was not totally aware, neither was he totally unaware of the way that things could be, when you thought of good and bad. But he didn't ever think that he would be involved in sorting that all out, making things go this way instead of going that way.

And he never knew before that there were people like he was, with the kind of skills and ways he had of being in the world, and now that he did know that, he was interested of course, in knowing more about them and knowing what they knew and seeing if there was something that was there that he'd been missing without him even knowing that he'd been missing it.

He was unsure, but he would like to see just what they had in mind. What did they want from him? What was it they expected? How much freedom would he have? He was a little bit unsure. He was used to having freedom.

They told him that they only, just, they only wanted to say hi, and to tell him what they were and what they represented, and they could see that he had talent and that he might help them out, and if he helped them out, then they could help him out.

Well, how could they help him out? They knew he'd like to know that. They were not sure just what it was that he might want or need, but they knew he might be interested in any opportunity to learn more about the world, and also to meet more people who were people more like him.

Also they would pay him and cover his expenses for anything he did for them. But they knew that what he meant was something more than just the money. They knew they had to offer him something that was meaningful.

There was the pride and satisfaction of doing something that was good. But if he didn't really know if what they did was good or not, or if it was a thing that actually was needed or only just a thing that was serving just their own interest, well they could tell him, they could say, they could offer him their knowledge and an access to their network, and he could freely check it out and see if it was good for him or a thing that he found interesting. But was he interested in that, was he interested in helping them for the sake of something like that? What would it take to make him interested in helping them at all?

Well, he didn't know for sure, but yes, he thought that yes, he'd help them out, a little bit at least, and check it out and see what's what and whether he was right for them and they were right for him. He was certainly, he said he was, enticed and genuinely was interested, and if the tiger was a sign of the quality of them, then he definitely could say that he was certainly quite interested in knowing more about them. The tiger was amazing and meeting her had meant that the world had gotten bigger and the world had gotten better and was certainly more interesting and was certainly exciting to be living in right now.

Everyone was wondering if they ought to talk about the snake. And that hesitation said a lot about the power of the snake. Finally, they said their piece and they said the things that he had heard when the tiger said the things she said, when she carefully, she told him what she knew about the snake. She was not sure about him and neither was the group and neither was the monkey and he said as much to them. But he said that he was curious and intended to find out. But his finding out might help them out. But he didn't bother saying that of course it might backfire, because it was, of course it was, quite obvious to everyone concerned.

This is when we gamble.

But he promised that he wouldn't say a word about them to the snake and he kind of let them think that he was maybe going to be for them a kind of double agent. But he wasn't really sure that he would actually do that. He wasn't really sure that he would ever take a side against the other. He didn't really want to.

They were not sure what he would do, but they hoped that he would do the things that they would like him to, and they guessed that it was worth the risk, even though it was a gamble, so they must of course be careful. And they also wondered now a little bit about the tiger now, as well. They would have to be more careful with the tiger now as well, because she clearly liked the monkey. So they would have to be prepared for any bad thing that might happen where she might be concerned.

Anyway the wheel's in spin. The die is cast and all that there. So off they go the lot of them to what will be the future of all of them to come. It was clear to everyone that a milestone moment had just come and that everything was different now and would be from now on. What will happen? What will come? Only time will tell.

39

IT'S EASIER THE SECOND TIME you do something that's hard; you're not as nervous when you do it the second time around. Especially when what's hard about it is in part the fact of doing it.

The snake's group was a different group. That was obvious. And the monkey's expectations were different as well. And because he thought they mostly were a shady group of people, he didn't feel as nervous, although perhaps he really should have.

If they were a shady group, and it surely looked that way, then they also were more dangerous, so he ought to be more nervous since he was surely more at risk. But he'd felt a bit more vulnerable when he met the tiger's group.

Perhaps because they were not shady, they fought for justice and were good, it made him wonder just how good he was, and that's what made him nervous. He knew that he was good in contrast to the snake's group, but in contrast to the tiger's group he wasn't all that sure. In contrast to the tiger's group he felt a little selfish and conceited, and he felt a little guilty about the fact of that, and because he couldn't totally commit to working with them or even to their cause.

He knew that probably the tiger felt that he had let her

down, but he could handle that. But he couldn't handle feeling that he'd let himself down too. Guilt was not a feeling that he was used to feeling, and he didn't like to feel it, and he tried to shake it off. In fact, it pissed him off that he was feeling it. And so, naturally, because of that, he was looking forward now to meeting with the snake's group even though he knew that they were shady, a little or a lot. At least with them he wouldn't feel that he was less than what they were, morally or otherwise.

The snake was not as nervous as the tiger seemed to be but he was quiet and absorbed and the monkey wondered what exactly this meeting meant to him? After his big meeting with the tiger and her group, the monkey had cut out on her, more or less. She seemed to understand that it was best to let him go and let him be alone and let him think about it all. Now, he wondered if the snake would be as understanding as all that, if afterward he split without having a discussion. Because that was what he planned to do, what he was sure that he would want to do.

So, the monkey meets the people who are the people that the snake works for. He doesn't work for them the way the tiger works for the people that she works for. The tiger works with people who are the people that she belongs to, or hangs out with, or something. She doesn't really work for them. Or maybe she does work for them and she only thinks that she works with them. Or maybe it's both, she works for them and with them. Maybe.

Both of them are definitely separate from their groups even though the two of them belong to their groups. They don't belong to them insofar as they are the kind of people who don't belong to anyone. But they are their agents; that's for sure.

But the snake is a different kind of agent than the tiger is. There is a way the snake is in his group that doesn't seem as comfortable as the way the tiger's in her group. But although it's not as comfortable, it's somehow more agreeable because it seems he has more freedom.

That might not really be that relevant to the tiger and her group. It might be that the reason that the snake seems to have more freedom is precisely just because the snake's relationship with his group is much more adversarial. If the snake must stake his freedom, his independence, as it were, then it must be only just because he needs to do just that. There must be something in his group that wants to take his freedom from him if he needs to take it for himself.

The snake's group was more cold. You could see that right away. The building they were housed in. The security up front. All the glass and all the metal, so shiny all of it, all showing reflections, all looks and views bouncing off of them. The monkey thought it was just like the neon lights in front of any strip club that you see. The garish flashing there makes it hard to get a fix on who the people are who go in there and the ones who come out too, unless you follow them or something.

The elevator had a person in it who was operating it. He had to use a key to select the floor they wanted. And they went up to the top floor penthouse and the elevator opened up and they were right there in a room, a single and large room with windows everywhere and a table like the table that you always seem to see in boardrooms of executives in movies and TV.

There also was a part of it with a layout like the clubs you also see in movies and TV. With the big leather chairs and men drinking scotch and smoking big cigars. The monkey almost laughed out loud when he looked at all of this. He felt like he was walking into a dangerous cliché.

Everything about this group said 'We Are Powerful.' But it was all so overstated that it all seemed quite unreal. The monkey couldn't help but feel a little smug about it all. Because power so conspicuous as this, that was ostentatious as this was, had to be a power that was merely bought and sold. It didn't matter who was at the helm to steer this battleship, it was driven and was steered by a need that any person could fulfill as long as they were willing.

The monkey realized that the snake's group was more than just a group; it was more like a machine. His interaction with them would be somehow more abstract. It was not the people that the snake needed to assert his independence from; it was the independent force and machinations of the group whose logical conclusions were subordination and subservience.

He thought he understood now why the snake was being quiet. You had to concentrate and focus to make sure you weren't sucked in.

Business people try to ingratiate themselves in a different kind of way from people who are trying to only fight for justice. And people who are buying you are also kind of different from people who are selling you, or rather, selling themselves to you. The monkey knew the snake's group was more like business people, but he wasn't really sure if they were selling or were buying, and he figured that they also were not so sure of that themselves.

Although, given that the snake had brought him there to meet them, he figured it was likely that they were leaning more toward some buying than they were toward some selling. But of course to do some buying, they would have to sell themselves a little as worthy of the purchase. Their position would be stronger if they didn't have to sell themselves at all. If they could bank on the monkey really wanting to be part of their machine, then they could buy him outright and do better in the deal.

This was interesting. There was some sussing out to do.

The role the snake was playing in this little game was rather different from the tiger's role, although it looked just like the same. They both were introducing a possible new member, but their responsibility for the monkey's actions or his capabilities and the consequences they would meet with if he failed to meet the grade were rather different indeed. The snake was risking more with his group than the tiger was with her group.

Well, they sat around and it was stuffy, kind of stuffy, kind of boring, even though they didn't say a thing, still it was quite boring, already it was boring, to the monkey it was boring anyway. It was something that he felt like he didn't want to do. And he hadn't even heard from them what they might like him to do, if anything at all. This was so boring. Why'd he bother, anyway? He didn't really care, one way of the other, about this stupid group.

He didn't really want this thing to happen, at some level. And he knew somehow, because of that, that in fact it would.

He didn't really care, one way or the other. But if pressed, then he would have to say that he'd rather be some other place, any other place, than in the place that he was in right now. At this moment, in this place, it was a really awful place. And couldn't he just — you'd think that he could just go outside and play somewhere. Go hang out. Go have a beer. Go watch TV, or dance around, or go chase girls, or tease some guys, or just do any of the things that he used to do.

The things he used to do. Those were things that were the things that always entertained him. They were things he found amusing. And what is wrong with that?

God, why get so involved in things that weren't at all amusing? — In things that could be dangerous?

Of course, things that could be dangerous could also be amusing. But these things that were dangerous were things that were just boring because they were so typical. They were just a job.

This was just a job. This meeting was an interview for just a stupid job.

Oh, jobs were necessary to put some food onto your table and make sure you had a table and some kind of home, some kind of thing to house you in, and clothes and all of that.

Well, they were mostly necessary to mostly everyone. But, of course, they weren't to him.

He'd never had a job before. He never needed one at all. He'd been provided for. He was lucky in that way.

So he didn't need to do this for the sake of money. He didn't care for money, not in any special way. He wasn't really someone who wanted to consume, to be a big consumer. So why'd he care in any case?

Oh, it was so boring, but he felt that he should do it, that he should go on through with it, and find out what they liked and what they wanted him to do, if anything at all.

And maybe he was really, not really so much bored, as he was nervous, actually. Perhaps, he was reacting to a kind of nervousness that he wasn't used to feeling, and so feeling it was something that was making him be antsy, and that was why he felt like leaving, and why he felt a bit exhausted, and felt frustrated as well. And all of it amounted to really feeling bored. Lately, there were lots of things he wasn't used to happening to him.

Of course they asked a lot of questions. He was not interested in that. Perhaps it was a way for them to try and break the ice. But he was not interested in that.

As you know, any time that anyone starts asking lots of questions, you get kind of suspicious — like, why are you asking me so many of these questions — What are you getting at?

You start to get a feeling that there's something there that's hidden, an agenda that is hidden.

It's like when cops in TV shows do interrogation — you know, they're always trying to get at something, and of course, they do, usually they do, get at what they're after.

Interrogation is a thing — most people find that they don't like it, really. It's like when you're a teenager and your parents ask you things, and well, they might not be the kind of things that are really bad to ask, but somehow still, if feels like they are asking something else behind the things they're asking. Of course, for them, they might be feeling just how defensive you can be, and they are tippytoeing all around you and trying not to set you off, but of course, that only guarantees that you will, in fact, go off. It could be like that.

So, they ask a lot of questions and he gets all uptight. And he sees the snake's uptight as well. In fact, he's been like that all night. So, the monkey tries to just relax and not get so uptight, because he does resent the fact that he is getting so uptight, and feeling like — how boring — and all of that, like that. Because it feels that when he's like that, that it's like — that they are winning. And he will not let them win like that — even if they are not playing that, even if there isn't any fighting really even going on, even if they're only trying to break the ice a bit.

Eventually, they start to talk to him and treat him like he is someone they think could be a new associate. One who has been recommended by a tried and true and valuable associate established in their firm. They value this associate so much that they are certain that he's bringing them a person who will be for them an asset of great value, there's no doubt.

Then they start to itemize, to make a kind of list of all the benefits of being an associate of theirs. And they do so, by way of saying so, and by granting him the things, whatever are the things, that he would need, whatever he might need. They are there to help him out. And you can see that the seduction's being poured on now. But in an ordinary way, a very ordinary way, an ordinary 'we are a company, and we are very interested in you working for us' kind of way.

They don't ask for anything from him. They're all about offering whatever he might want. And keeping it all casual. Yet, keeping it all serious, in the way that it's all full of promises and benefits that will come from their relationship; from their new working relationship that will mutually benefit everyone involved.

And it's all vague. There's no real indication of what he might be doing, specifically, that is. Just that they are interested. They're interested in him. They only want his expertise, to apply it where they might.

And they make it sound exciting. And they make him feel important.

He decides to play it cool and let them do the talking. He relaxes and stays quiet and lets them make their offer. He listens to their overtures and tries to look agreeable but keeps an attitude that says to them that he still is his own man.

The snake is very still and it's like he's waiting for something. And, in fact he is. He is waiting. The snake is very good at that. He waits quietly within a feeling of impatience.

The snake is waiting for the part when the group makes

recognition that the monkey is his find, is his partner and is his friend.

Of course they know, and of course he knows they know, that the monkey is his find, is his partner, is his friend. But he is waiting for the part when they make the recognition that he's the one in charge. He's the one they have to go through, to have anything at all, that is anything at all, to do with what the monkey does, when it comes to doing things that benefit any of their interests in any way at all.

He will nip it in the bud if they try to build their own relationship with monkey. The monkey's just a new part of his relationship with them. He's like an added bonus. He's a new development in what the snake is offering to them. They would not dare to cross him openly, there's no question about that. But there's no telling what they might try when he was not around.

Oh yes, the snake has an arrangement with his group that's rather different from the one the tiger has with her group. You could say that it's a little bit contentious.

The snake's group, of course the snake's group, is sensitive to this. Of course, they are quite careful when it comes to how the snake feels. If they think that he's uptight about anything at all, then of course they do pull back from whatever they are doing in order to make sure that the snake is well appeased.

So, they do acknowledge, in their way, they do make it quite plain, that the snake, of course he is the one who is bringing in the monkey, and that the monkey and the snake are in fact a team, and that the group is looking forward even more now to the benefit of working with the snake, because it seems that their best man has now become much better, he has increased his value more to them considerably now.

It's plain that he's accomplished this, and the group would like to let the monkey know that anyone the snake endorses is someone that is valuable to any operation that they are involved in. And they are looking forward to working with the two of them. And if there's anything at all that the monkey needs, he only has to say so, and the snake will let them know, and they'll take care of it.

They acknowledge that the snake's the one that the monkey needs to go through. And of course, this satisfies the snake. And of course, the gesture is transparent to the monkey and to everybody there.

But the monkey also notices that by making such a gesture, that the snake's group understands that there is value in the monkey that goes beyond his being part of what you might call a snake package. The monkey realizes that, there between the lines, is an open invitation to deal with them alone. And he wonders about that. And he sees that there's a weakness in the partnership between them, between the snake's group and the snake. And he wonders if there might be some way he could take advantage of that weakness.

Oh, the intrigue.

Interesting it is, and boring it is also.

And that was interesting as well. That tension was a thing that was an interesting thing.

Really, the more people that you knew, the more complex things became.

40

WHAT DOES IT MEAN to be together? To hang out with each other? What does it mean to be together and to work with one another? What does it mean to be a friend and work with one another?

They are now together and they are now they're quiet. It often goes like that. When something is established, it's like it's finished in a way. And when often when it's finished, when anything is finished one often does go quiet. It's a thing that often happens, it's a thing that people do, when they accomplish something, a little after that, they often do go quiet.

They walk along and they are thinking and the tiger now is following. Where did she come from, what's she doing there? She is being careful to make sure that they don't see her. But she can see from where she's hiding like she is, and following them too. Following and hiding are tricky things to do at both the same time like that. But we know that she is good. She's very, very good at stalking and at hunting. She is the tiger, after all. She can see that there is something going on between them because she sees that they are quiet and they're quiet in a certain way.

That quiet makes a sound it does that you can hear or feel or see or notice anyway, there's something there about it that you can calculate because you definitely can see it. You can see that there is something going on when they're being quiet like they're being. Something's going on. She is concerned.

Of course she is concerned. She is concerned because she is concerned about the two of them together. Whether they are quiet or whether they are loud or whether they are something else the tiger is concerned. And just a little jealous. That is something new. There are so many things that now are new to her. They later might be old, but now that they are new, they are exciting in a way. But now there are so many things it's a little overwhelming. Not all things are so great just because they're new.

You shouldn't try to squeeze things into things that they don't fit into. Anything can be a thing that is a thing you can imagine. And when you can imagine it, you can imagine it one way, and it can be another way, in fact. And when you try to make it be the way that you imagine it to be then that can be big trouble for anyone concerned, if there is someone concerned, and there usually is someone who is concerned, who is involved in some kind of way, in some way or another.

So the tiger watches and tries to keep her cool and tries to not assume and make an ass of you and me. But she sees that something's up and whatever it might be, that silence that she sees is a distance that's between them. That can mean any-thing. Something good, something bad, something neither good nor bad. But it does mean there is distance. It means there is a space there, a space that is between them that's defined as space between them and as a space between them, it naturally can be a space that's filled with something else, or someone else. And when the space between them is occupied by some-one, then that someone can have an influence on the nature of that space and the meaning of that space thereby.

Sometimes a thing can happen where you liberate yourself from the dilemma you are having by doing what you do a little differently. If what you do is something that when you normally you do it without having any trouble, but now you find that doing it is really quite a trial, then sometimes you can change it back to being something that is easy by doing it some more, the thing that gives you trouble, but in a different way. You go ahead and do that thing but with something else in mind, something different from the thing in mind you have when it's a trial. In fact, the best thing then to do is to let yourself just go, or let your mind just go and you go follow it. It's different when you follow than when you're trying to take the lead. This is why following is really such an art.

The tiger, you see, is following, and she is always good at that. But because she is concerned, she finds that she is really trying to actually take the lead. If she keeps that up, she will be found, she won't be hidden anymore, and she must be hidden for a while. While she's following the monkey and following the snake she can't be seen by them. She cannot try and take the lead because then she'll try and change things and try to make things happen in the way she wants them to, and that will spoil everything — especially her following after those two guys and trying to stay hidden while she's doing that.

She's really very good, you know, at seeing what she's doing, and that can be a problem just as much as it is good. But for the moment it is good because it makes her stop and see that she should change her tactic, and so that is what she does. She shakes off her compulsion to know what they are doing and her hoping that the monkey thinks the way she wants him to. She follows after them, but with a different thing in mind. Instead of wanting to catch up with them, she wants to stay away from them, she wants nothing now to do with them. She tells herself she only wants to know where they are going.

So she throws herself right into it, right into doing 'following.' She doesn't care what they are thinking, then. She doesn't care how they are doing. She only cares to follow them, to find out where they're going and to go along with them. And to make sure they don't see her, she follows her desire to be really good at following.

Oh, she feels a little guilty for even being there. Does she have issues with the monkey that can't allow her, then, to trust him? But she swallows all of that and settles in herself that the reason that she's following the monkey and the snake is because she doesn't know why; it's a premonition she is having. So she doesn't make assumptions. And she doesn't make her wishes. And she doesn't now feel bad about the fact that she is following. She doesn't now know why, but she knows she has to do it. And she has to do it right.

The monkey and the snake are walking and they're quiet. And so, of course, they're thinking. And the monkey and the snake have just come from their big meeting with the people that the snake works for — or with, depending how you look at it. But of course, the snake has thought, he's always thought, that he works with his group. But now he's not so sure about what is going on. Things now are beginning with the monkey and the snake, with both of them together, and the group that was the snake's group is now the monkey's group as well. So, things now are just starting, but because that was a start, it now feels like an end. And whenever there's an ending you often stop and wonder what it all has meant and what it does mean now and what's it going to mean when later it all starts up again. And it does, as it is, in fact, it's doing that right now, it's starting up again. But of course, it's different right now — and what does it all mean?

The snake is happy that the monkey is now part of his arrangement with the group and hanging out with him and doing stuff with him. It's cool to have a comrade. But on the other hand, although the monkey is a comrade, and that offers now some comfort and gives the snake some strength, he also is an equal, and that means competition. And that gives the snake a weakness that his group might use to their advantage.

What if the monkey went with them, and worked separately from him? That would give them leverage in their dealings with the snake, that could hurt the independence he's enjoyed with them up until now.

If the monkey were to be with him truly as a comrade, and not try to be on top, and not work a better deal by sneaking around the snake and going to the group without telling him, the snake, that he was doing that, then that would be just great. But if the monkey did go there and went behind his back to try to make a deal, then that would be a bad thing. It would be a very bad thing. And of course, it's not that much a stretch of the snake's imagination to think the group would like to try and do that very thing to him; to lure the monkey there to them and make some kind of deal with him that would compromise the snake.

The monkey figures that the snake's group will probably try this. The monkey knows the snake is thinking and because he is so quiet and feels so far away the monkey feels that distance and interprets it as worry and knows he should be careful. It will be interesting to see if the snake's group tries to see him to try and make a separate deal. But that's not what's on the monkey's mind as much as other things. Like, just what are the snake and monkey going to do and does it make a difference to him?

What is their assignment? What are they supposed to do? The monkey cares far less about any social drama than he does about this question.

With the interview now over the two of them have left and have gone into the world together as a team with no specific task, but with some kind of vague commitment to doing something that will benefit them all and which will also in the doing cement some kind of deal between the monkey and the snake and the monkey and the group.

Who's more interesting to him, the snake or the snake's group? The monkey wonders about that. And who is it that's more interesting, the tiger or her group? The monkey wonders about that. And who is it that's more interesting, the tiger or the snake? The monkey wonders that. And what is it that's more interesting, a friend, a boss, two bosses who do not like each other, two friends who have some bosses who are against each other — and so must be, in principle, against each other also — or solitude? The monkey wonders about that. But maybe what is interesting, is not the question he should ask.

Oh well, for now, the monkey goes along, and doesn't answer anything, but listens to the query to feel the heart of it. He keeps track of his own feelings, as complex as they are, as complex as each other thing — each thing there is to think about, each thing there is to feel about. And so he goes along as the snake and he go on, as they go out now together to both get into something. But into what, he doesn't know.

And so this is how the day begins? The work day now begins? Well, this is something new. Well, he's glad he doesn't know what he's supposed to do. Just be himself, he guesses. Act natural, they say. But when you tell yourself to do that, the act of doing it becomes unnatural. Because then you second-guess just what it is that is natural in you, and is the thing that you do naturally, and what you naturally would do, naturally.

But the snake seems to the monkey like he does have some idea of what there is to do. There is about him now, the monkey sees, a grim determination. He's more quiet than the monkey might have thought he might have been after meeting with his group.

The monkey kind of feels like he just went to a big party with a girlfriend and he flirted too much there and now it's after they have left and she is giving him the treatment. That makes him want to laugh, to think the snake's like that.

If that's a weakness of the snake's, it's important that he knows it. The monkey knew already that the snake was full of pride, and he knows that pride's a thing; they say it is a thing that comes before a fall. That was weakness number one. Now jealousy or envy — whichever of the two — would be weakness number two.

It's important that he knows about these weaknesses, of course. This is just a test. The monkey's not committed, at least not totally committed, to any of this stuff. He's just going along with it because it's interesting and because he is intrigued and because, maybe, he just needs this. And then again, maybe he does not. Maybe this is just the thing that is the last thing that he needs. But he's only going to find out by giving it a try.

The tiger's there behind them watching them and following and wondering and waiting. What will they do, she wants to know? Will they get into mischief? Are they only hanging out? Or are they on some kind of mission?

The first thing that the snake must do is to establish the monkey's presence. Just by hanging out with him, he's achieving this first task. They go to lots of places that are always public places. Some of them are restaurants and some of them cafés. One or two are small parks. A few of them are pool halls. And one's a bowling alley. They even hit a library. And then later they go to check some bars, and one big discotheque. They spend their day and afternoon and their evening doing this.

Each time they do the same thing. They hang around a little. They sit and talk a little; but they don't say very much. They sometimes have a drink or two, and sometimes have a snack. And each place that they do go to, the monkey notices that they are being noticed too by certain people there.

You can tell when people look at you, when they look a certain way at you, that seeing you means something. And the fact that you are there also does mean something. And the fact that you are with the person you are with means something most of all. The monkey saw this happening everywhere they went. It was such a subtle thing, but it was plain to see for someone who could see those kinds of things.

He knew, of course he knew, what was going on. But they didn't talk about it, the monkey and the snake. The monkey saw the people who made a point of seeing them, and by seeing how the snake would be, by how he gave off energy, by his own subtle response, the monkey could determine where each person stood, what their level of importance was and what level of respect was expected from each one.

The monkey understood that he was being introduced and

positioned in an order of importance above everyone he saw and that likewise, they were being introduced to him with regard to how they should be regarded and respected.

A lot can be established just by being with someone. Especially when they're showing you off to everyone. And when they're showing everyone that you are number one in their company; their number one companion who's in their company.

This, of course, was all the more remarkable because the snake had never done this with anyone before. So he was really doing something that was making lots of waves throughout his organization. And he felt, each place he went to, each time this ritual played out, that he was going further past the point of no return.

Was that good or was that bad? He wasn't sure. But, he knew that it would mean he was no longer in control the way he used to be.

It was interesting, and he was banking still that despite the sharing of some power, that his power overall had also now increased. And it was because he risked control that he stood to gain some more.

And it was also worth the risk because things were more dynamic now. Thing were far less boring now. And they would be more exciting now. That was worth this risk.

At last, he had a challenge. He never realized until now that he needed a good challenge.

He wasn't sure what he was doing, but he was pretty sure that he should do it. And so this is what he did. He showed the monkey all around so everyone would know that the monkey was around. And so that everyone would know that the monkey was with him. The monkey was like him. And they would have to treat him just like the way that they treat the snake.

The tiger was concerned and a little bit confused, but she pretty much had figured out what the snake had been up to. She figured that he must be giving the monkey the grand tour. It was interesting to see the different places that they went to. She knew her group already had mapped out the territory of the snake and of his group. But still she found it interesting to take this little tour from behind the scenes like this.

Each time they left a place, she tried to see if there was anything about the monkey she could see that registered as different.

By the middle of the night, when they came out of the dance club, the last stop on the tour, she could see there was a comfort there between them, that settled there between them, that gave her some concern.

When you go around to different places like the monkey and the snake did and you meet a lot of people that really only one of you does know, even though you meet them in a rather oblique way like the monkey did all day and part of the night too, and you don't have much to say, as the monkey and the snake did not, and it seems to be ok and you're comfortable like that, and the whole point of the exercise seems to be to show to everyone that you are some kind of twosome and you're comfortable with that, then of course it's not so strange, if after all of that you do feel that you've bonded and you are some kind of team. That was the objective, and it worked to some extent.

It seemed a little simple upon reflection maybe, but in spite of its simplicity it worked to some extent. The monkey did feel comfortable and he felt they were a team.

He felt he'd been committed. He didn't feel he had committed himself precisely, yet. But he felt it would be easier to do that when he wanted, and felt it didn't matter now if he did or he did not. He was committed by this deed. By this ritual he had become a partner of the snake.

The tiger sensed this in a way and it worried her a bit. She felt compelled to act, but was unsure what she should do. She waited and she watched as the monkey and the snake said goodbye to one another.

Which one should she follow, the monkey or the snake?

The monkey and the snake were parting company. It had been a strange day and it had been intense.

The monkey needs some time to let this all sink in. And he

needed to have privacy to see where he was at and what was what and what to think and what he felt and what he should do next. So he headed for his home but he wanted, actually, to go to the new place that he got — to his secret hideaway. But he wasn't confident enough that he could get there without being followed by someone.

He was actually exhausted by having seen so many people. How interesting it was that such a thing could tire you out. He was saturated with the feeling of those people, all those different people. He wouldn't now be able to sort out anybody who might be following after him.

So he would just go home and lock his door like he never used to do and try to go to sleep. He wondered if he could. He was tired but he was also all wound up. It was an unfamiliar feeling and it made him feel a little vulnerable and a little apprehensive and he didn't really like the feeling very much.

He would wait then, until he was well rested, to go to his new place. And he would exercise some caution and disguise himself again.

He would go to his new place, and he would stay there for a while. He wouldn't see the tiger and he wouldn't see the snake until he wanted to go and see them — if he ever did again.

He didn't feel like he could stand to see either of them now. But he knew that probably he would again and not too long from now. And the knowledge of that fact made him give a little sigh.

The complexity of these relationships really was a drag. And yet, he did have to admit that he liked it sort of, too.

He ran all the way home hoping it would make him so tired that he would just collapse right into bed and go right away to sleep.

The snake watched the monkey for a while and saw him break into a run. Then he headed for his own home — he also was fatigued. He wasn't used to feeling the feelings he was feeling. And he wasn't used to feeling different ways about something and being of two minds about what he ought to do.

This difference was interesting and it was very real and he didn't really want to resolve his ambivalence just yet. It might be more worthwhile to explore it for a while — to work it, actually, to see if there might be some advantage in the feeling; in being of two minds and irresolute like this.

But it certainly was tiring because he wasn't used to it and he was resisting it, in spite of his intention to try and work with it.

So he headed for his home so he could get some rest.

41

THE TIGER, WELL, THE TIGER has thought about it all. And she has felt the feelings that she has. And she has thought about those too. And she has weighed the differences between the way she felt about it all and how she thought she ought to think and act about it all. And she has found that when the scale had been examined and the differences made clear, that despite the clarity and the certainty of all her thinking on the matter which was based upon her knowing the recommended course of action that was best to take in such a case as the case there now before her, that however good and right and tried and true that recommended course might be, she knew she must ignore it and follow what she felt. And she must make the way she felt the basis of the course of any action she would take. And so she did decide to do that.

She did decide to go ahead and do what she would do because her heart did tell her to. This is something interesting. At least she thought it was.

She remembered how she heard it said that the final resting place in the progress of a discipline, of any discipline, including those for fighting, was, in fact, the heart.

It all started with the thinking of the concept and idea. And then the body took it on until it was like second nature. And then finally, the heart embraced it as a passion and as a deeper part of being, as philosophy and love, like something like religion, like a natural devotion. And that was when the discipline became an understanding that became a part of living, of the person's life itself.

So it was with trust and with belief in the progress of her knowledge and her understanding, which were a part of her own discipline, that she decided that although her thinking was at odds with where her heart was, that since in fact her heart was the last stage in the progress of her discipline — of it becoming manifest, that her heart was uppermost in the making of decisions. And so she did decide to do that which her heart did bid her do.

She went after the snake. She was going to fight the snake. She had to tussle with the snake because to tussle with the snake was the fastest way to introduce herself in a way in which he won't dispute, he can't dispute, her capabilities. So he'll have to take her seriously and treat her as an equal. And it was a good way also for her to get to know him.

She wasn't going to fight him for the reasons that might seem to be the case. She wasn't going to fight him because of jealousy. She wasn't really like that. She didn't think the monkey was a thing she needed to possess.

She wouldn't fight for ownership over anything. And a person wasn't something that she would call a thing in any case. But she never did feel jealous of anyone before and, truth be told, she felt that now a little bit.

She felt a little threatened in a vague, uncertain way by the relationship between them, between the monkey and the snake. But that was not the reason that she had to fight the snake. It was a new and very strange thing to feel a thing like that, and it makes her worry somewhat.

Still, she had the trust she needed to be sure and certain of herself and of her motives to know it was complex; the feelings that she had for the monkey and the snake. And to also know she knew her discipline was good and it was there to help and steer her down the proper path.

So off she went to get him.

The monkey and the snake had parted company. She had managed to elude their knowledge of her presence as she followed them around and kept an eye on them to see what they were up to. And she had done that, naturally, on her own reconnaissance, without the knowledge of her group, who would have liked it better, she was sure, if she had left them both alone and not tried to have an influence on the relationship between them, between the monkey and the snake. They wanted it so they could see it for themselves the way the monkey would do things when left to do them on his own.

So she didn't tell the group that she was going to go and follow them.

She often didn't tell them all that she was doing, or the way that she was doing it. Although, she always felt that she was doing it on behalf of their great cause. Nevertheless, this time it felt like it was different from the other times when she had gone and made an executive decision. This time she really felt a difference that was palpable between them, between her group's will and her own.

But she had never known before a person like her monkey, or for that matter, like the snake. And she felt a kinship with them, with the both of them, despite the fact that one of them might really be an enemy and a deadly one at that. She felt like they were all of them a rare, endangered species and they must somehow resolve the differences between them and come together somehow, and be as though they were a tribe, a clan and a family.

Perhaps it's strange to think that she intended to accomplish this by beating up the snake.

It would probably be natural to assume that such a thing

would not be normally the kind of thing that would be a thing that would endear you to someone you had just met, especially by way of introduction. It would pretty much assure an unfavourable impression. As first impressions go, it would not be a good one.

Nor would you expect it to make a good impression on the friend who is a friend, apparently at least, of the one whose ass you're kicking.

And then there is the matter of her estimation. Is it something over or is it something under her actual capacity to endure and then defeat the snake or to even bring it to a draw?

But she saw the monkey and the snake fighting once before. And she already had done this kind of thing when she introduced herself to monkey. But that was different in a way because she wanted to seduce him.

Oh well, was it different really? Wasn't this another case of seduction actually?

Probably, most likely, she admitted to herself, and felt empowered by it, surprisingly, perhaps.

Anyway, she figured, if the monkey could hold his own against the snake, then she could do the same. And it wasn't just because she was as good at fighting as the monkey. It was actually because her attitude, again, would be playful and seductive.

Your attitude in fighting is actually a thing that can be the thing that makes you either win or lose. You can't determine it abstractly. If you do, you well might lose.

It's determined by the truth of where your heart lies in the matter. Whether that does mean that you are frightened or enraged, apprehensive, self-assured, wish evil or wish good, feel love or only hate, think it is right or it is wrong, think it's playful, think it's sexy, or only necessary — it's the truth of feeling it and knowing it and totally embracing it that determines if your power is more or less what it can be.

Deny yourself, defy yourself, and only go against yourself,

then automatically you are outnumbered in the fight and it's harder then to win.

So it was, she must admit, another instance of the same thing that drove her when she went and introduced herself the first time to the monkey. It was seduction, finally. But it was a darker kind. This was something interesting for her to realize.

That she could have this feeling for someone that was similar to how she felt about the monkey, but was really rather different, was interesting to her and was really quite intriguing. How new! Who knew that she would feel this thing that she felt to start with.

With the monkey she was only just beginning to admit it to herself, the quality of feeling she was feeling for him now. And now there was this other thing. Perhaps it was just all her curiosity, and she ought not totally resolve within herself the nature of her feelings so completely just yet. But the whole thing did excite her.

The duplicity excited her. All of her relationships that were important to her were suddenly at stake because of rifts between them. But that somehow made them, all of them, all the more exciting and all the more important. Because they were more tenuous, they were also much more sexy to her. And that might not be a good thing. But then again, it might. And in any case, it was exciting, and she liked to be excited.

It might seem that it's very odd that such a break and near division could invoke and call upon her such a resolute emotion that it drove her now more pointedly in pursuit of her intention. But that was how it was with her right then. With great purpose, she strove forward. Eager now she was, to launch herself into the fray and face the consequences.

He wasn't far in front of her, the snake, and she caught up to him quickly. Of course you know how stealthy she can be and well, she still was, although you might think that her skills would be somewhat compromised by the pitch of her excitement. But in fact, the opposite was true; her skills were heightened and enlivened by the passion of her purpose. And of course you must remember that the snake is very tired.

He did not hear or sense her when she came at him both hard and fast and knocked him on his ass. She hit him from behind and tackled him right down. And the snake had never known a thing like that to ever happen to him before.

It was a shock, to say the least. But he recovered very fast.

At first, he thought it was the monkey playing games with him. Then he knew it was a woman and he was quite astounded.

The smell and feel of her hit him just as hard as her body had hit him. And the fact that he was getting an involuntary hard-on hit him also hard enough to confuse him quite a bit.

They were rolling on the ground, resisting one another's grappling and holding as they tried to pin each other and hold each other down. He saw her face and she was smiling. And he could hear her breathing, and it sounded like her growling. And she got in close and bit his ear seductively. And his cock got all the harder, which really did annoy him. The snake was always in control, but he wasn't at this moment and he was starting to freak out. He felt her breasts against him and he started breathing hard and his mind was clouding over.

He went into a null state and he clamped his teeth together. Then he gathered up his panic into a single purpose and he threw her off away from him. How he managed this considering the hold she had upon him, neither of them knew and neither of them cared.

He looked at her. She landed in a perfect cat-like stance upon her hands and feet, still grinning wickedly.

He dove beneath her twisting on his back. He slid between her legs and wrapped his arms around her legs and wrapped his legs around her waist. Quite supple and quite slippery you could say the snake was.

She felt his cock against her body. As he twisted her upon her back, she reached in and grabbed his hard-on and then grabbed onto his balls and squeezed them hard, but not too hard. — Quite resourceful was the tiger and merciless, as well. But she didn't want to damage him irreparably.

The snake had lost his hard-on but he didn't lose control. He ignored the pain and, bending forward, bit into her ass.

She bit into his ass.

That was pretty funny and the snake was getting hard again.

He grabbed her by the cunt.

They rolled around like that, attached like that. It was absurd. They were quite a sight to see, if anyone could see them.

They wrestled and they squirmed, and then the tiger started hitting him — not punching him — just hitting him. And he started hitting back. It was ridiculous.

They took the opportunity, while their hands were slapping at each other, to break apart and stand apart, facing one another.

Both of them were huffing, both of them were puffing.

He asked her who the hell she was and what the fuck she wanted.

She answered with a kick. It was so beautiful to see. It was one of them there kicks, the kind that spin around backward first and then come around the front, and if they manage to connect, then they can have such a force that they can really knock you right down on your ass.

The snake stepped back enough for it to miss him by about an inch. But there was another one that came up quickly right behind it.

The tiger came upon him spinning forward with these kicks. Three or four of them came at him before he tried to stop her with a sweeper. And he made contact. But amazingly, she did a backflip out of it.

She assumed a boxing stance, but an open-handed one. She called him on.

He thought about it for a moment. He sized her up. And while he did so, she moved in close enough to hit him. Then, without his even really meaning to, he punched her in the stomach.

She registered surprise, and she lost her wind. But still, she let a right cross go and punched him in the mouth. Some blood he tasted coming from the inside of his lip. He saw some stars.

The next few blows they traded, they each blocked each of them. Then they stood apart and stopped and looked at one another for a bit.

She said 'hi,' and he said 'yeah' — it sounded like a question. And she said 'yeah,' it sounded like the answer to the question. She just wanted him to know, she said, that he is not alone, just like the monkey's not alone, and just like she is not alone. And that maybe they could be, the three of them, together in some way — either independently, or in some other way — but together nonetheless. And she looked him in the eye and she smiled again at him, and then she ran away.

And he watched her run away. And he wondered, what the hell was that?

42

SOMETIMES IT CAN BE DIFFICULT to think about some things when you need to think about them, or you ought to think about them, but you'd really rather not. Sometimes you'd rather think about the things you like to think about rather than the things that you have to think about. Having to do anything you aren't inclined to do can really be a drag — and thinking is no exception.

It can be really hard to do it if you do not care to do it. And if you force yourself to do it, there's something false about it that makes it seem just pointless. Like, you are getting nowhere — and the point is to get somewhere when you're thinking something through or trying to make a plan.

This is what the monkey had to do, but he didn't feel like doing it. He had to make a plan, but he thought that was a drag.

A plan can be a drag when it's only just a thing you want to put in place. That can be sort of too abstract.

Some people like it when it's like that. That's the way it ought to be, as far as they're concerned. That's the way it should be. So if it's any other way, well then, that way is the wrong way. There's just one way to do it, and that is how they do it. And if they do not do it that way, then they spoil the plan.

And then they spoil everything.

Sometimes it looks like they are more concerned about the plan than what the plan is planning to achieve. Following the plan is more important to them then succeeding in the plan. That can be OK, if that is what you're used to. But that could be a drag, if you are not used to that.

The monkey was not used to that. He liked to think that he could do it. There was something about doing it that seemed a little sexy. Just the thought of doing it (and getting it accomplished) and what it meant to be like that, to be someone who could do that, to be all that together and controlled like that, was, it seemed, a good thing and a sexy way to be. But it wasn't real for him; it was a fantasy. He couldn't really do that. So it wasn't really sexy; it was actually a drag.

The best things that he likes to do are things that he just wants to do because he likes to do them and he doesn't even really know the reason why he likes to do them. But he does. And he likes it when it is like that. He likes it like that best. Everything just seems like it is — everything's OK, and everything's all right and everything is just the way that everything should be when he doesn't have to force himself to do whatever it may be.

Oh well, you might avoid it some times. With some things, that's the way that some things are sometimes. But when they do not have to be that way, then why then go and let them, or go and let yourself go ahead and let them be that way? Why then go and do that if you do not have to? — if you really do not have to, if nobody is forcing you?

There are so many things.

Well, sometimes you just have to wait and let things run their course. And the best thing you can do if you are the monkey, and you otherwise would only be impatient and wonder why you bother, the best thing then for you to do, is to let yourself do nothing and just daydream a little. Maybe just do that. That's a very good idea.

If you daydream while you're waiting, then you're not really waiting any more, you're doing something else. Because well, why wait if you have something better you could do? And that is something better; daydreaming is something better for him to do at least.

There is a part of him that doesn't really care to get so much involved with everyone and everything. Like it's all too much, it's all just work. He is a lazy guy and he really does admire that trait within himself and in anybody else. If you're lazy, then you only do the things you really want to do or like to do. And that is something rare, if you let yourself be lazy, really lazy, and you celebrate the fact.

He is not too much a fan of the prevailing work ethic. He doesn't like to work just for the sake of working. But he can apply himself. He does apply himself. He can be rather rigorous in the way that he applies himself. But he doesn't value work as only something in itself as something that is valuable only in itself.

So he doesn't make a plan; instead he just only daydreams. What does he dream about? — Nothing in particular. He stares off into space and he roles around on the floor and he doesn't think about them, about the tiger and the snake, or about their groups. He forgets all about them. It is a drag to think about them. They are too much in his mind. Already he is feeling like he's been living with them for too long, like he's been too cooped up with them and spent too much time with them.

It is exciting overall. Yes, overall, it is exciting. But it also is a drag.

Maybe it is like the feeling you might have when you are planning a big party and you're getting all prepared and you're getting all excited, but when you think about it all, about everyone who's coming and all you have to do to manage everyone and everything, then maybe suddenly you see that it will be lots of work and a little bothersome and it makes you kind of nervous. And although you'll probably enjoy it, and you'll probably be glad, perhaps you'll have to wait until the party's over to really understand that you did have a good time because maybe while it's happening you'll be a nervous wreck. That was where his head was at with respect to all of this. He was starting to get nervous. Like, excited nervous. But still, he didn't like it.

He needed to be by himself. Just to be himself. Not to plan and think things out. Just to be himself. And not do anything that was specifically related to the stuff that lay ahead.

That was the best thing he could do to prepare for what was coming up ahead. Nothing.

He could daydream sure, and roll around, and hum a tune, and just be just whatever, just however, just like this and just like that.

Other people were exhausting with their agendas and all that. So this was how he would relax and recharge his batteries, by forgetting all about them and throwing out his care about them and throwing out the other things that he was getting all involved in.

So there he was inside his place, in his secret hideaway. He was well rested. He felt very confident that he had got to there without being followed by the tiger or the snake or by anyone at all. The night before when he got home, he locked the door, he had a drink, he went to bed and he fell asleep.

When he woke up he felt fine, but he had to get away. He had to find some solitude.

That was interesting. He never needed that before. And well, of course why would he? Knowing people helps you know things and it changes lots of things.

So he went to get some solitude and to let things sit a little to see how things did sit.

He put on a disguise, inside a public washroom. Then he walked around a bit. Then he took a taxicab. Then he walked around a bit and pretended he was shopping. Then he took another cab. Then he walked to his new place.

He was sure he wasn't followed. He felt like he was inside of an adventure story.

It felt great to be inside his place, his secret hideaway. It was so open and so clean. Not clean as in not dusty, but clean like with no drama vibe.

For a while he just enjoyed it, being there like that. He moved around. He rolled around. He jumped around. He lay around. He had a little snooze.

The sun came through the window and was warm; the light was warm upon him where it lay upon him.

But there was something pressing that he knew he had to deal with.

43

THE MONKEY PLANS ON IMPULSE. That doesn't work for everyone, but it kind of works for him. He's never planned that much
before he fell in with these guys. Now he feels compelled to plan.
But he doesn't really like to plan, so he kind of plans on impulse.

It's a funny thing to do, but he's a funny kind of guy.

It's a risky thing to do, but that makes it much more interesting.

Of course, he couldn't really stand it if this got to be all
that much more interesting than it was already for him. It was
interesting enough right now.

Anyway, you know what? The monkey does just what he does.

He's just never done that much before that really did
involve any other people, not in any real way, anyway. So he
never really thought before about the consequence of action.
Which means he never had to think before he did something
before. He's just not used to it.

Have you ever played chess? Do you remember the first few
times you played it? Do you remember learning how to plot and
how to plan?

The monkey was quite good at chess. But he wasn't sure that
he would say that playing people was the same thing. But, it's

just the thought that planning was a thing that you had to learn to do like you did when learning to play chess. It was sort of similar.

Anyway, after he hung out awhile at his secret hiding place, he went to see the snake's group. And he went without the snake. He went to see what they would say if he went there by himself.

He had a feeling they would welcome him. And welcome him they did. In fact, they seemed quite happy to see him by himself.

They asked him how he was and if he needed anything. Was everything OK? Did the snake show him around? He should feel that he was welcome to come and see them any time. They certainly did value someone like the monkey. How was he fixed for money? If he needed to be driven to anywhere at all, they could provide him with a driver and a car.

That made the monkey realize that the snake, as far as he could tell, did not use a car and the tiger didn't either. And the monkey never ever had ever used a car either. He never needed one. He never thought of that before. It was kind of interesting.

So no, he didn't need a driver and a car and he was all right, in fact, for money. The snake had done a fine job of showing him around. He remembered what a strange and enervating thing that was. And as he did remember, he paused then for a moment. And as he paused, he frowned a bit, which they took to be a sign that there was some kind of problem there between them, between the monkey and the snake.

Perhaps, they thought, the monkey thought that the snake was just as presumptuous and volatile as the snake's group thought he was. But that was their projection, and a bit of wishful thinking.

They started talking all about the opportunities there were at the company for a person like the monkey. They saw great value in him and they wanted him to know that they were open to his input. And, if he had ideas about what he'd like to do, they were more than willing then to listen and give him their support.

If he liked, they could facilitate any plan he had. He only had to tell them. They were also certain that they had some choice assignments for him that would interest him a lot. They felt that they could offer him lots of opportunity for adventure and excitement.

Of course, they totally respected the relationship between the monkey and the snake. And they wouldn't want to compromise any covenant between them that they might have made. But they did want him to know, that as far as they're concerned, their relationship with the monkey was both separate and distinct. So if he didn't feel like clearing something with the snake that he might do for them, or sharing something he might do for them — that was all right by them, as well. They all could work to each and everybody's gain and benefit, mutually of course.

The monkey said, he thanked them, he said that they were gracious and were generous, but that he just came by to say hello. And also just to say that he was looking forward to working with them too. And he thanked them for their offer and once he was more settled, if anything came up, he would like to talk about it. He would see them again soon, he said, and he was glad that he was welcome to come there, and he looked forward to the next time.

And the subtext was of course, that he would come there on his own and see them on his own and work alone with them. That is what he wanted them to think. And he knew that they had wanted to think they could think that way. So he let them think that way.

And then he went away and left them and went straight to see the tiger's group.

It was going to be a day — an impulse-planning day.

44

WHAT WAS THAT MONKEY UP TO?

When he left the snake's group, he went to see the tiger's group.

What is subterfuge? What is being sneaky? What, exactly, is betrayal? And when is it important to do things for yourself, and do them secretly?

The monkey never had to work these issues out before. Now, he sort of had some friends, and some would say a girlfriend — although the monkey wouldn't say that, and the tiger wouldn't say that. But they would both agree that they certainly were close. They would all agree that they were close, the monkey and the tiger and the snake. And they would also all agree that because they all were close, they were each of them empowered. Yet also each of them was now limited in ways they weren't before. So of course, now, these issues were apparent.

The monkey had been fine before he met those guys. He didn't feel alone before. But now he could. He had discovered that.

But he could live with that. If he had to live with that, he could do that.

Anyway, he had no problem with them, with the tiger and

the snake. But each of them was more than just the tiger or the snake. They were also both a group. And the groups were where his trouble truly lay.

The groups were all too much, as far as he could figure. Ever since the groups came in, he felt like going out. The groups were what he thought were really limiting the scope of possibilities of what he felt that his relationships with the two of them could be.

He felt like he had just been hired to work for different companies with different ideas and different things to do. He never had a job, and now he did have two. He never did have friends and now he did have two. He liked the friends. Although they were a little troubling, they were fascinating too. But did he like his jobs? And did he like his companies? He wasn't sure of that.

Of course, he'd only just been hired. He hadn't even done a day of work for either one. But he had a dreadful feeling about working for these groups. And he wondered if there were some way that he could get these groups to work for him instead.

Was it too late to quit them both and merely go away without them coming after him? Probably it was too late to simply fade into the background and live the way he used to.

He felt nostalgic for that time. And it was kind of odd to feel that. He wasn't used to feeling that. But he might get used to feeling that. He had a feeling that he might get used to feeling something like that.

The whole thing made him frown. And then he sighed, and carried on.

He went to see the tiger's group. They were surprised to see him. They seemed a bit concerned that he was there to see them. They asked him where the tiger was? And when he told him that he needed to speak with them alone, they seemed to be suspicious of his motives right away.

That was interesting to him. The monkey found it interesting, the differences between them, the snake's group and the tiger's. But in spite of what were differences between the ways they did receive him, he still knew that they both did have their very own agendas which would both be better served without the mediation of either of their agents, the tiger or the snake.

So he knew that their suspicion was a temporary thing. As soon as he revealed to them the reason he was there to speak with them today, their reserve would fade away and they would be intrigued. And of course he was, you know he was, you know that he was right.

When he told them where he'd just come from, well, of course, they were intrigued. They listened with attention, and they listened with great care, while he told them all about what had just transpired there at the snake's group's place just now, just then, and he told them also about when he went to see that group the first time when he went to see them with the snake.

They could contain themselves just barely when he told them all of this. And then they jumped to some conclusions that the monkey figured they would jump to.

They assumed the monkey brought this news to them to help them fight the snake's group, and to also help them figure out if the snake could be on their side or if they'd have to deal with him in some other way.

They did commend the monkey for having such resourcefulness, and they said they were impressed. They had been waiting for the tiger to make this kind of contact for a while. They had confidence in her but they never dreamt that things would ever go this quickly.

They said that he had taken risks, of course, by doing this on his own initiative. In fact, he was right now quite likely very much at risk. So now he ought to take advantage of their network of intelligence and draw upon their resources, which were greater than his own, and part of which included, naturally, the tiger.

The monkey listened quietly in awe of just how quickly things could go when you let them go ahead and go the way they wanted to. He listened and he nodded and looked agreeable about everything they said, as they made their plan for him. And he thought that sometimes maybe, the best way that there was to plan was to let the others make it for you. And then you just adjust it and conform it so that it will suit your own needs best.

They were careful to include the tiger in their plans. But they did so in a way that was vague enough to leave some flexibility in their relationship with the monkey. They were showing loyalty. But they were also illustrating that their desire to get results influenced their willingness to risk a compromise in the arrangement and relationship that they had between themselves and the tiger.

This of course he had suspected would be the case with them. They wanted him to be a double agent for them. And he wondered about agency as he agreed to do this for them.

45

WELL, THE MONKEY sure is having a very busy day.

He heads over to the snake's place. He leaves the tiger's group's place and heads straight over to the snake's place. He thinks about the tiger for a moment then heads over to the snake's place.

What will everybody think? He doesn't know, and doesn't wonder much about it. He's just going now that's all.

Ever watch those movies, the ones they call black movies, they call them that in French, partially in French, they call them film noir movies. That's like saying black film movies. But they keep it in the French because then you think less about the colour and more about the darkness. You think of darkness and dark shadows and nighttime in the city and high contrast black and white and gangsters and detectives.

And the detectives in these movies, they always move one way at first and then when it gets to be nearer to the end, suddenly you see that they are moving differently. And they don't say what they're up to, but you can tell they're on to something then. Everything speeds up and they change from being vague and full of nihilistic irony, to being singular of purpose and full of just conviction.

And when they've got it all sewn up, they tell everyone about it and they solve the mystery. And when they do the telling, they seem really hard and tough and angry in a way. But not in an explosive way, more like in an ethical and intellectual kind of way. And when they're finished, they seem soft and sad again. It's kind of just like French existential sex.

Well, if you know those movies, then you know about the way detectives move when they are moving suddenly, moving with conviction, and not saying much about it, just being kind of anxious and determined with a beauty and precision in the way that they are moving and the way that they are being. Well, if you could imagine that, then you could also then imagine the way the monkey moved and how he might appear to be if you saw the monkey moving as he headed for the snake's place, see?

But if you think that it's unlikely that the monkey could possess the complexity of life that could produce the complex feelings and weird psychology that drives the poor detective, that sort of anti-hero (if there really is a thing that really is an anti-hero in the movies called film noir), then you would be right. But still, he moved like that.

What does that mean? Well, that movement has a way of being constituted by the state of being that you happen to be in.

You know: if you feel sad, you move sad. If you feel glad, you move glad. And if, suddenly, you come to have something like conviction where there was none before, and you make some kind of plan from it that you can't articulate, that you really can't explain, but you know now what to do, and each moment that you follow your inarticulate conviction is another moment your conviction grows a little stronger, then suddenly you might find that you are moving seemingly faster with seemingly more purpose, with a determination that seems more singular and also more direct; more certain of itself. That's how the monkey looked.

His feelings weren't all that complex, but he felt duplici-tous. Perhaps he was a double agent of himself. Well, his agency was singular but it was diverse. And he was an agent of himself foremost. His associations and his relationships with all of these new people were yet to be determined in any way conclusively. But he knew that he would work for no one but himself.

He wanted to hang out with the tiger and the snake. He didn't want to work for them or for whom they worked for either. He didn't want to play any 'I Spy' games of subterfuge or espionage. He didn't want to be some kind of secret service stooge posing as a hero and fighting for something that was totally abstract to him.

He liked his fights to be more personal. In fact, he'd rather they be frivolous. He didn't really like either of these groups. They were too serious for him. He didn't want to be involved in either of their trips. But he liked the tiger and the snake.

Maybe they identified too much with their respective groups to play with him alone? Well, soon he would find out if that were really true.

So he went to see the snake.

And when he arrived, he was electric. And it made the snake feel funny. It felt a bit contagious but the snake resisted it.

The snake, of course, was thinking still about his meeting with the tiger. And he wondered if he should and how he should broach her as a topic with the monkey.

The monkey came right out and told him that he went to see the snake's group. He told him all about the way they had struck an independent deal with him to work apart from his association with the snake.

The snake felt all enraged by this and wondered what his game was, what the monkey's game was, in going there to see them behind his back like that.

Well, shouldn't it be obvious that he went there to be certain about what they both suspected was anyway the case? This group could not be trusted to respect the deals they made.

The monkey was not interested in any kind of deal, in any sort of an arrangement, with this group in any way. He'd like to hang out with the snake but he didn't need a job.

He had never met before he met the snake someone who was the way he was, like how the monkey was. And that was very interesting. He never knew that there were people like he was before, and that had changed things for him in a way that was significant.

He thought the group would be a large community of people more like him, at first. And to be involved with them would mean things would also be more interesting. There would be discovery of others that would lead to different things about himself that he would learn or that he would grow into. But of course, he quickly saw that they were ordinary people who wanted just to use him for their profit and own gain. They were entrepreneurs trying to exploit the skills of the monkey and the snake so that they all could make some money and gain some power and control in a society which he, the monkey, was not even part of and had no interest in.

The monkey and the snake were only soldiers to that group. And they only would be given just a small piece of a pie that they helped most of all to bake. The group would always profit more than them and their gains would be more lasting — giving money to their soldiers while they would gain an empire.

Whatever they might want, said the monkey, was totally their business. And what the snake might want was his. But the monkey didn't want it and the monkey didn't need it. And the monkey didn't want to help the snake's group get what they might want.

But the monkey liked adventure. And so he'd like to hang out with the snake, whatever he might do. But the monkey only wanted to do things that he thought were interesting to him. He didn't care to make more money. That wasn't interesting to him because he didn't really need it. He had enough of it. He didn't need some more of it. Making money was just something that you had to do in order to survive. He could do that on his own. He wanted to have fun and he wanted to be challenged.

The snake was still enraged that his group had dared to do this, to betray the snake like this. But he didn't dwell on it. It was useful information and he thanked the monkey for it, and also for his candor. The snake was one cool customer; he was as cool as a cucumber.

The snake did not think of himself as someone working for his group, like some kind of hired hand. But he did have to admit that the monkey had a point. And there was something running through his head. It was something that the tiger said about him not being alone. And he thought of what the monkey said about community and it all fell in together that those two must be together or at least must know each other, the monkey and the tiger because otherwise it was too coincidental. He remembered the girl in the stairwell that he thought might be the monkey's girlfriend. Was that then the tiger?

Nothing ever was too coincidental as far as the monkey was concerned. He loved coincidence. But it made the snake feel edgy, and he would rather know what the connection was. So he told the monkey all about his meeting with the tiger. And the monkey was surprised, but he really had to laugh. And so he did, he laughed out loud.

The snake was getting used to that kind of odd reaction that the monkey was prone to. So instead of getting aggravated or being all annoyed or being kind of puzzled, he simply understood it as a confirmation that the monkey knew the tiger. And he also took it as an indication that the monkey was delighted by what the tiger did (which happened to be true, because the monkey never thought that she would do what she had done, and that did delight him truly). This meant that there was more to this, to the meeting that he had with her. And it meant that he was probably right about who he thought she was and what she meant to the monkey. And he wanted now to know all there was to know, but he mustn't seem too eager.

This was funny to the monkey. He could tell the snake was eager and was trying to keep control. He was so different from the snake and it fascinated him. The monkey would, of course he would, be as eager as he pleased. He would not hide the eagerness he had for anything. But that was just the way he was. And the snake was how he was. And the monkey liked the difference. He found it interesting.

So of course, he did admit that he did know the tiger well. Well, he felt he knew her well, kind of pretty well. She was in some ways, well, you might say that she was kind of like his girlfriend in a way. In any case, they did hang out and they'd been together a few times. And they seemed to like each other. He certainly liked her. He thought she was fantastic. He'd only met her recently. About as recently as he had met the snake.

He never knew before that there were people like the tiger and the snake, but he was really glad there were. And he was glad that he did meet them. And it was something. And it really was really something strange and something wonderful. Where did they come from? What were they all about? It was a mystery. And he liked a mystery. And that was why he thought, he hoped, that there were more of them, that the snake's group (and the tiger's group, but he didn't mention them) was comprised of maybe more of them, because it really was amazing that there were any of them, really.

But the snake did want to know. Who is she? What is she? How does she fit? How is she a part of any of all this?

It's an interesting thing when it all becomes an 'all of this.' The snake's world just got bigger, right after getting smaller. And that contraction then expansion had a profound effect on him. He realized that there were many things that could be possible. And all those possibilities were things that were uncertainties, and he did not like uncertainties. He liked to know about the things out there that he had to deal with. Now he thought, he realized, that there might be something out there that he didn't know about, that was interested in him. He saw a correspondence between him and the monkey because the monkey had found something that was out there that was interested in him. And he hadn't known about it either. Maybe there was something else out there that was interested in all of them. He had to think about it.

But he had to know, was there another group?

Yes, there was another group.

Were they interested in him?

Yes, they were interested in him.

In the same way that the snake's group had been interested in monkey? Something like that way, but they weren't into money, they cared about the way that people did things and about who should be the ones who go and say who should be doing what.

That was intriguing to the snake, who was all about control.

Was the monkey part of that group too?

The monkey wasn't part of that group, and he wasn't part of this group. He wasn't part of any group, at least not yet, in any case. But they wanted him to be.

Was that group against this group?

Oh, most certainly. They were against each other, yes.

That was interesting. And they were interested in him, the snake?

Yes.

In recruiting him, or in having him defeated in some way?

Yes, either way, depending.

Was the monkey then, an agent of this group? Was he supposed to do this thing: to recruit him or defeat him?

They thought he was, but he was not.

What did they want him for?

To fight for good against the bad.

That really made the snake laugh.

The monkey was amused and he was amazed by how much there was unravelling and how it would change everything that it was unravelling. It felt like things that were blocked up were moving once again. What is held in silence gathers force, and he saw the force dispersing. Some forces you do like to hold on to if you can. You like to let some go. Sometimes it really does feel good when you let them go after you've held on to them for a little while. The monkey felt much better answering all these questions. The secret information was a burden and a bore. Secrets ought to be more enticing and intriguing than these secrets were. He was starting to feel free again, but there was still more to be done. But he felt encouraged by the strength of his convictions, vague though they might be.

Was the tiger part of this group too?

Yes, she had introduced the monkey to them.

Was her mission any different than the monkey's was?

It was pretty much the same as far as he could tell.

Was she ambivalent like him?

He couldn't say for sure, but it sure did seem that she was more committed to her group, the way the snake was more committed to his group. Maybe even more, after what the snake knew now. But the monkey had to say that his feeling was that she was more ambivalent than he the monkey was because he was not ambivalent, he was absolutely sure that he was no one's agent, except perhaps his own.

He didn't tell the snake that he did prefer the good guys more because they were, well, good — and he thought that good was good, mostly more than bad.

The snake had kept the part about his hard-on out of his account about his meeting with the tiger. He kept all the sexual details to himself. It often is important that you keep something as yours, and you keep it to yourself. And what you keep is often something private just like that. Like something sexual or like, who you do like more between two people or two groups.

But the air of some seduction was apparent anyway in the telling of the tale, and the monkey knew how playful, how seductive and of course, how deadly, the tiger really could be.

Had the monkey told the tiger all the things he told the snake? No, but he would do so, more or less, in any case. Presently, he would. The important thing to know, that is, for him to let them know, was that he was an independent agent.

The snake asked him now to go; he had some thinking he must do. He thanked the monkey once again for being candid with him. What the monkey told the snake, the snake really found most interesting. It was most interesting, indeed.

The monkey split and hit the street and felt unburdened and elated, but he also felt a little sad and he wasn't quite sure why. And he didn't get a chance, not much of one at least, to figure that one out because he didn't get too far before he ran into — guess who? — That's right of course, the tiger.

She had been waiting outside there. She didn't know he was in there. But she'd been out there waiting for the snake to come out there. And then she saw the monkey come out there. And then she went to catch up with him there. She overtook him there and was in front of him now there. And she said to him, 'hey there.' And she laid a big fat kiss right on him there.

Ah, the tiger was fantastic. What was she up to now? The monkey kissed her too. He was up to something, too. She stayed standing very close to him. She had an impish grin. She said, 'yeah?' after everything the monkey said.

'I just saw the snake.' 'Yeah?' 'He said that he saw you.' 'Yeah?' 'He said that he met you.' 'Yeah?' 'He said he met you in a most unusual way.' 'Yeah?'

(She said it just a little differently, every time she said it. But every time she said it, you'd think that he was telling her the things he liked about her and the things he'd like to do with her if they were making love. It was like then she was saying playfully, 'oh yeah? I dare you then to do that.' Or, 'you think so, do you? Why don't you try it?' — It was a little disconcerting, but it also turned him on. And even though it felt like she was maybe only doing it to try and throw him off, he kind of liked that too.)

'It sounded like he met you, in a way, like I met you.' 'Yeah?' 'Yeah.' 'Yeah?' 'Yeah.' 'Yeah?' 'And I saw your group today.' 'Yeah?'

Now, of course, she changed a little bit. Now, she looked at him. But still she stayed real close. Her breath seemed somewhat hotter. And she didn't answer 'Yeah?' after everything he said; she didn't do that any more. But the monkey missed that now, and he wished she would continue to keep on saying that, to keep on saying 'Yeah?' Because now that it was gone, the playfulness that went with it also was now gone. And he liked her playfulness, although it also threw him off. But that was how the dance went.

Of course, she wanted to know what he was doing there by going there. Why did he go and see them? She didn't feel suspicious, but she felt a little worried.

And he told her that he saw them because he went to see the snake's group, and the snake's group wanted him to work alone with them, to work without the snake with them, to work exclusively with them, and of course, behind his back. So he went to see the tiger's group to see how they would be with him when he was there without her there.

He told the tiger's group about the snake's group's offer, and they asked him to become a kind of double agent and try to trap the snake. Whatever that might mean. And he wasn't sure what that might mean. But he had some kind of an idea what all of it might mean. They both wanted to use him. And it didn't really matter about the tiger or the snake, who each of whom before him were their special agents first. Each of them had worked to establish things with each of them before the monkey came around. And now the two groups seemed like they were willing to jeopardize relationships they had already established with their special agents, the tiger and the snake, for the sake of their own interests. What do you think of that?

What did she think of that? She wasn't sure what she did think. She felt a bit conflicted. And she stepped backward just a bit. But she kept looking at him.

Then he told her that he told the snake what he had just told her. And she stepped back a little more and she frowned a little bit. She felt a little bit depressed, but she didn't feel surprised. In fact, it kind of all made sense, and she resigned herself to that. She felt odd about the way she felt. She kind of felt a bit deflated. Have you heard of this expression: head them off at the pass? It was like she was the one who was at the pass and who they just had headed off. But that was, actually, OK.

She began to see already that the monkey, no doubt unwittingly, might have indirectly helped her to be successful in her plan. But what was her plan, exactly? What did she mean to have accomplished by coming on like that, the way she did when she decided to present herself like that, to the snake like that? Wasn't she intending to insinuate herself between the monkey and the snake? So that two would then be three? Which would turn them into one, that is, into a kind of gang? And then she might have influence on their disposition as a gang, as their own kind of a group?

She now was pretty sure that the monkey would like that, for them to be in their own gang. And she had been prepared to pretend to want and like that too. But now she thought that maybe she wouldn't be pretending. And the only thing she really would have really been concealing was her own complicity. And she may have only been concealing it only from herself. But now it was all out there in the open. It barely had a chance to live at all as subtext.

Well, in a way, it all was good, but she didn't have control of where everything was going. But that could be OK; there could be advantages in not being so responsible for absolutely everything.

She told the monkey she would like to meet the snake with him. And he told her that he did plan to set up such a meeting.

She took him by the hand, and they went over to her place. They talked a little more about everything that night, but mostly they did not. They mostly fooled around. It was a little different for sure, because the ground was more uncertain. But that uncertainty just added a kind of earnestness that made it seem to be as if it felt more intimate.

The conflict was romantic in a way.

46

THE SNAKE. OH, THE SNAKE. Things have never been much stranger. There's something to be said for when things are status quo. Strange things can be interesting. When things are strange, it can be cool. Things can be exciting when things are really strange. But it also can be weird when things are strange. It can get too weird to take. And then you start to miss the way that things were going when they were going normally, the way they usually do go.

So that's the way the snake felt. He felt a little bit like that. Like, he wished that things were going a little more like that. Like how they used to go before things got to be so strange. And he had a funny feeling — not funny 'ha ha' but funny strange — that they were going to get still stranger, even stranger than they were right now, which was already pretty strange.

There's never any guarantee that things will stay the way they are. In fact, it's really not that likely. And you often only value the way that things were going when they're not going that way now. And then you wonder if they could be? And you kind of wish they could.

Romance loves the past because everything has happened,

there's nothing to anticipate, or immediately deal with. So you're free then to interpret things in whatever way you feel like. And if someone does contend with the version you come up with, then you can try to rest more easy with the knowledge, or should I say conviction, that everybody has the right to understand the story, that is, the meaning of the story, in whatever way they like, that is, in the way that suits them best. You have a right to your romance. A romance is, after all, only just a kind of story.

But the snake was not the kind of guy you'd think of as romantic. But still he felt like things before were not so complicated. Well, who could say that he was wrong? Things were a little easier before the monkey came around. And now there was the tiger, and the tiger's group, which complicated things some more. And maybe even made things dangerous.

He didn't mind about there being danger in his life. There was always danger in his life. But any danger that was in his life before was much easier to deal with than the danger he faced now, that he potentially faced now. At least he thought so anyway.

He was all about the way things were. The way they used to be. He didn't like to be like that. He was a now, right here, right now, type person. And he was really good at making plans for dealing with the future. He was not the type to dwell upon the past or be nostalgic. And yet, here he was to contradict the way he thought he was.

He was struck by how things were, compared to how things are. And he was struck by realizing that he didn't plan and think things out the way he should have done. And he was struck by realizing that even now, right here, right now, that he didn't have a plan and that he hasn't thought things through and that he doesn't really know just what it is that he should do. That isn't much like him. That also then, is strange.

There are so many things now that are strange since the monkey came around.

And now he wondered what to do about his group and all of that.

Well, he guessed that he would go and see them. And so he went to go and see them. He was a little more impulsive than he used to be.

And while he was heading over there to see his little group (not that they were little, but he was a little angry, and sometimes you will call something a little something when you are a little angry, like when someone used to say, oh, the little Jesus, when some boy was mischievous), he tried to think about it all. But he didn't really want to. How odd. But, there you are. He was still calculating; he just decided that he should put his feelings into order before ordering his thoughts.

The snake could work with how he was. He didn't have to force himself into some preconceived idea of how he ought to be. He could change, and he could flow with it. He could master anything. He was a master of control, which actually demanded that you be open and be flexible, and be capable of riding sudden tidal waves by surfing safely to the shore.

And thinking wasn't only done by talking to yourself. Thinking was perceiving, and it was feeling too. And it was sorting through the knowledge that you had all over you. Your body had knowledge all over. Your senses had knowledge all over. From sensing and perceiving, and from feeling and by learning, from everything it does and everything that's done to it.

Your will is thinking. Thinking's not just talking. It's dreaming and it's knowing and it's touching and it's feeling and it's loving and it's looking and it's listening as well. Thinking's tasting and it's walking and it's making gestures with your hands, and it's making music too. Thinking's what you are and what you do. You are always thinking, like you are always dreaming.

In this way the snake came back from where he thought he had gone to, back to where he thought he'd like to be. By thinking with conviction, his conviction did the thinking. And so he put himself in place. And he got himself together. And he went to see his group. He was all now here we go.

So the snake tells his group that the monkey came to see

him, and that the monkey told him that he wasn't interested in working for the snake's group at all in any way. And the snake's group was not sure that they should believe him. They were not sure he was not trying to pull a fast one on them. Maybe he was jealous and felt threatened by the monkey and so was saying this to them to see what they would say, what they would want to do and how they felt about it all. But there was something in the way the snake told his group what the monkey said, something in the way the snake himself was when he told them, that let them know that it was true, that the monkey really did say that. And it made them really mad.

Never mind their own betrayal of the snake, they were too preoccupied with their feelings of betrayal by the monkey. And they wanted him to die for that. Can you imagine that? They wanted him to die for that and they would like the snake to kill him. They asked the snake to kill him. They said that he should kill him.

They said the monkey came to see them and they thought that he was up to something. They said they thought that he was trying to double-cross the snake. They said he must be up to something. Maybe he was working for some other company, or some other agency. Or perhaps he was some kind of spy, or some kind of secret agent, or just some kind of wise guy, or just some kind of jerk who thinks that he can pull a fast one and can put one over on them. Well, he wouldn't get away with this. They won't let him get away with this.

They said they thought the snake should watch out because he might be in some danger. Who knew what he was up to, what this monkey guy was up to. He was up to something, sure. This wasn't innocent, his sudden change of mind.

They must protect their interests. Someone with the skills and capabilities of someone like the monkey must be up to something. Why would he want to be strictly independent? What did that mean, in any case? Independent of what, exactly? What did he mean by that? He must belong to something or to someone and they probably knew whom, they bet that they knew whom.

They knew about the tiger's group and they had heard about the tiger. They had never seen her, but they had heard about her. And this could be somebody who was an agent of this group. Perhaps he was the tiger. They had heard she was a woman, but maybe not.

Of course, if he was an agent of this group, the group who was against them, the group they knew who was against them, then he wasn't really doing what you might call a good job. But perhaps his task was limited to meeting with them only, to get a look at them and get a good fix on the snake. Perhaps the snake was more his target.

The snake had better watch out, the monkey might be crafty. He came to see them on his own to make a deal with them, independent of the snake. There's your independence for you. He was trying to divide them, to play one against the other, so that he could isolate the snake and somehow then entrap him.

The snake should really kill him before it was too late.

The snake said well, he thought it was a thing that they should know; that the monkey came to see him. And that the monkey told him what the snake just told them was the thing the monkey said. He told his group they need not worry. He would take care of this business. He would sort all these things out and make things right again. He was in control of this. Their safety was not compromised. He had only come there now to let them know about what the situation was, and to let them know that he would take care of this. There would be no problem. He was sorry that he brought the monkey there to see them, that he brought him there to meet them. It always was a risk to bring in someone new. It was perhaps a worthwhile risk, but it didn't quite work out. He apologized for this. But this wasn't serious.

He told them that he didn't really think the monkey had the nerve to do the kind of work they did. And he didn't think that he could be the spy or saboteur that the snake's group thought he might be. If he were, then obviously, he wouldn't lay his cards out on the table. He wouldn't tell the snake what he had told the snake. And he would have kept a lower profile.

He may have meant to be a spy or to be a saboteur, or to double-cross the snake, but the snake said that he did believe that the monkey didn't have the nerve. The snake said that to his group, and he told them he would deal with it. But that's not what he was thinking. That was not what he believed. He led them to believe that he would kill the monkey ruthlessly. But he wasn't going to do that.

The snake owed no loyalty of this nature to his group. They were associates in business. He wouldn't kill the monkey, not on their behalf. Just because they were embarrassed? Just because they had been caught with their pants around their ankles? That was their problem.

It wasn't a surprise to him that he shouldn't trust his own group. They shouldn't trust him either; if they ever knew what they should know was ever good for them.

Whatever. The snake and the snake's group had a partnership that worked. And for now, the snake would try and stay and let it be the way it worked. But the monkey was another thing.

He hadn't worked that matter out for himself just yet. And he didn't need to yet. But he would need to, soon. He would need to warn the monkey. He might not be in danger from the snake, but he could be from his group.

Everyone pretended that they were all placated, but they really weren't at all. And they all knew that they weren't. But they left it that way anyhow. And that was it for now.

The snake bid his farewell to them, and then he went back home to have a drink and think and wait and see what happened next.

47

WORD TRAVELS FAST is what they say, and they say it for a reason. Often when they say something, they say it for a reason. And normally the reason is because it seems to be that way so often and so much that it makes them go and say it. And yet, they always seem surprised, just a little bit surprised, that it happened once again and once again it proved the same old saying, whatever it might be. In this case, word travels fast is what they say. And they were right again.

Of course, what is fast to one is still slow to someone other, and the other way around. So what they say is often contradicted by what they say as well.

But as far as the monkey was concerned word had travelled fast because the tiger knew already, because her group found out already, that the snake had gone to see his group and that his group had said the snake should go and kill the monkey. So everyone knew everything. And it seemed to monkey that was fast. Someone told the tiger's group, and they had told the tiger, and she now told the monkey.

The tiger wasn't sure. But she was getting used to that. She wasn't sure how sure it was that she used to be, but she thought that she was sure before more than she is now. It wasn't something that she ever thought about before. But recently it struck her, there were some things she was unsure of, and more and more things like that kept on coming on as she went along. As she went along it was happening more often. She was at first, she was perhaps a little disconcerted by it all, but she was getting used to it. And so now, it didn't bother her. She started now to see it as a part of everything. It was just another factor that you had to take account of; the uncertainty of things that you might wish were more certain.

She was so cool, the tiger. It was hard to ruffle her for long. The monkey did admire her. She didn't seem upset at all by the things that she had told him.

He wasn't sure to what extent she may have been planning on her own, and how her plan may have differed from the plan her group did have. But as far as he could see, all her group's plans were forsaken, and new ones now were called for. And this didn't seem to please her. And he did admire this.

He also was impressed by how she wasn't disappointed — or didn't seem to be, at least — by the actions of the monkey.

The monkey wasn't much for plans, but it seemed that all his actions had some sense of purpose. It might be that his reasons were a little bit obscure, perhaps even to him. But the tiger kind of liked that because, regardless of the reason that might explain the things he did, they remained a thing that was consistent with who he was and what he was, right to the very core. And the tiger did admire that. It was like his actions and his being were transparent to each other.

She might be going slightly overboard with that. But even if that were the case, as much as she admired it, there was something that it did not change, and that's the fact that he's in danger.

The tiger and her group were not the same. They didn't feel the same way about all of this stuff. They were a little disappointed and they had their doubts about the monkey. But they didn't want to hurt him. They didn't think that he was bad.

They just thought he was undisciplined and irresponsible. And if the snake's group were against him, then chances were that he was good, or that he could become someone who's good, if they kept an eye on him and helped him out a bit.

The monkey was impressed by this gracious gesture. It was magnanimous, for sure. And he could tell the tiger also was relieved that they had conveyed this attitude toward him and asked her to pass it on.

It was apparent she still liked him, since they were at his place and they were together there in bed. In fact, their affection for each other seemed more real to him since all of this went down. There was no point now of a seduction that wasn't personal.

He was pretty sure the snake and he were cool. The snake's group may have asked the snake to go and kill the monkey, but the monkey doubted he would do it. He might. But the monkey thought that probably the snake would likely not do that. It was perhaps more likely that somebody else would try to do that. And the monkey wasn't sure about what he thought or how he felt about any of that yet.

It was kind of cool in a way, in a weird and fucked up way. He felt like he was either an outlaw or a hero. But he didn't really think that he was either of those things. He wasn't even certain that he even was in danger, really. Maybe they were only trying to put a scare in him, trying to intimidate him to make sure he didn't bother them at all in any way at all.

Well, the tiger wasn't sure. Maybe she was getting used to that, in a general way, but still she did not like the fact that she was uncertain and unsure if the monkey would be killed or not by the snake or someone else. And so she would feel better if he would let her help him try and stay alive.

The monkey told her that he wasn't going to join with her group either, but he would like to hang around with her. If she would like to do that too, it would be really great. He thought it would be great, in any case. And he still would like the three of them, the monkey and the tiger and the snake, to try and have a meeting.

She wasn't sure about that, but she thought that they should do that. It could be interesting, and maybe in some way it could help the monkey out.

Indeed, he thought it might just help, but he wasn't necessarily thinking about help in the same way that the tiger was.

How was he thinking about help, then? He hadn't thought it through, yet. It was a feeling that he had.

The tiger said her group would help the monkey too, even though they knew, of course, he wasn't going to join them. She said she wasn't sure that they'd ever let him join them now however, even if he wanted to. But, like she said before, they would help him out a bit.

The tiger and the monkey said all they had to say for now.

In the morning when she left his place she thought it would be good to check in with her group again and try to clear a few things up. Maybe not directly, by telling them directly, the things that she might do, like go to meet the snake with the monkey, but to talk around the concept to see how they did feel about her hanging out with them, with the monkey and the snake. And she also would then test her group to see what they would think about an idea that she had for working, in a way, a bit more carelessly, to see if that might work out more successfully.

She would see — and so shall we.

48

THE SNAKE WON'T HURT the monkey. If it need be known, and it should be known. Well, they think that it should be known. The snake thinks that it should be known, and the monkey's glad he knows it.

The snake can't guarantee, of course, that his group won't try to hurt the monkey, or to outright try and kill him by using someone else. But the snake won't help them do it. He doesn't need to do that. He doesn't want to do that. He likes the monkey — see? And it's best for both of them for it to be this way now between them. But of course, it would be better if the snake's group weren't so pissed. It's just because they found themselves with egg stuck on their face. They might get over it — or not.

The monkey wasn't worried, not really all that worried. He might have worried if the snake was on his case at all. But the snake seemed happier; in fact, he seemed relieved by all of this.

Actually, the snake now saw that he had been mistaken to introduce the monkey to his group. Why had he ever done that? As soon as he had done that, he wished at once that he had not. He realized he foolishly was making competition where there always had been none before. Why did he not see that? That was not like him. But he never did know anyone who could be the competition before he met the monkey.

He only did what he did do to try and pull him in. It was the sort of thing that he would do with anybody else. But the monkey wasn't anything like anybody else. Of course, he was like no one else at all. And he wasn't pulled in anyway by any of the stuff that other people were pulled by. He didn't want the kind of things that other people wanted, and other people needed, so that they could feel important. And he didn't need to have those things to make him feel like he finally belonged somewhere. Like he had found his family, his gang. Other people got that feeling when they were brought into the group.

But the monkey didn't need to be seduced into thinking that he'd found that through the largesse of the group because he already had found it, because he already did feel it, because he had discovered kinship without the limo ride. So the snake knew that the monkey was already on his side because the monkey saw himself as being friends already with the snake.

The snake did not have friends, and it could be interesting to have one. It tugged at him, somehow. He wasn't sure he liked that. The snake was not the kind of one to be easily seduced, if seduced at all, by anything at all. He was a seducer, but that was just a game. This was not a game and that was what was funny. And he wasn't sure he liked it being outside of a game. But it was interesting. And there was no denying it. It was pointless to deny it. He didn't know yet how to manage it, but he could see the value of it. And for once he felt like everything was not so damned predictable.

That could be good. That could be bad. But he liked the risk of it. He liked to see all angles. But it was a little boring if he saw them all too soon or saw them all too easily and figured them all out without any kind of challenge. He liked to have a challenge. It was quite a novelty.

He did like to play games, the snake. And he still liked to play games that he easily could win. There was still some satisfaction in feeling just how simple it was for him to win. But a challenge was a new thing and he welcomed it as well. It was time to shake things up a bit.

Perhaps the monkey was not playing what the snake would call a game, but he was still a part of one. The monkey was inside the game, but as the necessary blind spot that made the game as such — like blind spots do in vision. The game was just a game because there was the monkey now.

And what about the tiger? He did not know about her yet. She was a question mark. But he was inclined to think that she was a variable both in the game and out.

If the monkey was the blind spot, then perhaps the tiger was that thing they had at science centres that enabled you to see the blind spot in your vision that helps constitute your vision. She might be the device that allowed the snake to see the monkey in the role the monkey played, and to see the play of roles in general, to see the game in general.

It was a strained analogy, but it was interesting to see the snake reaching in this way with a species of philosophy that was transcendental and metaphysical. But you know, the snake does love abstractions, and this just might be his way of accommodating both the monkey and the tiger in a way he understands with a style of thinking that's consistent with an inside/outside view. — Something like that.

At least, it seemed to be the thing that was going on with him. The snake was mapping out relations, their functions and their meanings. He was a strategist, and now he was confronting anti-strategy as a moment and a movement, as a gesture and position which displaced all of those things while at once still being them.

It's all well and good to think that, to imagine it and to believe in it, but it's really something else when you see how it is done, and understand that you can do it, in fact that you have done it, or that it's been done to you.

For the snake, it was potential. He could do it now, he thought, because he thought that he had seen it done in retrospect by what the monkey did. He thought perhaps the monkey didn't see what he did do as something he was doing, but rather just as something that he surrendered to. And he thought that was the trick. Although 'trick' might not be the word that was the right word he should use. And yet, it suited monkey somehow. — That tricky little monkey.

It was strategy by principle, and it was very powerful. Because of course, it worked just by virtue of being what it was. What it was, was what was working, and that was why it worked, and why it was so powerful because it was working right away. As soon as you gave into it, it would soon give way, and you would have your way because your way was it.

The monkey was quite valuable for the snake to have around. He was a kind of spur. He was a moving point of some departure from one thing to another. He was a living predicate.

The snake did need his group, but he needed the monkey too. Maybe for a different kind of reason, but a reason just as valuable. In fact, maybe even more so. — For the moment, anyway.

49

THE TIGER IS GOING THROUGH SOMETHING because she's disappointed.

She's surprised and she's a bit shook up by what her group has told her that they now want her to do. They suddenly had changed their position from before when they said that she could reassure the monkey that they would lend a helping hand if ever he did need it. It seems they were not truthful when they said there were no hard feelings that they had toward the monkey, even though they were not happy with the way that things worked out.

Now they've changed their tune. Now they wanted her to try and use the monkey to try and trick or trip and trap the snake and disempower him or bring him over to their side.

It wasn't like her group before to compromise her methods and to challenge her approach. And she felt unexpectedly divided by it all.

You could say, she could say, anyone could say that she was competitive and she liked to win. There aren't too many who really like to lose. But there are some who do not care too much to be the one who is the one who always wins. There's a notion there that sometimes it's how it's played that really counts. If the play is good, then that can be considered to be winning in a way, as well. That is, in a different way, for sure. But still, it still is winning.

She likes to win, she really does, the tiger likes to win. And if she doesn't win, she's pretty sure she's lost. And she doesn't like to lose. She can accept her loss. She can lose most gracefully. At least, theoretically she can. It has to be conjecture because she never really loses; she really always wins, whatever that might mean. And of course, it does mean different things. But whatever it does mean to her, she always seems to win. Good for her.

But maybe she might lose this time. She doesn't like the thought. She does have the potential to take her losses well. But that is so abstract. That is all so well and good for things along the way. The things that do not mean that much and that don't add up to much and that are only small parts out of some big picture can be things that you can win or lose without you really caring much because you still have the big picture.

What about that picture? What if you lose that picture? Can you lose that picture? Oh well, if you lose one picture, chances are that you can get another one. Not everybody can, but the tiger can.

It's not about the picture, really. And it's not about the things that make the picture, either. They're not the kinds of things the tiger would ever really care about ever really losing. If she lost her trust in someone, that would make her sad perhaps. Or that would make her mad perhaps. But she wouldn't lose her will to trust; she wouldn't be incapable of trusting someone sometime once again.

She sort of felt a little bit like she was disappointed in her group. This was itself a new thing for her, but she also felt a little bit like she had lost some trust in them. Their intentions and their interest were after all, it seemed, a little bit more selfish than she thought they were before. And well, for all of that perhaps hers were as well. And maybe there were different types of selfishness for different types of selves.

It was interesting that feeling that she had of knowing they were different, her group and she were different. They weren't completely different, but there was a difference there, somewhere deep in there where it's important there.

And that difference made there be a thing that was a thing she could not lose, or would not like to lose. It was not a thing that she could win, but it was a thing that she could lose. And if she lost it, then she would be a loser. And so she wouldn't be a winner, despite the fact that it was not a thing that she could ever win.

She could only lose it if it was taken from her somehow by someone or by something that was capable of that. She did not know who could do that, or what could do that either. But maybe someone could, or maybe something could, and she would have to be prepared because they would have to fight for it and she would have to win.

But how could it be taken when it is a thing inside of her? How could it be taken when it is a thing that is her? How could it be taken when it is a part of who and what she is?

It could not directly. It could not be taken. But it could perhaps be lost somehow on account of something else or someone else who is responsible for that, for that something else. She knows that's true because it is a thing, this difference she has. It is a thing that she does know. It is a thing that she does feel. It's vague, that's true, but still it is a thing because she's made it be a thing. And she's made it be a thing that's inside of her. She's made it be a part of her, and a new thing that she's found.

This thing is her difference. It is a thing that is a new thing that makes her be somebody, and makes her be somebody else as well. She put it there by seeing it, in the way that she does see. And so of course, she made it be a thing that also can be lost. And now it won't be lost, because she will always save it. And that is how she'll win.

This might all be confusing. It's an origin of things. And the reasons for these things can always be confusing. But it gave her a resolve and a whole new way of feeling about who and what she was. And that did give her strength.

She always was a something with her group. But now the tiger had her own trip. She still had their trip too, but now she had her own trip. Perhaps she always had her own trip, or perhaps it was just recently that it came to be and she only now can see it, and now seeing it has given her an epiphany.

That doesn't really matter though, if she had it then, because it's christening was now. And that was what now mattered. That was what was celebrated now, and it was done so in a quiet and a meditative way not in a trumpeted triumphant way.

It's that small but blissful moment when something simple that you've hoped about yourself is true, turns out to be true. It's your confirmation you were waiting for, though you didn't think you were.

Her group was now caught up in the specifics of the things that they wanted to acquire: the monkey and the snake. They had their eyes upon the prize. And they were so eager and intent upon getting hold of it, that they were going to compromise their basic principles.

She understood the root of what they wanted her to do, but she couldn't do it for them the way they wanted her to do.

Maybe she could do it though, in some other way. Maybe she could do it in a way that would still be in the spirit of the way that they usually did things. And then maybe in that way, she would obey the heart of their desire, if not the details of her duty. But what exactly would that look like? What exactly she would do, she had not figured out yet. But she was sure that she would soon.

50

THE MONKEY STARED into the void. He stood upon one foot with his other foot straight out. And his arms extended up, straight up, but kind of off a little to one side.

He stayed like that and stared out into space. It wasn't hard for him to stay like that. He could stay there for a while. But he didn't stay that way for long.

He dropped down to the floor and rolled around the room, the nice big open room. He rolled around the hardwood floor and while he did he did a bit of thinking. While he was rolling back and forth, he thought a little bit about: what was thinking, anyway?

Thinking was a thing, he thought, and that was very interesting. It was almost just like everything, but it wasn't really quite. But being as it was almost just like everything, that meant that it could be one thing while being at the same time another different thing. And almost just like everything, it could happen by itself, or it could be made to happen. It could be steered and it could steer itself.

But it was most unusual in the way it knew itself. It knew itself in the same way that it knew everything it knew; by thinking that it knew it by way of thinking of it. So it knew itself, of course, by thinking of itself. But that was kind of strange because, if you gave some thought to it, it was something like two mirrors facing one another. It was like a mirror trying to see itself by looking into another one.

Well in a way, it seemed to work. That was most unusual. At least the monkey thought it was.

Of course, it was quite common. It happened all the time. But he thought it was unusual when compared to other things. It seemed that thinking was the only thing that seemed to know itself by thinking of itself.

They say the body knows itself by knowing what it wants and what it needs. And sometimes they will say something that's sort of similar about Mother Nature too. They say they both react in certain adverse ways when they are deprived of what they want and what they need.

But thinking is not like that. At least, it doesn't seem to be. Not to the monkey, anyway.

Could thinking be like that? Does thinking know itself by what it wants and by what it needs? Are there any wants, or are there any needs, that thinking ever has? What is thinking, anyway?

The mind is thinking, but thinking's not the mind. Sometimes thinking doesn't mind, but the mind is always minding.

The mind now, that's a whole and other thing. That's for another time.

But now thinking, that is strange, because it doesn't seem to know itself by what it wants and what it needs. It doesn't seem to have a thing that it wants or needs. A person wants or needs to think sometimes, but what does thinking want or need? It doesn't seem that there is anything, not to the monkey anyway. And he thinks that's interesting.

The monkey stood upon his head and felt the blood rush down. It felt good to feel that feeling. Then he thought about the way that thinking was a thing that you could control and that someone else could too, that is, control the thinking inside you.

Then he thought about the way that thinking also could control you. Your own thinking could control you.

It was interesting how sometimes you could make your thinking go, and sometimes you could not. And sometimes you could make it stop, and sometimes you could not. That was really interesting, when you couldn't stop your thinking. That really taught you something that you didn't know before; that you and your thinking were not the same thing really. They were not identical. They belonged to one another. But they weren't identical.

There was you and your thinking, and your knowledge and your feeling too, and your spirit, and your body, and your mind, and your heart, and your soul, and your sense and sensibility, and your energy, and of course your sexuality, and naturally your instinct too. All of it was part of you. But it was not identical to you. That was how you owned it, that's what made it yours.

And you, what were you? Goodness, gracious, what were you? That was something that you could only just determine, and someone else could too.

The monkey often felt like he didn't really know and he was making it all up as he went along. But he never felt so much confronted with himself before the tiger and the snake. And he never did do so much thinking about so many things before he met those two. Before, he mostly let his thinking go ahead and do what it did do, on its merry own. Now he thought deliberately about a lot of things. And he sort of realized that he was always thinking, really, and that he always had been thinking. He thinks so, anyway. But there were different ways of thinking.

Of course there were different ways of thinking that were different points of view, like opinions you might have that were contradictory. But that was something else. What he realized about the different ways of thinking was that thinking wasn't always just like talking to yourself. In fact, thinking and just talking to yourself could be completely different things. Thinking could be talking. And talking could be thinking. But they could be different things as well.

Then the monkey wondered while he was doing cartwheels all around the room (it's good to not have furniture, when you like to do such things), while he turned around and went around and round and round the room, he wondered if his hands ever did some thinking?

It seemed that they had memory. Sometimes when he had trouble remembering a phone number, his hand or more specifically, his fingers, could remember it for him, by dialing it for him. Of course, memory and thinking weren't really the same thing.

But could his body strategize? That was more like thinking.

He did a little Tai Chi, and while he did, he wondered about sometimes when he was sometimes fighting and he made a move that saved him from something or turned the tables in his favour without thinking about it, did his fighting spirit think of it? He didn't really know, but he found the thought intriguing.

This was all because of tiger, and all because of snake.

Their groups were not that interesting. They didn't make him think of much or learn that much, except they helped him figure out what it means to be belonging to some people or some place. His place was here alone like this, and his people were the tiger and the snake.

They were not the same, and he was not the same as either of them either, but he felt he did belong with them and they belonged with him.

At first, he thought their groups and they were like a package deal. Now he knew it wasn't so. He wasn't sure they would agree if he said that yesterday, but he thought they might today or that they might tomorrow.

Their groups were threatening, but that didn't worry him. The tiger and the snake were too valuable to them, and he was now their friend. And he was pretty sure that they were thinking and were feeling something similar to what he was thinking now and feeling. He had changed as many things for them as they had changed for him. They all might have what they do have as distinct from one another, but they also now could have something that they would only have by being now together. By knowing one another now, everything had changed.

They were a force together, though they were not joined together. They had not joined together yet. And they might not have to either, not in any formal way. But by acknowledging each other, it might just happen naturally. That would be interesting.

Time was all so different; now that there was now and there was the way it was before. There never used to be a 'now' and 'a way it was' before. And so now of course, there also was the way it is and how it is and how it might be too, as well as wondering and waiting and saying what it is and what it was and what it might be too, and how it could still be.

All around there was a sense of things that was different from before.

He thinks a little bit about everything he's done and got himself into and what he might do next.

Other people were exciting, but they also could be trouble. They could kind of wear you out because they were exciting, and because you cared.

It's a strange thing when you, suddenly, you realize that you care what people think. That is, when they're certain people and they are also thinking about you. How did that happen, anyway? How did it happen to the monkey?

It sort of just did happen in no specific way. When he found that he was not alone. And then that he could thereby also then feel lonely. But so then also feel he did belong, but not to groups of people, only to a few, to just these two in fact, although he wondered if there might be more of them out there, somewhere. Of course, there must be more of them out there, somewhere.

Well, while all of that became the way that things have now become at no specific time, but rather in the midst of time, that is when it happened. And he realizes now that this is the case. And it never was the case before with anybody else, except for with his parents, maybe. But that is different always. In any case, now it was the case that they, the tiger and the snake, could really make a difference. It mattered to him what they thought of him, and how they felt about him too.

Not that he would go and do something like go and change himself just to please those guys. The point was that he already had gone and had been changed by them, by just the fact of them. And he thought that was OK.

There is always something there to have something there to say about today. And now there's always someone he can say it to as well. It doesn't matter if they're there or only in his head. He could save it up for later when they actually are there, or he could say it to them now by playing in his head, in his imagination, like he was talking to them, like as if they were then there. That was interesting. He could have an imaginary dialogue with imaginary versions of people that he knew well enough to guess what it was that they might say in response to what he said. A common everyday occurrence that was just fantasy and was quite new for him.

Now he could have fantasies of talking with his friends.

He must get them together. The monkey made a resolution to get them there together, the monkey and the tiger and the snake.

He opened up his eyes. It was now dark in there. The lights weren't on in there. The light outside was gone. The light outside had faded. He still was lying on his back. He still could see the sky. He felt a little sad. He didn't quite know why. But he didn't really mind it. He kind of actually liked it.

And he fell asleep like that. And it kind of did feel good.

51

THEY ARE WHO THEY ARE and they are there together. They are all together. The monkey got them all to gather there together: the monkey and the tiger and the snake.

They are at his place. They are at his new place. It seemed that it made sense. It was a gift of trust, although he didn't tell them that. He didn't need to tell them that. He just had to do it, for them and for himself. It was an invocation in order that there be more trust around amongst them there.

It might be tricky, just the same.

What about the tiger and the snake? Their only meeting was bizarre and it was even stranger now, knowing who they worked for and how different they were and how they were supposed to be dealing with the monkey for the people that they worked with in a way that was not friendly. So it was a little strange, and that's to say the least.

But they were who they were and they were there together. And they knew everything. And everything was clear. It was rather simple, really. They were who they were and they did what they did do for whoever they did do it for, for a group or for themselves, but they wouldn't hurt each other or go against each other because they were there together like some kind of family.

This is what the monkey said, and it had the ring of truth like it was a good idea. But it was harder for the tiger and harder for the snake to commit to one another as if they were another group. This group was different, yes, and of course it was quite thrilling. It was like they had their very own secret kind of club. But it seemed kind of half-baked, even if it was appealing.

The monkey's in the middle. He has no association, other than with them, that he could compromise. But there was still a risk of danger for him coming from the snake's group.

The tiger and the snake had lots to compromise. Plus, they also were supposed to be the other person's enemy. At least, their groups were enemies. But they didn't feel that way. It may be strange to say, but they did not feel that way. They didn't feel that much about each other either way. They didn't know each other, but they were willing to find out.

Would they get along? They might all get along. They might be very friendly with each other. Maybe they would not. But there was already respect there between the two of them. There was respect there all around.

Maybe it is not so much that they are like a family as they are some kind of species that is special and is rare, who have recognized each other and see that it's important that they somehow bond together. The ostensibly contentious differences between them may just be abstractions, or they may amount to something that is very real for them. Only time will tell how well the tiger and the snake can deal with one another.

But the monkey — oh, the monkey — it is essential that he be free to do whatever he likes and yet still hang out with them, with the tiger and the snake. And he hopes that they can do that. He thinks that if the three of them ever came together and did something together, that they could be very powerful and it could be totally amazing.

They are three and they are there together, the monkey and the tiger and the snake, and that is something else. And they wouldn't be there like they were if they weren't in some agree-ment with what the monkey said. There was a force and they felt it, and they only could agree that for them to bond together could be interesting. It was already interesting that there was in fact, a force. They could feel the force. And they would check it out.

The monkey would lay low. And they would all hang out. And they would see what they would see.

And this made the monkey happy.

52

THIS IS THE BEGINNING of their relationship. Beautiful it may be. It may be something else. It will be many things, because it already is that. And it hasn't been resolved, because it's only starting after all.

There are many things.

And these are some of them.

Fin.

ACKNOWLEDGEMENTS

I would like to acknowledge the invaluable feedback and support of my dear friends Sandra Dametto, Ravi Rajakumar, Joe Hiscott and Dayna McLeod. I am extremely grateful to the inimitable Zab for her beautiful work and for suggesting Pedlar Press and Beth Follett to me, and to Anne Golden for paving the way. Thanks to my family. Thank you, Beth Follett. I wish to acknowledge the inspiration I received from the following people: Gertrude Stein, Steve Ditko, Lao Tsu, Derrida, Doctor Seuss, Jet Lee, Sui Meng Wong and Buffy the Vampire Slayer.

Michael Boyce was born in Ottawa in 1958. He grew up in New Brunswick, and lived in Toronto and Montreal for many years. When he was kicked out of high school he turned to music, literature and film as a means of education and self expression. After earning a Ph.D. in Humanities from Concordia/McGill Universities he concentrated on independent video production. He is Irish Catholic/Scottish Presbyterian by lineage and Pagan/Taoist by nature.